The Resolution

The New Homefront, Volume 4

By Steven C. Bird

The Resolution: The New Homefront, Volume 4

Written and published by Steven C. Bird at Homefront Books

Edited by Sara Jones at www.torchbeareredits.com
Final review by Carol Madding at hopespringsediting@yahoo.com
Illustrated by Keri Knutson at www.alchemybookcovers.com

Print Edition (4.20.16)
ISBN 13: 978-1514313886
ISBN 10: 151431388X

www.stevencbird.com
www.homefrontbooks.com
www.facebook.com/homefrontbooks
scbird@homefrontbooks.com

Table of Contents

Disclaimer

The characters and events in this book are fictitious. Any similarities to real events or persons, past or present, living or dead, are purely coincidental and are not intended by the author. Although this book is based on real places and some real events and trends, it is a work of fiction for entertainment purposes only. None of the activities in this book are intended to replace legal activities and your own good judgment.

Some items in this series have been changed from their actual likenesses to avoid any accidental sharing of Sensitive Security Information (SSI). The replacement values serve the same narrative purpose without exposing any potential SSI.

Dedication

To my loving wife and children:

Monica, Seth, Olivia, and Sophia

From the beginning of my writing career you have been my motivation and my inspiration. To this day, you still inspire me and drive me to accomplish all I can. It is my constant desire to protect you and provide for you that drives my imagination in ways that allowed me to create this story, and to continue it into a series. Not only has this series come a long way since The Last Layover, we too, have as a family, as well as with our own desires and goals to be more self-sufficient, just like the characters in the book. With your continued love and support, we will continue on this journey together as a family, and someday, our hard work and investments in ourselves will pay off big.

~~~~

Additionally, I would also like to thank all of my friends and colleagues who have helped me get this far. One of the things I love the most about the writing community, at least in the post-apocalyptic/SHTF/dystopian/prepper genres, is how close-knit fellow authors, editors, and designers are, and how willing everyone is to promote and help each other along. It truly is a “rising tide lifts all boats” type of community and I’m proud to be a part of it. Thanks to everyone and I hope and pray we all continue to see success in our present and future ventures.
~~~~

Continued from (Chapter 30) *The Blue Ridge Resistance: The New Homefront, Volume 3*

Introduction

As the country continued to struggle amidst the fallout from the orchestrated collapse, the United Nations and other foreign entities continued to increase their influence, taking advantage of a nation desperate for order. Introduced as "peacekeepers" by the current administration, armed foreign troops occupied U.S. territory for the first time since the Japanese invaded the Aleutian Islands in Alaska, occupying the islands of Kiska and Attu in 1942-43.

Initially, the UN established itself in major metropolitan areas such as Atlanta, New York, Seattle, and Los Angeles; once seen as a legitimate government presence, they began to venture out into rural areas to quell any potential resistance to their true intentions—enjoying the spoils of a war they did not even have to fight. America and its valuable resources were ripe for the picking, or so it seemed.

The one thing the occupiers did not count on was the will of the American people, a people born into a freedom that was handed down to them since the founders pledged their lives, fortunes, and sacred honors to resist the tyranny they faced under King George III. The patriots of today may face a different foe, but the struggle to hold on to their natural, God-given rights is the same as their forefathers. Human nature will always go in one of two directions: those who will give up freedom for security, and those who will give their lives in the struggle for freedom.

Chapter One: The Encounter

The stormy weather of the previous day had completely given way to a beautiful East Tennessee morning and provided them a gorgeous view of the Blue Ridge Mountains. For the next few miles, things were relatively quiet. They stayed on their guard, but enjoyed the scenery of the new life the spring season always brings. Their only distractions were the occasional abandoned car on the side of the road. As they approached, they would slow down to take a cursory look, but from what they saw, most simply seemed to have been abandoned there, as if they had run out of fuel trying to cross the mountains.

As Ed looked out one of the openings on the side of the livestock trailer, he turned to Nate and said, "Welcome to North Carolina."

"Really?" Nate replied.

"That's what the sign says, at least," responded Ed.

Nate stood up, hanging on to the side of the moving trailer next to Ed, and said, "Hopefully, we'll make good time the rest of the way to Hot Springs. We've been away for long enough. I can't help but feel like it was a bad idea to leave the homesteads as short-handed as they are without us."

"Yeah, I've been thinking the same thing. On the bright side, though, Charlie and Jimmy should be home by now. That gives them better coverage."

"True," Nate said as he stared longingly out the window, wishing he was back home with Peggy.

"Besides," added Ed, "I can't help but think we were meant to find the Gibbs family and make our way to Sabrina. We needed each and every one of us to pull that off. I honestly think at times the bigger picture steers us in the direction we need to go."

"You mean God?"

"If that's how you want to look at it," replied Ed as he looked up at the sky. "What the *hell*?"

"What is it?" asked Nate as he followed Ed's gaze, attempting to see what he was focusing on. Once he caught a glimpse, he said, "Crap. I wonder if that's the helicopter from the bridge last night."

"Nate..."

"What?"

"Either I'm losing it, or that's a Hind."

"No, Ed... you're not losing it. That's an Mi-24, alright."

As the helicopter arced back around as if to get a better look at them, Ed said, "Man, that thing has UN markings on it."

"What the hell..." Nate began to say as the tractor came to an abrupt stop, throwing Ed and Nate forward against the gear packed into the front section of the trailer.

Dazed, but uninjured, Ed and Nate scrambled to their feet, looking out of the back of the trailer to see a Humvee pull across the road behind them, blocking their retreat.

Several armed soldiers got out of the Humvee armed with AK-74M Russian service rifles. The AK-74M is the modern Russian service rifle for its ground forces. It is an updated version of the famous AK-47/AKM platform, but chambered in the 5.45x39 Russian cartridge with a synthetic stock and handguards, instead of the traditional wood of the previous models. The helicopter landed in the clearing off to the right of the tractor and they could now see that another Humvee was blocking the road in front of the tractor, explaining their sudden stop.

Just then, they heard a message from Jason come over the handheld radio. *"Just comply. Only fight if you must."*

As the tractor's diesel engine shuddered to a stop, the soldiers in the rear of the trailer took aim at the back doors, while several other soldiers gathered alongside the tractor to deal with Evan and Jason up front.

One of the soldiers, focusing his attention on Ed and Nate, said in a choppy East European accent, "Slowly open door and exit vehicle with hands on head."

Ed opened the door and, doing as instructed, he and Nate stepped out onto the ground with their hands on top of their heads.

"Three steps forward and drop to knees," the soldier then said.

Complying with the request, Ed and Nate knelt down while another soldier came from behind, stripped them of their handguns and knives, then pushed them down onto the ground, their faces hitting the hard blacktop surface.

Ed attempted to pay attention to what was happening with Evan and Jason. He couldn't turn to see what was transpiring, but he could hear that Evan's defiant tone wasn't getting him anywhere.

In perfect English, with a standard American accent, one of the soldiers gave Evan and Jason the order, "Place your hands on your heads and climb down."

Evan replied, "But I can't climb down with my hands on my head; I need them."

"Would you rather stumble and fall with your hands on your head or be shot for non-compliance?" asked the soldier.

"Damn it," Evan mumbled.

"What was that?" the soldier demanded.

"I said 'damn it,' damn it!" Evan said in an angry tone. "Who the hell are you, anyway, and why the hell are you pointing guns at us? This is a public road. We have every right to use it as U.S. citizens."

"I'll determine what your rights are," the soldier replied. "Right now, you are suspected domestic terrorists and insurgents. You will be treated as such, in accordance with the Insurrection Act, until cleared. Is that understood?"

Biting his tongue, Evan reluctantly muttered, "Yes."

Hearing several of the other soldiers talk with a thick accent amongst themselves in the background, Evan asked, "You sound American, but who the hell are those guys, and why are you working together doing this?"

"We are here under the direction of the President of the United States, in accordance with his orders and at the direction of the United Nations. We are operating as peacekeepers to quell the violence and instability caused by right wing extremist insurgents," he answered. "That's all you need to know for now. Your compliance is mandatory. Resistance will be treated as hostile intent. Do you understand?"

"Very much so... traitor," answered Evan with contempt.

The next sound Ed heard was a deep thud and that of Evan's body dropping to the ground. Flinching out of reflex, wanting to help his friend, Ed was quickly reminded not to intervene, as the muzzle break of an AK-74 was shoved forcefully into his face by one of the soldiers standing watch over him.

Searching the trailer's contents, one of the soldiers shouted something in what sounded to Ed like Russian. The soldier who appeared to be in charge responded by joining him inside the trailer.

Ah, hell, Ed thought. *We've got those damn guns in there.*

After a brief conversation that he could not understand, Ed heard scuffling coming from Evan and Jason's direction, as the soldiers in the rear began to zip-tie his and Nate's hands behind their backs. They were then forced to their feet and marched to the waiting Mi-24 helicopter that was parked in the clearing. Ushered aboard at gunpoint, they were joined by two of the soldiers. The door was closed and the whining sound of the helicopter's two Klimov TV3-117 turboshaft engines began to bring the rotors to life.

Chapter Two: The Relocation

As the helicopter lifted off, pitched forward, and began to accelerate, Nate asked the soldiers, "Where are you taking us?"

"Do not speak unless required by us," one of the soldiers said.

Okay, then, Nate thought to himself.

After a one-and-a-half-hour flight in the troop compartment of the Mi-24, the helicopter landed. Ed and Nate were quickly ushered inside a large one-story building located about fifty feet from the helicopter. On their way into the building, Ed attempted to get a look around to try to piece together an idea of their location. While taking mental notes, he was jabbed in the back by the muzzle of an AK-74, followed by the forceful command, "Eyes front!"

Complying with the order, Ed looked straight ahead, saying to himself, *One story, newer construction, large blue awning out front, looks like a government building, sounds of an airport, a UN flag flying above the American flag on the flagpole. Rat Bastards!* He and Nate were then led inside.

Entering the building through a side door, the soldiers led Ed and Nate down a long hallway and past what appeared to be lower-level administrative offices. At the end of the hall, they entered a room with several large boxes stacked in the corner. Looking them up and down, a soldier in the room visually sized them up and acquired an orange prison-style jumpsuit for each of them.

"Off with your clothes," the soldier said in a heavy Russian accent. "Everything comes off. Shoes, socks, undergarments—everything off."

Ed and Nate shared a concerned glance, which was quickly interrupted by the soldier shouting, "Now!"

Begrudgingly, Ed and Nate complied, as they had no other options at the time. As Nate lowered his pants to the floor, the soldier holding the jumpsuits noticed his prosthetic leg. Pointing at Nate, he said something to one of the other soldiers in what appeared to be Russian. The soldiers shared a laugh as he nodded his head.

Once Ed and Nate were stripped of everything, another soldier came from behind them, gathered all of their belongings, and placed them in a bag. The soldiers shared a few words in Russian before they turned their attentions back to Nate. Giving an order to the guards standing in the back of the room, the soldier walked up to Nate as two of the guards grabbed him by the arms, holding him firmly in place. Nate's first reflex was to struggle, but given the circumstances, he quickly decided to comply with them... for the time being.

As the guards held Nate, the soldier who approached him said, "Remove your leg."

"Excuse me?" Nate was caught off guard by the demand.

"That is a very clear order. Remove your leg."

"What... why?" Nate said, starting to protest as the soldier punched him in the gut, folding him over in pain.

"Hey!" Ed shouted and almost immediately felt the butt of an AK-74 strike him in the back, knocking him to the ground. With a rifle muzzle pointed at his head, Ed quickly put an end to his resistance.

The soldiers then wrestled Nate to the ground, removing his prosthetic leg by force. "You have no need for this at the moment," the soldier said. "We can find it a better home." Tossing an orange jumpsuit onto Nate as he lay naked on the dusty floor, he then said, "This is all you need for now."

The soldier turned to Ed and tossed him one as well. "Compliance is not optional. You will learn that the hard way if you force our hands. Now, get dressed and help your friend here get up on his one good leg. You have a long day ahead of you."

Chapter Three: Returning Home

Leaving Quentin and the Blue Ridge Militia behind to head for home, Evan and Jason were blessed with the gift of two horses, given to them by their new friends in the resistance. They set out under the cover of darkness to head for the Homefront. Armed with their battlefield pickup AK-74Ms and a supply of AK magazines loaded with steel-cased 5.45x39 full metal jacket ammunition, also given to them by the resistance, they were more than prepared for the journey home. “Thank God for these horses,” Evan said. “My feet definitely weren’t up for a long-distance hike.”

“Quit being soft; it’s only about fifteen more miles,” Jason quipped.

“That’s easy for the guy who didn’t walk barefoot through broken glass to say.”

“Ah, you’re just gettin’ old.”

“Well, that’s the first accurate thing you’ve said. Do you think we should stop by the church before we head on up to the Homefront?” asked Evan.

“That’s what I was just thinking. Pastor Wallace seems to have his finger on the pulse of the area. That and we could get an update on Sabrina and the Gibbs family. They may have seen or heard of Ed and Nate passing through, too.”

“Exactly.”

~~~~

As the two men saw that they were approaching the Wolf Creek Bridge, which they needed to take to cross the French Broad River, Jason slowed his horse and said, “Looks like the sun is coming up. Do you want to press on through in the daylight, or wait until nightfall?”
~~~~

"The anxious side of me just wants to gallop on home as fast as I can, but the side of me that keeps getting shot at wants to play it safe. Let's bed down in the woods and get some sleep. With just the horses, we can get off in the brush and bed down out of sight," replied Evan as he pointed to the brush and trees on the south side of the road. "If we are up on the hill a bit, whoever is on watch can keep an eye on the bridge during the day as well. Any traffic coming through this area needs to use that bridge. It will also help us spot any trolls."

"I'm glad you always agree with what I'm thinking. That sure saves a lot of arguing."

Evan chuckled. "Ha. Yeah, well, being on the same page is probably what's kept us alive this long. But the way I see it, it's you who's agreeing with me."

Jason nudged his horse to get him moving and said, "Whatever makes you feel better about yourself." He rode off into the trees, ducking down to clear the low-hanging branches. Evan laughed and followed closely behind.

As the terrain got a little too steep for Jason and Evan's comfort level, they dismounted and led their horses through the thick brush on the side of the hill to a reasonably level spot that overlooked the bridge and the river.

"This will do," Jason said, as he tied his horse's reins to a tree, freeing him up to get a better look around.

Following suit, Evan hiked up the hill to get a bird's-eye view of the situation while Jason began to set up camp. Wishing he had binoculars, Evan squinted to see as far as he could in the faint light of the early morning as the sun began to rise.

Rejoining Jason down at the camp, he said, "It looks like there are a few houses on this side of the hill, a little closer to the bridge. There's also the railroad tracks that follow the riverbank along the south side of the river. I almost forgot those tracks were there; when we came through here on our way to Hot Springs, it was so dark and rainy that it was hard to see anything that wasn't right in front of the tractor."

Jason looked through the trees at the road below and said, "I'll keep an eye on it while on watch. I'll take the first shift. You get some rest, old man."

"You do realize I'm only one year older than you, right?"

"Yeah, but you slow me down like it's ten."

"I'll remember that the next time I have to save your ass," Evan said while adjusting his hat. "Before I sack out, though, I'm gonna slip down to the river and get some water for the horses. Just cover me from here."

"Cover you? There isn't much covering I can do from here using an AK with iron sights, but I guess when you hear the random gunshots, you'll know to look out. The most you can say I'm doing from up here with this thing is guarding the horses."

"That's true. I'm gonna miss having you as overwatch with your Remy."

"Don't remind me... I miss her already."

"I'll make sure I tell Sarah which one of the loves of your life you thought about while we were gone," Evan said with a crooked smile as he slipped off into the woods, heading down the hill toward the road.

As Evan worked his way back down the hill with his injured feet sliding inside of his slightly oversized boots, he thought, *I really should have sent him to get the water.*

Reaching the road, Evan paused to look and listen. With the morning mist rising off the river in the distance, it was almost silent. Appearing safe, Evan slipped across the road and into the brush on the other side, which separated U.S. Highway 70 from the railroad tracks. As he stepped onto the tracks, he began to look around for something to carry water back up to the horses. *Thank God for litterbugs,* he thought as he saw a plastic milk jug in the brush on the riverbank. *One man's trash is another man's treasure.*

Holding the jug underwater while the air bubbles were forced out the top by the incoming water, the *gulp, gulp, gulp* sound almost mesmerized him into not noticing the sound of approaching vehicles. *Crap!* he thought as he quickly pulled the jug from the water and placed it in the bushes. He crept up to the edge of the tracks, remaining exposed in the brush; to his horror, he saw three military vehicles approaching. As they neared the bridge, he could see an MRAP in the lead with two Humvees following closely behind. Appearing to have once been U.S. military equipment, they now wore the letters *UN* on the sides.

Jason watched in horror from above, not knowing Evan's exact proximity to the traffic. Clutching his AK-74M, he felt helpless, as the traffic was at the edge of the minuscule 5.45x39's effective range. This would make any sort of fire from his position a spray-and-pray evolution rather than being any sort of precise shooting. Providing a distraction to allow Evan an opportunity to fight back or escape was the most he could hope to accomplish with what he had.

Evan remained perfectly still as the three-vehicle convoy rolled on by, pausing just before the bridge for one of the soldiers to make a cursory inspection before proceeding. Once the threat was out of sight, Evan grabbed his jug of water and slipped back across the road and up the hillside to Jason's position.

When he arrived back at camp, Jason said, "Holy shit, man. That was close."

"You're telling me! I've had enough of those guys lately. That's the last thing I wanted to see heading in the direction of home."

"With only three vehicles, it's obviously just a patrol of some sort, but still... that's not good," Jason replied, beginning to pace back and forth with frustration.

"With them out on the roads, traveling in broad daylight is definitely out of the question," Evan added. "And to that same point, I think Highway 70 is out of the question as well. Those railroad tracks lead all the way into Del Rio, right?"

Pulling a map given to him by the militia from his pocket, Jason said, "Yep, it's off the beaten path in some places, but follows right alongside Fugate Road a large part of the way."

"That's still a less-traveled route than Highway 70. Let's take the tracks to Fugate Road, and then just take Fugate Road from there."

"Roger Roger!" replied Jason sharply. "Now get your old ass some sleep. I have a feeling once we get going again, things could get rather busy in a hurry. We'll head out again at sunset. I'll wake you when it's your turn to stand watch."

Chapter Four: Friend or Foe

Shoved violently into a small ten-foot by twenty-foot room, Ed and Nate fell to the floor with the door slamming behind them. Ed looked around to see a few old GSA (Government Services Administration) workplace posters as well as a poster produced by the state of Georgia with information on workers' rights, the minimum wage, and equal opportunity. There were marks left on the tile floor from what appeared to be vending machines directly in front of a series of power outlets.

"I can't believe those bastards took my leg!" Nate shouted as soon as their captors were outside of the room. Then he and Ed helped each other back to their feet.

"I guess they figure you're easier to deal with this way," Ed replied as he visually scanned the walls. "Looks like an old break room."

"I guess we're on break, then," replied Nate with sarcasm in his voice.

Ed continued, "Based on the amount of time we were airborne, the average speed of a turbine-powered helicopter such as a Hind, the general direction we seemed to be heading, and the sounds we heard outside, I'll betcha we're in Atlanta—on the airport grounds somewhere."

"That makes a lot of sense, considering all of the reports we've heard of them using Hartsfield-Jackson as a staging area."

Looking around the room for items they could use, Ed noted the emptiness of the space. "They didn't leave us much to work with."

"I'm sure that was part of the plan. Anything not nailed down can be used as a weapon," Nate said, shifting his weight and letting go of Ed's shoulder. He hopped on his leg over to the wall, placed his hand against it, and slid himself down to the floor to sit. Leaning back against the wall, he said, “Now we wait, I guess.”

“But for *what*? That’s what concerns me,” replied Ed.

“I hope Evan is okay. That bastard hit him pretty dang hard with that rifle.”

“Yeah, he dropped like a ragdoll. I wonder where they are.”

“There wasn’t a second helicopter, just Humvees, so I doubt they brought them this far. I can’t believe this is happening.”

“Me neither,” said Ed as he stood and walked over to the door, holding his ear to the wood.

“What’s up?” asked Nate.

Ed replied silently, placing his finger to his lips to ask for Nate’s silence. After a moment, he said, “Someone’s coming.”

Hurrying back over to Nate, he sat down next to him as the door opened and three men entered the room. Two of the men wore the UN Peacekeeper military uniforms, while the third wore pleated gray slacks and a tucked in, button-up white dress shirt.

“Hello, gentlemen,” the man said with a perfect American accent. “I’m sorry about all of this, but considering the hostile insurgent activity we’ve experienced, we can’t take any chances. I’m sure you two will check out just fine, but we’ve got strict protocol to follow.”

“Who’s *we*?” asked Ed. “And what part of your protocol required your friends here to confiscate my friend’s prosthetic leg?”

The man in civilian clothes looked at the two soldiers inquisitively and replied, “I’ll check on that for you. I’m not quite sure why that happened, but I’ll get to the bottom of it. Oh, by the way, my name is Chad Robbins. I’m with the Department of Homeland Security. I’m here to assist our friends from the United Nations as they help us work through these trying times.”

"They haven't been our 'friends' from what I've seen. They're more like an occupying force. I mean look at us, we are law-abiding U.S. citizens just struggling to survive in this messed up world, and here we sit in orange jumpsuits, being held by a foreign military force. What the hell kind of help is that?" said Ed, becoming more irritated by the moment. "And where the hell are we, anyway?"

Looking Ed squarely in the eye, the man said, "It is my understanding that you may be involved with a right-wing radical insurgent movement that's threatening the stability of the nation and its recovery efforts. Until we get that straightened out, you're not really in the position of being considered a law-abiding citizen. As for our location, we are safely in the hands of the United Nations at a secure location. That's all you need to know for now. More will come eventually, but we need more from you, as well."

"That's all a bunch of bull!" Ed snapped. "My friends and I were trying to find other people in the area who may want to establish some sort of trade and barter system, when we were ambushed and taken prisoner by your blue-helmet-wearing thug friends. Unless you want to try and squeeze us for sales tax or some bullshit interstate commerce thing, we haven't done a damn thing wrong. And how do you justify detaining us against our will without even telling us where we are?"

"Like I said, details will be disclosed as the situation allows. We have very strict protocols here that we must follow. Back to your involvement with the insurgency... if you are not, then how do you explain the stolen weapons?"

Pausing briefly, remembering the weapons taken from the gang that took Sabrina and her family, Ed replied, "We recovered those for you from some villainous scumbags. We don't know where they got them. All we know is they were using them against innocent people and we stopped them, as any good citizen should. I'm starting to feel like we need to see a lawyer to protect our constitutional rights."

"Rights? Under the Insurrection Act contained in Title 10 U.S.C. 331-335, we are acting entirely within our authority, granted to us by the president and by law."

"That's bull. There is no insurgency, just Americans trying to hold on to what is left of their own country."

"It's a new world, my friend. You are what we say you are. Now, I'll give you two a little time to think about how you want to proceed. You can cooperate with our investigation or face indefinite detention until some point in the future, when you can be prosecuted formally. The path you take from here is your choice." Turning to leave, Mr. Robbins stopped just short of the door, turned back to Ed and Nate, and said, "We'll be seeing you soon. Think about what I said and proceed carefully."

The two soldiers followed Mr. Robbins out the door, slamming and locking it from the outside behind them.

"What in the hell is happening here?" asked Nate, confused at how their lives had taken such a turn.

"I don't know," Ed said softly, in case there were listening devices in the room. "But whatever they do, they aren't just going to let us go for cooperating. And on top of that, we don't even have anything to cooperate with. We told them the truth already."

Nate whispered, "Whatever we do or say, we can't give anything away about where our homes are. We don't want them paying a visit to our families."

Ed nodded in reply and leaned back against the wall. "We are from Knoxville. We stayed in a tent city near Newport with other refugees before moving on," he said with a whisper.

Nate nodded. "I doubt that will match up with what Evan and Jason said if they were interrogated, but we will try."

"We barely knew those guys. We were hitchhikers."

"Roger that."

"Speaking of them, I just hope they are okay. I hope that even if we don't make it back, they do. It was stupid for so many of us to go on a supply run and leave the homesteads shorthanded. We should have stayed put and simply done without."

"Hindsight is twenty-twenty, my friend. We thought we were doing the right thing at the time. You're damned if you take action and damned if you don't. All we can do now is keep up the fight for home."

"Amen, brother. Amen."

Chapter Five: Fugate Road

Feeling something bump his foot, Evan was startled awake; he grabbed his rifle lying next to him.

"Whoa... throttle back, man. It's just me. It's your turn to stand watch," Jason said, holding his hands in the air in jest.

Regaining a grasp of his surroundings, Evan said, "Sorry, man. My nerves are getting shot. A man can act as calm and collected as he wants on the outside, but if this stuff doesn't get to him on the inside after a while, something is wrong."

"Yeah, this world is only fitting for a psychopath or a scoundrel," replied Jason. "I feel the same way. Every time I hear so much as a twig snap, I flinch and expect all hell to break loose."

"What time is it?"

"Four o'clock. Just wake me when the sun goes down."

"Damn, man, you should have got me up to relieve you sooner."

"Nah, man; you were sleeping well. Besides, I probably can't sleep, anyway. I can't stop worrying about Charlie and Jimmy, Ed and Nate, and the folks back home. We don't know anything about anyone but ourselves at this point, and that's not okay."

Standing to stretch, Evan yawned and said, "Well, give it a try at least. I'll wake you at sunset if nothing comes up between now and then."

Jason begrudgingly complied as Evan used a Sterno can and a stainless camping mug to warm a cup of instant coffee given to them by the Blue Ridge Militia. *Thank you, Quentin,* he thought as he smelled the aroma of the coffee as it began to heat.

The next few hours were uneventful, yet time felt as if it stood still; like Jason, Evan was anxious to get home. He felt responsible for whatever situations their friends and family might be in, as he was the one who led them away on the supply run to Hot Springs. He was haunted by the unknown, fearing the worst, but hoping for the best. *If nothing else, at least we were able to help Sabrina and the Gibbs family. But at what cost?* He asked himself. *Please, God. Let it be worth it. Let everyone be okay. Please let our families and friends be safe.*

As a tear rolled down his cheek, Evan's thoughts were interrupted by the sound of an ATV approaching at a rapid pace. Looking toward the direction of the sound, he saw a four-wheel drive utility ATV barreling down the railroad tracks, heading away from Del Rio. Clenching his AK74, he expected a pursuer to appear at any moment.

The rider was clearly throwing caution to the wind as he blasted down the tracks at full speed. Hearing rustling behind him, Evan turned to see Jason joining him.

"What's going on?" Jason asked.

"Not sure yet. Just a man on a quad in a hurry to get somewhere. He looked like he was coming from Del Rio. He was on the tracks going as fast as he could with no concerns of stealth."

"A lookout, perhaps, on his own personal Paul Revere ride?"

"Hmmm, could be. Off to warn the Blue Ridge Militia about the patrol into Del Rio, maybe?"

"Let's hope that's all it is..."

After a few moments of silence passed with no further activity, Jason said, "Damn, it's only six-thirty?"

"Yep. Let's get something to eat, saddle up the horses, then work our way back down to the tracks. It'll be getting dark by then. Then we'll get on the move."

"Roger that," Jason replied. "What's for dinner?"

"I've got dibs on the spaghetti with meat sauce MRE."

"You bastard. I wanted that one."

"Oh, you can have it then. It really doesn't matter to me. I was just kiddin' around," Evan said, as he chuckled at Jason.

"Nah, man, you called it. That's how it works. I was just bustin' your chops."

~~~~

After they had eaten, Evan and Jason saddled up their horses and led them back through the thick brush down to the road. Before stepping out into plain view, they listened carefully for a few moments. Being unable to see or hear any potential threats, they led their horses by the reins across the road and down to the railroad tracks.

Evan looked up at the sky and noted the bright, moonlit night. "At least we won't have to turn the headlights on."

"Ha... yeah," replied Jason with a chuckle. "Your jokes get worse and worse as time goes on."

"Probably because there is less and less to laugh about," Evan replied as he mounted his horse. "Besides, a good comedian draws from his audience, and you're all I've got to work with."

Replying with a crooked smile, Jason threw his leg over his horse, nudged him softly in the sides, and said, "I'll take point," as he passed Evan.

Evan allowed Jason to get about twenty-five yards ahead of him, then he nudged his horse and followed along. They had decided to keep a safe distance between them in the event they had to react to a roadblock or ambush; this would give the second man a chance to return fire and engage the threat from a different position. It would also allow the opportunity to provide cover for the other to facilitate an escape.

Passing under the bridge, they began to follow the tracks along the edge of the river. They took it slow, allowing their
~~~~

horses to navigate the large gravel and the railroad crossties. The railroad tracks were less than ideal for a horse, but it gave them a direct path and kept them off the road and out of direct view, while making reasonable time. The moon allowed ample light for the horses, making traversing the rugged railroad at night possible for Evan and Jason, who were relatively inexperienced riders.

Reaching the point where the railroad tracks merged with Fugate Road, Jason brought his horse to a stop and gave Evan the signal to join up with him. Arriving at Jason's side, Evan asked, "What's up?"

"From here on out, the road and the tracks pretty much run parallel to each other the rest of the way to Del Rio. We might as well stay on the road from here on in. We'll make better time and it's easier on the horses."

"Not to mention, easier on the horses means easier on my back."

"Damn, Ev, you're fallin' apart on me."

"I swear, I feel like I've aged ten years in the past one year," Evan said, twisting his torso to stretch his tight and achy back.

"You probably have. Not to mention you've had to work awfully hard to keep up with me."

"Yeah, that's it," Evan said with a chuckle. "How much further?"

"Ten miles or so."

"That means we're passing through Del Rio in the middle of the night. We've gotta go right past the church to get up in the hills to the Homefront. I think we should take the few extra minutes to stop and check in with Pastor Wallace. I hate to wake him, but slipping in at night may be the best way to not bring attention to ourselves, considering the patrol that came through earlier. We don't want to contact him by radio and give them a bearing on us with DF equipment," explained Evan.

"Agreed. It's probably not a good idea to bump into a UN patrol while carrying Russian-issued AK-74 service rifles just like theirs. We've already gotten into enough trouble being caught with stolen guns."

"These aren't stolen. They're battlefield pickups. That's a legitimate practice as old as war itself," Evan said jokingly.

"Yeah, let's just remind them that we killed their buddies back at the farm. That's probably what they are patrolling all the way out here for, anyway. Looking for evil, right-wing insurgents like us."

"Well, lead on then, brother. All this chattin' is gettin' us nowhere."

"Yep, let's get on with it," Jason said as he nudged his horse back into action.

After a few more miles, with Jason taking the lead, they came around a corner as the road veered to the left and saw two Humvees parked in the front yard of an old farmhouse. Jason gave Evan the signal to halt and then led his horse off the side of the road and into the brush and small trees following along the left-hand side of the road. With the river and railroad tracks off to the right and nowhere to take cover, their options were limited. He then signaled for Evan to join up with him at his position.

Evan slowly crept his horse up alongside Jason, and with a whisper, he asked, "What's up?" Then he saw the Humvees. "Oh... Shit."

"Yeah, exactly," Jason replied. "We can't just ride right through here on the road or the tracks if they are UN. I can't see any markings from here. Let's backtrack to the last side road on the left and find a place to ditch the horses while we take a better look and put a plan together on how to get around. We can't risk one of the horses making a noise up close."

"Good call," agreed Evan as he pulled on his horse's reins, turning its head to go back the way they came.

Approaching the road, Evan looked back at Jason and signaled for him to follow. About a hundred yards up the road, he dismounted and led his horse behind some trees, tying its reins to a large branch. Jason joined him and hitched his horse in the same fashion.

"How's your feet?" Jason asked.

"Could be better, could be worse. The extra gauze is padding the stitches pretty well. Luckily, I didn't have any lacerations on the balls of my feet; they're mostly on the heels and arches, so I can adjust my weight if it begins to give me problems. I would just prefer not to run."

"We'll take it slow to the farmhouse, then. You lead, so if they start giving you trouble, you'll set the pace."

"Roger that," Evan said as he slung his AK-74 over his shoulder. He double-checked that there was a round in the chamber and that the magazine was fully seated. He checked his Glock in the same manner, then said, "Let's go."

Replying with a nod, Jason took up the rear position as Evan led them through the trees and across one of the farmer's fields towards the house. Between them and the house was another tree-and-fence line separating the two fields. Evan planned on using the tree line as an observation point to assess the threat from a safe distance.

Wading through the knee-high field grass toward the tree line, the night's dew collected on their pants and boots, with wet seeding grass clinging to them like fleas on a dog. Annoyed at first, Evan thought, *On the bright side, we can drop to the prone position and disappear out here if need be.*

As Evan arrived at the tree line, he motioned for Jason to take a knee and wait. Scanning the area and determining that it was safe to advance, he signaled to Jason to join him at the tree line.

Slipping quietly beside him, Jason asked, "So, what do we have?"

"I've not seen any movement outside of the—"

A loud scream and the slam of the rear screen door of the house interrupted Evan's statement. They watched as a man was dragged into the backyard by two UN soldiers, with a third holding back a frantic woman who was trying to get to the man. Before Evan or Jason could comment to one another, one of the soldiers un-holstered his sidearm and, with a loud *POP* and a flash of light, executed the man. The woman instantly collapsed to her knees with a painful sob. Giving the woman no time to grieve for her husband, the soldiers dragged her back inside the house, her body limp, with no will to continue fighting their aggression.

"Damn it to hell! What the... Shit!" Evan exclaimed quietly.

"What the hell, man?" asked Jason.

"Damn it! Damn it! Damn it!" Evan repeated under his breath.

"Plan?" asked Jason smartly.

"We are clearly not in a position to just assault the place. Two battered and bruised homesteaders versus two Humvees full of commie bastards."

"How do you know the Humvees were full? Two guys could be in one and the third guy may have been solo."

"Possible, but doubtful," Evan replied. "They probably wouldn't have brought two vehicles with only three men. That would leave the second Humvee defenseless in the event they came under attack while on the move. There is probably a minimum of two per truck, but we'd be smart to assume more."

"Agreed," Jason replied.

"We've gotta get them outside. We can't just assault the house. How would we avoid hitting innocents?"

"Why do we keep getting mixed up in something every time we turn around? We're supposed to be on our way home, and here we are, planning another altercation."

"You couldn't live with yourself if you turned a blind eye to injustice, and neither could I. I guess that means we are just gonna keep getting into the middle of stuff until this world straightens itself out."

"Oh, well... live by the sword, die by the sword, right? You've gotta go somehow and that sure as hell beats slipping and falling in the shower, I guess. So again, what's the plan?"

"The first step of the plan is to try not to die by the sword tonight. The second... I dunno. We need to draw them out without alerting them to our presence. Ideas?" Evan asked.

"We could risk a horse."

"Risk a horse doing what?"

"We could rig up some sort of makeshift noisemaker. A bell would be perfect, but in lieu of that, we could use our stainless camp mugs tied together, then hang them beneath the saddle from a strap underneath. We could lead the horse over here, then send it running in front of the house. Surely, they'd check out the rattling noise out front."

"What if only one soldier comes out to check on it? If we took him out, the rest would hunker down and wait for backup."

"True. What are you thinking?" asked Jason.

"Steal a Humvee."

"Huh?" Jason asked in a curious tone.

"If these guys are lower-level soldiers... uh, I mean peacekeepers, out on patrol, they'd have their asses handed to them if they went back without a Humvee. How would they explain that? No, I think they wouldn't want to deal with that. I'm thinking they'd go after it in a panic."

"And just how do you propose doing that?"

"Piece of cake," Evan said with a sneaky grin, his face illuminated by the moonlit night.

Chapter Six: Deprivation

Unable to sleep with thoughts and fears for Peggy, Zack, and their families back home, Nate lay on the floor of the former break room-turned-confinement quarters, staring at the ceiling. He wondered what time it was. With no windows and no watch, he could only guess it was the middle of the night. Ed had been asleep for several hours, snoring loudly, which made Nate feel good, knowing his friend was getting some much-needed rest. The next morning would undoubtedly bring a long and trying day.

As Nate closed his eyes, resolved to catch at least a nap, a loud banging sound against the door startled both him and Ed. The men sat up, dazed and confused as to what had just happened. They stared at the door, awaiting the unknown... but nothing. Nate could hear his heart pounding in his chest, as the silence was deafening. His and Ed's excited breathing were the only sounds audible over his beating heart.

"What the hell was that?" asked Ed.

"I don't know. It sounded like something smacked up against the door."

"Probably just some jerk Blue Helmet screwing with us."

"Yep," replied Nate quietly.

After several minutes of silence, Ed lay back down on the floor and said, "Screw those bastards. I'm going back to sleep."

"Good luck," replied Nate. "What time do you think it is? I'm getting hungry."

"Hell if I know. I was asleep for a bit; it's got to be late. I hear ya, though. I'm starved."

"I wonder what's for breakfast?" asked Nate jokingly.

"Stress Benedict with a side of hard time... I would imagine."

"Mmmm, my favorite."

"But seriously, I'm far from that point yet, but at least there are lots of cockroaches in here to live on for a while... if it comes to that," Ed said, pointing to Nate's arm.

"Damn it!" Nate shouted, knocking a roach to the floor. "I freaking hate those disgusting little bastards."

"Me, too. I think I'll sleep with my fingers in my ears to keep them from laying eggs in my brain."

"Damn it, Ed! Why did you have to go and say a thing like that? Now I'm gonna be paranoid."

"It's good to be paranoid in this world, my friend. Fear and paranoia can be valuable tools when managed." Ed put his arms behind his head and closed his eyes. "Not that I'm not enjoying the company, but I'm gonna try to get some sleep."

"Cool, I'll stand the first roach watch," Nate said, creeped out by the thought of sleeping on the floor in a room with a pest problem.

~~~~

Giving way to his roach phobia, Nate's heavy eyelids began to close after what felt like several hours of paranoid insect vigilance. As soon as he gave in to the relaxation of the onset of sleep, loud music startled him awake. "What the...?" he said, immediately sitting back up and looking around.

"Is that classical music?" asked Ed, again confused and cloudy-headed from his rude awakening.

"It sounds like Russian folk music or something like that. I can just picture some guy in a furry hat with his arms crossed jumping around doing that funny dance."

"Oh, those bastards. I swear they are just trying to get under our skin."

"Well, I'd rather be tortured with music instead of getting beat with a rubber hose, or worse."
~~~~

"Ha. Yeah, good point," replied Ed with a chuckle. "This must be some new UN-approved torture technique since they disapprove of good ol' water-boarding and stuff."

"Screw these guys, I'm going back to sleep," Ed said, talking loudly over the music. "Good night, John Boy."

"Good night, Paw," replied Nate.

"Paw? Hell, I'm not old enough to be your Paw."

"Sorry, man; that show pre-dates me. That's all I've got."

"You didn't watch it on re-runs?"

"Nope, I was probably watching the cartoon channel about the time that show finally faded away."

"Damn Generation Z's, or whatever they call you. You guys missed out on all the good stuff. When I was a kid, we had quality cartoons, where a big rooster would beat the crap out of a dog with a two by four, or a coyote would get an anvil dropped on his head. You guys got a talking sponge or whatever that damn thing is."

"We must have been in here longer than we thought," replied Nate.

"Why?"

"Because we're being held prisoner by an occupying foreign military force, and we're arguing over old TV shows and who had the better cartoons growing up."

"Good point. Then again, maybe we actually got killed in the ambush, and this is just limbo. And for the record, it's not an argument. My generation wins hands down."

Nate chuckled. "If this is limbo, it appears the UN are the ones staffing hell, and they are waiting for permission to escort us there."

With a mutual laugh, the conversation faded away as both Ed and Nate attempted to ignore the loud music to get some sleep.

~~~~
~~~~

Running through a field, trying to escape, attack dogs were gaining on Nate as he attempted to keep up with Ed. "Come on, Nate! Run! They're gaining on you!" Ed shouted as he pulled away from Nate, who was having a hard time running at full speed with his prosthetic leg.

"Just go! Get out of here!" yelled Nate as one of the attack dogs lunged forward, pulling off Nate's prosthesis, causing him to crash to the ground as several vicious dogs piled on top of him, tearing his orange jumpsuit from his body and... "Help me!" Nate screamed aloud, sitting up, realizing that he was still in the old break room.

"Relax. Relax. You were just dreaming," Ed said, trying to calm him.

It was then that Nate realized there was a real dog barking and clawing at the break room door. Ed looked at him. "I guess they realized the loud music wasn't working. That dog has been at it for about ten minutes."

"Holy crap, that was a messed-up dream," Nate said, catching his breath.

"What was it about?"

"I'll explain later. What's with the dog?"

"I don't know. You'd think there was a steak tied to the door, or something, the way that thing has been going at it. It scared the crap out of me at first, but I figured they would have turned it loose on us by now if they were going to."

"Why didn't you wake me?" asked Nate.

"Ah, hell, you were finally getting some sleep. Besides, if they did let it in here on us, I figured you'd rather die in your sleep, anyway."

"Ha, ha," replied Nate.

Ed and Nate sat in silence for the next ten minutes, staring at the door, wondering if the dog would be let inside any minute. Rational thought told them it was just a psychological game, but these weren't rational times. Eventually, it sounded like a handler led the dog away down the hallway.

"What's next?" asked Nate, frustrated by the strangeness and uncertainty of the situation.

"I don't know, but I'm starting to just want to take the rubber hose beating and just get it over with."

Listening intently for what seemed like an hour, Ed and Nate waited for the next game their captors might decide to play with them. However, there was only absolute silence. The silence they thought would be welcome was maddening, as their minds raced through all of the possibilities of what their next day or even their next moment may bring.

"I wish we could at least turn the damn lights off," grumbled Ed.

"You know, this seems like pretty steady electricity, and I don't hear any generators, either," added Nate.

"If this is Atlanta—and a major staging area—I imagine they have probably restored the basic utilities for their own use."

"You know, it's funny..."

"What?"

"All this time, wishing we could have good and steady electricity, now that we have it, we just want to turn it off," said Nate with a chuckle as he laid his head back on his hands and closed his eyes.

"I just hope those bastards come back soon."

"Why?" Nate opened his eyes and turned to Ed with a confused look.

"Because I've gotta see a man about a horse," replied Ed.

"You've gotta what?"

"I've got business to take care of."

Still confused, Nate said, "Huh?"

"For God's sake, man! I've got to take a dump, and we don't have a restroom."

"Oh... Yeah, please don't do that in here."
"Trust me, I'll try."

Chapter Seven: Unavoidable Conflict

Crawling through the overgrown grass, Jason had to stop occasionally and peek his head up to get a view of his progress, as well as check the house for signs of activity. *Only twenty more yards to go,* he thought as he pressed on through the wet grass.

Keeping his eye on the front and east side of the house in order to provide cover for Jason if trouble were to arise, Evan found himself wishing he had a red-dot sight or a scope with an illuminated reticle. The black iron sights on the AK-74 were lacking for nighttime engagements beyond CQB (close quarters battle) distances.

Finally reaching the Humvee, while still lying in the grass on his stomach with his neck stretched back and his head up, Jason read the stenciled UN logo on the door and thought, *United, my ass. Unwelcome Nazis is more like it.*

The Humvee was parked at an angle to the house, helping to conceal his view as he got up on his knees, opened the door, and slipped inside. Leaning his rifle on the passenger front seat with the stock on the floor, he scanned the vehicle for things that he may find useful in dealing with its owners once they heard him drive away. His search rewarded him with a zip-up, olive-drab canvas bag containing at least ten AK-74 magazines loaded with steel-cased 5.45x39mm ammo. He tossed it on the passenger seat next to his rifle for easy access when his time for retreat arrived.

Continuing to search the rear cargo area, he found a Russian RG-6 grenade launcher, along with a case of 40mm grenades. *Jackpot!* he thought as a smile came across his face.

"Now, back to business," he whispered, attempting to prepare himself for the shit that was guaranteed to hit the fan. Jason was familiar with the M998A1 configuration of the

Humvee from his Army days. Quickly re-familiarizing himself with the controls, he rotated the rotary ignition switch to the RUN position, waited for the wait-to-start lamp to extinguish, and then held the switch in the start position while the diesel engine quickly shook itself to life. Releasing the switch back to the run position, he released the parking brake, threw it in gear, and tore out of the front yard like a madman before any weapons could be trained on him at such a close range.

Evan watched as two soldiers immediately ran out onto the front porch and began to yell inside the house, as if shouting orders.

Jason drove onto Fugate Road, jerked the wheel hard to the right, and sped away in Evan's direction. Wanting to disable the vehicle, Jason then yanked the steering wheel to the left; the Humvee exited the pavement and crashed hard into the railroad tracks. The sharp impact nearly bounced Jason out of his seat as he continued toward the river, where he dropped off a three-foot high ledge, hi-centering the vehicle as its front tires dangled in the water.

Shaken by the impact of his body slamming into the steering wheel, Jason quickly regained his composure, grabbed his rifle, the canvas bag, and the RG-6, and then headed out the driver's side door. As he leaped out of the vehicle, his foot slipped off of the ledge, raking his shin against the sharp and jagged rocks of the riverbank.

"Damn it," he mumbled from the pain. Gathering his cumbersome load, he ran thirty yards over the uneven terrain beyond the truck and hunkered down behind a mound of rocks and brush. Unzipping the canvas bag to get his newfound extra magazines within an easy reach, he flipped his AK's selector switch to the center position for fully automatic fire. Leaning the rifle against the rocks, he then removed the RG-6 launcher from its case, loaded six rounds into the cylinder, rotated it shut, and set it next to himself on the rocks.

Now all he could do was wait. Leaving the Humvee running to create a distraction and to cover the noise of his own movements, Jason could hear his heart pounding out of his chest over the noisy idle of the GM 6.5L diesel engine.

Evan watched as two other soldiers exited the farmhouse and joined their comrades. Now totaling four soldiers, they ran for the remaining Humvee. One of the men shouted orders to the others in what sounded like Russian, then they split up—two on foot and two inside the remaining Humvee.

Tracking the soldiers with the barrel of his rifle, Evan watched as the Humvee crept down the road toward Jason, one man on foot on each side of the vehicle. From his hidden position in the tree line, Evan cautiously awaited the proper time to initiate the fight, unaware if other threats remained in the house, which was moving into his six o'clock position as he turned to visually follow the immediate threat.

Reaching the crashed Humvee, the man in the passenger seat motioned for one of the soldiers on foot to move ahead and check it out. The soldier cautiously approached the noisily running vehicle; the last thing he saw was a flash of light further down the rocky river bank. The shot ended his life before he even heard the crack of the round's report.

Witnessing Jason's opening shot, Evan opened fire on the Humvee as it sped away in reverse, leaving the remaining foot soldier exposed as Jason's fully automatic barrage of sixty-grain, high-speed 5.45mm projectiles riddled his body with holes, dropping him to the ground.

Evan continued his barrage of fire on the Humvee as Jason picked up the grenade launcher and lobbed a 40mm grenade toward the retreating Humvee. Coming up short, the round exploded three feet in front of the vehicle.

Evan was certain he had killed the soldier giving the orders in the passenger's seat, yet maintained his fire to keep the vehicle on the defensive and to maintain the two-pronged attack that had caught them off-guard.

Jason fired another round, this time adjusting his trajectory and scoring a direct hit on the hood of the vehicle, sending aluminum sheet metal and fragments into the windshield of the Humvee. Jason fired another grenade as the driver, battered and bloodied, opened the door and fell onto the ground. The second grenade went directly inside, destroying any chances of survival for the remaining occupant.

Feeling a searing pain rip through his side, followed by small impacts off to his left, Evan rolled onto his back and returned fire toward the house. A fifth soldier was standing on the front porch, sending bullets randomly into the tree line where Evan remained concealed. *Shit, shit, shit,* Evan said to himself as he felt warm, wet blood run down his side. Still concealed from the shooter, Evan focused his eyes on his front sight as best he could with the available moonlight. He aimed a little low and fired a short fully automatic burst of four rounds at his attacker. As the recoil made his barrel rise, several of the rounds whizzed by the soldier; however, two of them were planted firmly into his torso, dropping him to the porch and taking him out of the fight.

As he focused on the house, Evan heard Jason shout, “Clear!”

Evan responded, feeling a sharp pain in his side as he shouted, “Covered!” He didn’t want to relay to Jason that the scene was “clear,” just in case another shooter remained inside.

Advancing toward the tree line, Jason arrived at Evan’s position and said, “Report.”

“A fifth man was in the house; he’s down. He sprayed the tree line with random suppressing fire and hit me.”

“Holy shit, where?” Jason asked.

"My left side. I felt around. I think it went straight. No organs. Just muscle and tissue. My love handles will never be the same."

"Hell, you'll be lucky if someday you can live life lazily enough to get your love handles back. So what's with the house?"

"Other than him, I haven't seen any activity. We'll have to clear it and check on the woman. By the way, how the hell did you take out the Humvee like that? What did you use?"

"I found a gear bag full of prepared '74 mags, as well as a cool six-shot RG-6 grenade launcher. I'll get the house. You stay here and keep still in case that wound is worse than you think. You'll just be a liability hurting and bleeding all over the place. I'll come back and get you and we'll check you out and dress the wound. Just cover me the best you can from here."

"Roger that," Evan said, wincing with pain as he held pressure on his side with his left hand.

Jason slipped through the tree line and carefully worked his way to the house. He kept his rifle at the ready and the safety/selector lever on semi-auto, as he didn't want to let any rounds fly without complete accountability for each, knowing that innocent people could still be alive inside. He crept around the back of the house, up against the siding, slicing the pie as he went. Reaching the back of the house, he scanned the windows, which were just above his head due to the house's tall block foundation. Seeing no apparent threats, he stepped onto the porch and took a knee by the back door, staying clear of any windows and the door itself. He then yelled inside, "This is the Blue Ridge Militia. The house is surrounded. Your comrades have been captured; make yourself known and exit the house, unarmed, with your hands above your head, and you will be spared. Resist and you will die."

After a moment of silence, Jason heard a woman's voice mutter, "Please... Please don't hurt us."

"No one is gonna hurt you, ma'am. Are there any more UN soldiers in the house?"

She sniffled and replied, "No, they all ran out when their truck drove away."

"Do you know how many there were total?"

"Five, I think. I don't know. I have no idea what just happened. They killed him. They killed my husband—they killed her father," the woman said as she broke down into tears.

It was then that Jason heard the muffled sobs of a crying child. "Ma'am, we got them all. They can't hurt you now. I'm coming in, but only to double-check your house and make sure it's safe."

"Okay," she said with a strained voice.

Jason slowly stood up and peeked into the house. Seeing no threats, he stepped inside with his rifle safely pointed at the floor, but ready in case he needed it. Stepping into the living room, where a fire in the fireplace was lit, he saw the woman. The young mother, in her late twenties or early thirties, held her preschool-aged daughter tight. The young, terrified girl cried silently, with the only sound being her short, interrupted breaths as she nearly hyperventilated. The mother's shirt had been torn open, her bra mostly exposed and her face red and swollen—clearly from abuse.

He continued through the small, two-bedroom house, clearing each room as he went. Once he was satisfied that the threat was gone, he returned to the living room. "Is that your husband?" he asked, pointing at the back of the house.

She wiped the sniffle from her nose and nodded. "Yes." Once again, her eyes welled up with tears.

"This place isn't safe right now. They may have friends on their way to help. Do you have somewhere nearby that we can take you? A safe place, with family, maybe?"

"My father's place is only a mile from here," she said, beginning to stand.

"Can we get there without using the main road?"

"Yes; well, not by car, but we can cut across the mountain," she said, pointing at the mountain ridge behind her property. "We have a trail through the woods we use to get there. It's quicker than driving around and no one can see us back there. It's an old log home near the top of a hill all to itself. We have an ATV in the barn that we usually use to get over there."

"Good. Get some things for your daughter and yourself. I'll get your ATV and my friend. Are the keys in it?"

"The electric start hasn't worked for years. My husband bypassed the key and just uses the pull starter on the side of the motor. It's kind of a piece of junk, but it works for us. After you get it running, you have to rub the loose wire that's taped to the handlebars against the metal to ground out the ignition to kill the motor. That, or shut the gas off, but it's harder to get started back the next time if you do that."

Jason stood there looking blank for a moment, caught off guard by the level of detail in her explanation.

She then asked, "Your friend? You mean there is only one other militia member with you?"

"We're not really militia. We've got some newly acquired friends there now, though. My friend and I live in the hills just past Del Rio. We're trying to get home while avoiding the new international presence in the area... not so successfully, I might add."

"Are you..." she paused after starting to ask a question.

"Are we what?"

"Are you The Guardians?"

Pausing briefly, he said, "That's just an urban legend. I'll be right back. Get your stuff. We've got to get moving."

Chapter Eight: Power and Persuasion

As the door opened, Nate flinched with the realization that he had finally fallen asleep; his heart raced for the moment it took to regain his situational awareness. He sat up as he heard Mr. Robbins say, "Gentlemen, I apologize. They were supposed to bring you some fresh bedding and some cots. I can't believe you had to sleep on the cold, hard floor. I'll have a talk with them about that."

"You need to have a talk with them about a lot of stuff. Those bastards tormented us all night," Nate said with a raised voice.

"Tormented? How?"

Ed stood up. "They banged on the door, played annoyingly horrible music at full volume, they had a dog scratching at the door and barking. They were intentionally screwing with us."

"I'll check on all of those things, gentlemen, and I do apologize. We aren't here to harass and punish you. We just need to check you both out and get a little more information from you. Now, I know you've got to be hungry. These two security professionals behind me," he said, motioning towards his UN escorts, "are going to accompany you gentlemen to the facilities to freshen up. They'll then bring you to my office where we will chat and have lunch together. It's almost noon; you must be starving."

Ed and Nate looked at each other, not trusting a word Mr. Robbins was saying, but desperate for a meal and personal relief.

Mr. Robbins then said, "Okay, then, that's the plan. I'll see you gentlemen in a few." He turned and walked out the door.

Ed helped Nate up to his good leg, put Nate's arm around his shoulder, and followed their escorts out of the room and down the hall to the restroom.

~~~~

Mr. Robbins looked up from his desk as Ed and Nate were led into the room. "Gentlemen. So nice to see you again."

Mr. Robbins nodded at their escorts, who then quickly left the room. They closed the door behind them, leaving Ed and Nate alone with Mr. Robbins.

"Here you go, gentlemen," he said, as he retrieved a pizza box from behind his desk, opening it for Ed and Nate to see a sausage and pepperoni pizza with extra cheese and black olives.

Ed and Nate looked at each other in disbelief. They hadn't seen a pizza delivery box in longer than they remembered.

Mr. Robbins, noticing their silence, said, "Oh, I forgot something. I'll be right back." He got up and left the room, leaving Ed and Nate alone.

"Dude, this is like a *Twilight Zone* episode. Freakin' delivery pizza..."

"I know, man. I'm afraid to touch it. I'm starving, but I don't believe it's really sitting right here on the desk in front of me. I feel like I'm gonna wake up any minute with one of those damn guards banging on the door or something."

"Yeah... me, too," Nate replied as Mr. Robbins re-entered the room.

Laying dinner plates and napkins in front of each of them, Mr. Robbins took a slice of pizza for himself and said, "I know it's just pizza, but there is no reason not to be civilized. Dig in, gentlemen."

Nate looked at Ed, shrugged his shoulders, and took a slice of pizza, devouring it almost instantly. Ed followed suit, both of them becoming lost in the bizarre moment.

"There is a pleasant little mom-and-pop pizza place just down the street from here. They make the best pizza and
~~~~

calzones," Mr. Robbins said with a smile as he took another bite.

Looking at Nate with a raised eyebrow, Ed turned to Mr. Robbins and said, "You mean like a pizza business, with electricity and everything you need to operate?"

"Um... why, yes; the people here are quite pleased with the government's presence. Their lives have virtually returned to normal."

"Virtually," replied Ed with a skeptical tone.

"Yes, well... on a local basis at least. We make sure they have what they need and they take care of us in return."

"I'm sure the Nazis got that same treatment from the local merchants everywhere they occupied, as well," Ed replied with contempt.

With a rather unpleasant look on his face, Mr. Robbins paused before taking his next bite and said, "Excuse me?"

"Oh, nothing; I was just rambling. I'm just a history buff."

Mr. Robbins brushed off the comment and got back on track. "So anyway, I checked up on things and the security officer for the facilities here assured me you would be getting proper bedding very soon. He asked that I extend to you an apology on his behalf. Also, as for the things you heard last night... I hate to downplay it, but it appears that perhaps the stress of the situation may have simply gotten to you both. He assured me no one was banging on the door on purpose. Perhaps one of the cleaning personnel bumped the door with their janitorial cart as they passed by. They do work the third shift. The dog you heard was probably just the explosives detection dog we have here on site. As for the music, our guys get a little lonely and bored and just let loose sometimes. You've got to keep in mind that they are away from their friends and families back home to help keep us safe and restore order here. They are making quite the sacrifice on our behalf.

He assured me, however, that he would try to keep things quiet in the future."

"So, what's next for us and how long is this future you're referring to?" asked Nate.

"That depends on the results of just a few little matters we need to take care of."

"And what would that be?" asked Ed, crossing his arms and leaning back in anticipation of what might be coming next.

"We're going to need to take some photographs of both of you for one, and secondly, we will need to extract some DNA samples, preferably from saliva. And lastly, we need to take some basic fingerprints. It's all to match with the growing amount of evidence we have in regards to the insurgency. Being apprehended while in possession of stolen restricted-use weapons puts you both at the top of our list of concerns."

As Ed began to speak, Mr. Robbins interrupted. "And just so you know ahead of time, this is not a request. We will be taking the photographs and samples regardless of your consent. The only variable is how easy or difficult the process will be for you. Now, before we go any further, I need written and signed statements from both of you, with as much detail as you can provide. We need to know how you came to be in possession of the stolen weapons, as well as any and all cases of your involvement with insurgent groups like the Blue Ridge Militia, the Southeast Militia, or any other group taking up arms against the government.

"In front of each of you, you will find pens and paper. I'll leave you for a few moments to allow the two of you to discuss between yourselves the level of your cooperation. It's simple, really; we treat people well who treat us well. Those who choose to work against us will find us doing the same—only, we have much greater strength and resources. I'll be back in about twenty minutes. The security personnel will remain by the door should you need anything."

Watching as the door closed behind Mr. Robbins, Nate asked, "So what the hell do we do?"

"We eat every bite of his damn pizza, then tell him to kiss our flag-waving, freedom-loving, gun-and-religion-clinging, patriotic American asses... that's what," replied Ed, as he reached for another slice of pizza.

Unable to take such a flippant stance on the heavy-hearted subject, Nate said, "I have a feeling that no matter what we do, we're screwed."

"Of course we are. They're playing the good cop game right now. I'm sure we'll meet the bad cop soon enough. Every damn word that man says is part of a well-choreographed game. He's a professional. Now hurry and help me eat the rest of this pizza before that treasonous jerk gets back."

Chuckling to himself, Nate reluctantly replied, "Yeah, I guess you're right."

~~~~

Exactly twenty minutes later, Mr. Robbins returned to the office to find Ed and Nate full from gorging themselves on the entire pizza. Not even a piece of crust was left.

"I see you enjoyed the meal. I'll make sure I pass along my compliments to the proprietors of the shop that prepared it. Now, let's see what we've got." He sat down, donned his reading glasses, and slid Ed's paper closer to him so he could read it. Quickly looking it over, he gazed at Ed over the top of his reading glasses and began to read aloud. *"We found the weapons. We did not steal them. We were going to give them back. Thanks for the pizza. Love... Ed."*

Leaning back in his chair, Mr. Robbins sighed while removing his glasses, rubbed his hands over his face with frustration, and said with a well-rehearsed smile, "Well, gentlemen, if that's all you have for me, that's all I needed to
~~~~

know. There is no sense in me wasting any more of your time. The gentlemen at the door will remain there until our technician comes by to take your samples. Have a nice day, gentlemen," he said as he stood up and walked to the door. Reaching for the knob, he paused, turned to Ed and Nate, and said, "If you think of anything else you may want to share with me, just let the security personnel know and they will find me." And with that, Mr. Robbins left the room.

"You know what?" Ed said, turning to Nate with a sneaky grin.

"What?"

"This is like the times as a kid when you really pissed your parents off and you expected them to jerk their belt off and tan your hide right there, only to have them just walk away. The unknown was always worse than just taking the whooping."

Chapter Nine: Tipping Point

Arriving back at the farmhouse with their horses, Jason dismounted while Evan remained in the saddle, due to his injury. He noticed that she had changed into a new shirt and had a bag for her and her daughter ready by the backdoor. He began to introduce Evan to the woman and her daughter then paused. "I'm sorry, ma'am, but I didn't catch your name."

Still wiping tears from her eyes while holding her daughter close, she said, "I'm Vanessa Taylor, and this is my daughter, Audrey. My husband was Bill Taylor. What—" She interrupted herself to wipe her eyes and clear her throat. "What are we going to do with my husband? We can't just leave him out there like that," she said as her daughter buried her face in her arms, refusing to face life's new cruel reality.

"I'll get him in the barn while Evan stays here with you. We can work out something more permanent once we reach your father's place. For now, though, the most important thing is to get a move on and get away from here before any of their friends come looking for them. Why don't you two go into the house for now? Evan will keep an eye on the house from his horse and when I'm ready for you, I'll come and get you."

Nodding yes, she led her daughter back into the house and closed the door. Evan looked at Jason. "Are you sure you don't need my help?"

"You'll only hurt yourself worse. Just stay put; I'll be back."

Evan nodded in reply as Jason headed off to deal with his tasks at hand. After about fifteen minutes, he came back to the house and said, "Mr. Taylor is taken care of for now, but the four-wheeler is a no go. I just can't get the damn thing to start. We can't keep dickering with it, either. Can you haul the little girl? If so, I can give Mrs. Taylor a ride. We'll leave less of a trail that way, too."

"Sure thing. If she'll let me, that is," replied Evan.

Jason stepped onto the porch and knocked on the door. Mrs. Taylor answered and Jason explained the situation to her in detail. Vanessa shook her head no and said with a rugged defiance, "I can get it started. We aren't leaving it. We might need it later."

"Okay, ma'am, but—"

"No buts!" she exclaimed as she marched through the backyard toward the barn with young Audrey in tow. Reaching the barn, the mother and her daughter went inside and out of sight.

"We'll at least let her try," said Jason in frustration. "I tried everything, though, and it just wouldn't start. We can't stick around here messin' with it much longer, either."

Just as he finished his sentence, they heard the ATV rev to life in the barn, followed by Vanessa riding out with Audrey on the back of the seat behind her. Evan chuckled and said, "Tried everything, huh?" He had a sly grin on his face, but it was followed immediately with a pain-filled wince.

"Keep it up, funny man, and I'll poke you in the side."

Pulling the ATV alongside the back porch to retrieve her bags, Vanessa said, "I don't know what your problem was, all I did was flip the choke on, made sure the ground wire wasn't touching anything, and pulled the cord a few times."

"Ahhh, the choke," Jason said, smacking his own forehead with the palm of his hand.

Strapping her bags into place on the ATV's cargo racks with bungee cords, Vanessa rejoined her daughter on the seat and said, "I'll lead the way. I'll try to go slow so you can keep up. Be careful; it's slick and rocky on the trail."

"Lead the way, ma'am," Jason said with a tip of his hat.

With that, Evan and Jason both nudged their horses and off they went, trying their best to keep up with Vanessa. *This is supposed to be slow?* Evan thought as every jolt from the horse's stride sent pain shooting through his side.

~~~~

As they entered the woods, Vanessa slowed to a stop to allow the men to catch up. Pulling their horses alongside her, Evan looked back, pointed, and said, "See those lights off in the distance?"

"Yep," Jason replied.

"Probably the friends of Vanessa's not-so-welcomed guests back there. Let's keep moving."

Jason nodded in agreement as they all slipped off into the darkness of the trees.

~~~~

After navigating the rugged hillside trail with just the moonlight to guide them, they popped onto an old gravel road. "This is Daddy's driveway," Vanessa said as she pressed the thumb throttle of the ATV and proceeded up the road.

"How you hangin' in there, old man?" Jason asked Evan.

"I'm hangin', but it's sure as hell not fun," replied Evan, trying to get a peek at his wound through the tear in his shirt.

"Quit poking at it; we'll get you taken care of. Let's keep moving," Jason said as he kicked his horse into action and raced off to keep Vanessa in sight.

"Damn it," Evan mumbled under his breath as he followed Jason's lead.

After a few more bends in the road, they came to an old two-story log home that appeared to have been built a significant time in the past. The rugged old structure had a character that just couldn't be found in modern construction. The large log home had a natural rock chimney on each end of the primary structure, which Evan immediately noticed; such a layout hadn't been used extensively since the power grid was established and everyone began to rely on modern furnaces to heat their homes.

As Vanessa brought the ATV to a stop, two tall, rough-looking men stepped out onto the porch. Vanessa lifted Audrey off of the ATV and ran to the open arms of one of the men while the other kept a watchful eye on Evan and Jason, his hands clutching a lever-action rifle with a classically styled walnut stock.

Erupting into tears, Vanessa began to explain in detail the events of the night to her father. A seriously distressed look came over his face as he pointed towards Evan and Jason saying, "Get those two inside right away." He turned and walked back inside, carrying Audrey in his right arm and his left wrapped around his daughter's shoulder.

"Come on in, gentlemen," said the second man while gesturing for them to follow.

As they entered the home, a woman in her mid to late fifties ushered Vanessa and Audrey into the back room while the men remained in the living room to discuss the events of the night. "Fellas, I've got to thank you for what you did back there. It's devastating what happened to Bill, and we will no doubt have a breakdown around here once it all soaks in, but I'm just thankful those bastards didn't get any further. There's no telling what they would have done if you hadn't come along. If that had happened, I'd be a dead man tomorrow because I would have snapped and set out to kill every damn one of them myself. My name is Carl Dennison. This is my brother, Ted Dennison," he said, gesturing to the other man.

"No problem, sir," Jason replied. "We would want someone to do the same for our families."

"Speaking of your families, where are you two from and how did you stumble across my daughter's home in the middle of the night?"

"It's a long story, sir."

"We've got time," replied Carl. "Besides, Vanessa's aunt—Ted's wife—is getting some things together to patch up your buddy here. Vanessa told us he was hurt. Catch us up while we wait."

Acquiescing to Carl's request, Jason told the tale of their journey from the Homefront with Ed, Nate, Charlie, and Jimmy, as well as their altercations with the UN peacekeeping forces. He kept the details of their location vague for security reasons but told him just enough to ensure the integrity of his story. Considering what they had just witnessed back at Vanessa's home, he felt confident that he and Evan were in good company and that they shared a common foe with this family.

"I was afraid it was gonna come to this, eventually," added Ted. "Those sons-of-bitches have been cruising all around Del Rio lately, knocking on doors, harassing people, looking for information on any militia activity. I imagine part of that is compliments of you fellas?"

Evan spoke up and said, "We're not fans of theirs, that's for sure. And they aren't peacekeepers at all. They're a damn occupying force and nothing more, here to carve out their own slice of the American pie."

Carl's jaw clenched as he gritted his teeth with building rage. "Well, those bastards are in the wrong place if they think the people of Del Rio will simply roll over on their own friends and neighbors. A lot of folks here have been quietly linking up with the Blue Ridge Militia, and we won't put up with this crap. What they've done tonight is an act of war. I don't give a damn if they are here by authority of the president; that man is nothing but a complicit traitor, anyway. It's an act of war on the people, and the people will take things to whatever level those bastards take it. What you two did tonight was only the beginning."

"Are you two affiliated with the militia?" asked Evan.

Looking at Ted before he answered, Carl replied, "We are familiar with them."

"Oh, by the way," Jason interrupted. "We saw headlights rolling into Vanessa's place as we left. Looked like another Humvee from a distance, but I suppose I could be mistaken. Anyway, I put Bill in the barn, in one of the stalls. I didn't really have anything appropriate to put him in—we were sort of in a rush. I know you'll want to go back a take care of him properly, but I highly recommend against that for now. They're gonna have eyes on that place. They'll want to make an example of anyone involved."

"Understood," replied Carl. "Bill was a good man. He wouldn't want anyone risking their lives when there is nothing we can do for him, anyway. The best way to honor him will be to stand strong and not let those bastards think they can treat our neighbors like this."

Just then, Vanessa's aunt entered the room and said, "I'm all set up for Evan. I believe Vanessa said that's his name."

"Yes, ma'am, it is," replied Evan, standing to be courteous and respectful.

"Evan, this is my wife, Patricia," Ted explained. "She'll get you patched up for now. Then you two guys can rest up before you head out. I'm sure they'll be flying overhead searching for the culprits in no time. Those damn drones are quiet, too, and can observe from a distance. If you aren't careful, they'll follow you home and that would not be a good thing. I know you're almost home and are anxious, but don't get sloppy and blow it now."

"Thank you, sir. We'll take you up on that," said Jason as Evan was led into the next room.

Chapter Ten: In-processing

As the forensics technician who collected the DNA and fingerprint samples from Ed and Nate left the room, Nate looked at Ed and said, “Now what?”

“Whatever it is, I wouldn’t count on our situation improving any. We didn’t make any friends today. Not that anything we could have possibly said could have truly served us well. We were being used, regardless. He was trying to play us like a fiddle—wax our strings, tune us up, and then expect us to play his tune.”

Nate nodded in agreement as the door behind them opened abruptly, with three soldiers walking into the room. “Up!” ordered one of the soldiers sharply. Ed and Nate complied, Nate balancing on one leg and leaning on Ed with his hand.

As Ed helped Nate out of the room, the soldiers following closely behind, Ed began to turn right to return from the direction they came, only to be corrected sharply by an AK74 muzzle brake to the back, followed by the order, “No! To the left.”

Here we go, Ed thought as he and Nate complied with the short, but forceful command. *The vacation must be over.*

They were then led out of the building for their first time since their incarceration. “Into the truck,” the soldier commanded, pointing in the direction of an awaiting cargo van. The soldiers led Ed and Nate to the truck and shoved them inside; the doors slammed shut behind them, leaving them in total darkness.

As the truck began to move, Ed said to Nate, “Here we go. If we get separated, keep up the fight. If you get out of here someday and I don’t, keep up the fight. No matter what, keep up the fight. If people like us just lie down and take the hand that is dealt us all across the country... let's just say I would hate to even imagine things going down that way."

For the next few minutes as the truck drove over bumps and swerved around turns, every move exaggerated by their lack of sight, Ed and Nate sat in silence, contemplating the myriad things that may await them at their destination. As the van pulled to a stop, both men sat up and covered their eyes, temporarily blinded by the sunlight shining in on them from the opened rear door.

A figure stood in the doorway, obscured by the light. "Out!" the figure ordered. Ed and Nate hesitated, causing the man to repeat his order with an even more forceful tone.

"Okay. Okay. We're coming," replied Ed as he helped Nate out of the van. His eyes adjusting to the light, Ed looked around and saw ten-foot tall sheet metal walls with multiple rows of razor wire across the top. He saw a large cargo plane at a low altitude on climb-out, apparently having just taken off from somewhere nearby. A sharp jab in the back urged him forward as a large steel door built into the wall slid open.

"Inside," the rather unfriendly escort ordered.

Leading Nate inside, their escorts were relieved by two men in solid-blue utility uniforms resembling military BDUs. Both appeared to be unarmed with the exception of tasers and batons. One of the men was of African descent, while the other appeared to be a Latino-Caucasian mix. Ed noticed this detail, as he was surprised to see personnel on this level who were not Russian, which had been their experience until now.

"Right this way," the Latino man said with a very American-sounding accent.

Sounds like a Jersey accent to me, Ed thought, still taking mental notes.

Looking around, trying to get a grasp on their situation, Nate said, "Hey, guys, we need to slow down a bit; since they took my leg, I can only go so fast, even with his help."

"You had a prosthesis? Who took it?" asked the man of African descent, also seeming to be an American by his speech.

"Your Russian buddies when we first got here. Any chance I can get it back?"

"That wouldn't be standard procedure, but there isn't much we can do about it. Those guys basically do their own thing through a different chain of command."

"Yeah, man, we just work here," answered the other man.

"That's above our paygrade, anyway. Our job is to get you in-processed. After that, you'll be assigned to a dorm leader who will be your point of contact for the duration of your stay in the camp."

While Nate was conversing with the two men, Ed took advantage of the distraction to glance around. He noticed that inside the wall, there was another similar wall, set back approximately thirty feet from the first one, with two steel doors, one on the left, and one on the right. This inner wall had razor wire coiled around the top as well. "What camp? Where the hell are we and why are you two helping them?"

"Just doin' our jobs. You'll have to direct the rest of your questions to your quad leader."

In reply, Ed grumbled, "What the hell is a quad leader?" He then continued to assist Nate.

The men ignored his question and led them to a camper-style trailer parked in the far right corner, in between the two walls. Reaching the trailer, Nate took hold of the grab handle by the door and hopped inside on one leg, with Ed and the two men in blue following closely behind.

"Who is this?" asked a man inside the trailer wearing a similar uniform. He appeared to have more authority, however, as he wore a sidearm on his belt.

"1242 and 1243," answered one of the escorts.

Thumbing through a stack of folders, the man with the gun replied, "Okay. Yep; got it right here."

The Latino man took a position at the door, blocking any egress while the other man stood alongside Ed and Nate.

"Take a seat," suggested the man with the sidearm. "I've got a few things to get done and your cooperation will make your lives much easier."

Complying, Ed and Nate both took a seat on plastic and metal folding chairs positioned in the middle of the room. The man with the sidearm then did a cursory visual check of Ed and Nate's physical condition. He looked down at Ed and Nate's feet and asked, "Any sores on your feet? Most people have issues from going without shoes."

"We'll survive," responded Ed sharply. "May I ask who we have the pleasure of dealing with today?"

"For you, my name is *sir*. Respond *yes, sir* or *no, sir*. That's all you need to know." Looking down at Nate's one bare foot and amputated leg, he chuckled and said, "I guess you aren't getting away in a hurry."

Staring at the man, Nate clenched the arms of his chair tightly, trying to control his rage. It was one thing to have an occupying force treat them with such contempt, but having his own countrymen do so filled him with negative emotions he would have to work hard to contain.

"Do either of you have any infectious diseases we should know about? For the safety of the other detainees, of course."

"No, sir," Ed replied in a firm tone.

"Well, at least you've got my name down. Now, give me your left hand," he said reaching out to Ed.

Reluctant to comply, Ed asked, "What for?"

"Have you already forgotten the simple piece of advice I gave you?" the man said, putting his hands on the table to lean down to look Ed directly in the eyes. "There are things to get done, and they will be done. The condition you are in when it's all over is the only thing you have control over at this point, and you don't have that control for much longer. Now, give me your damn left hand," he said insistently, reaching out to Ed.

Ed looked at Nate, still not complying with the order when an electrical shock went through his body, sending him falling to the floor, unable to control his muscles.

Feeling a hand around his throat as he began to regain control of his body, Ed attempted to resist, but realized that the other two men were standing on top of each of his arms. The man with the sidearm was breathing directly into Ed's face, squeezing tighter and tighter, making it impossible for him to get more than an occasional gasp of breath.

"I told you what was going to happen. Now it's going to happen like this."

Releasing his grip on Ed's throat, he picked up a device that resembled a rivet gun, put it around Ed's hand, and popped the handle, sending a stinging pain into the meat of his hand. He then leaned back down into close proximity of Ed's face, his foul breath reeking of onions and the smell of putrid meat, and said, "Now resist me again. Please... give me an excuse." Patting Ed on the cheek, he stood up, looked at Nate, and said, "Your turn, cripple boy. Give me your left hand."

Begrudgingly, Nate complied.

The man picked up a second device, verified a piece of paper lying next to it on the table, and then clamped it onto Nate's hand, popping it, and sending the same pain sensation through him. Nate felt as if a nail had been driven through his hand.

Removing the device from Nate's hand and inspecting the small red mark it left behind, he looked at Nate and said, "See how much easier it works around here when you just do as you're told?"

"Yes, sir," Nate responded with a flat, monotone voice.

"Now, you two will be assigned to quad two. The gentlemen here standing on your friend's arms will escort you there and get you checked in." Looking back at Ed on the floor, he continued, "And if you don't immediately comply with any orders they give you, they have my permission to beat you to within an inch of your life. Lose the tough guy shit before it gets you killed. Do you understand?"

Ed nodded to the affirmative as the guards released the pressure from his arms, allowing him to recover to the seated position of the chair.

"Now, you'll be staying in quad two as I said. You'll have a quad leader that changes with each shift rotation, but while on duty, he is your God. You will be fed twice each day. Your quad will eat together, sleep together, and use the toilet together. You'll do nothing without your quad, and it will all be at the discretion of your quad leader. The quad leader's decisions are final and will not be challenged. Now that we have all of that squared away, do you have any questions?"

"Yes sir," replied Nate.

"Go ahead."

"We still don't really know what's going on. How long are we going to be here, and what is the legal process that will determine that?"

"Good question, but that's not the concern of anyone here. You are here indefinitely as far as the leadership of the camp is concerned. If someone well above our pay grades wants you out, you'll get out; otherwise, consider it home. Now, if that's all, these gentlemen will escort you to quad two."

"But how can someone detain us indefinitely without due process? Is this not still America? Do we not still have our basic constitutional rights?

"Subsections 1021–1022 of Title X, Subtitle D of the National Defense Authorization Act was signed into law on December 31, 2011, and has been reaffirmed every year since. Like it or not, it's the law of the land. If the government expects that you are involved with terrorist activities, you can be held indefinitely, without trial or due process."

Nate knew the answer long before it was given. He had been studying the actions and trends of the government before the collapse. He just wanted to hear it directly from this man, who now seemed to wield total authority over him. And with that, Ed and Nate were led out of the trailer by the two escorts without another word being spoken. Ed stepped down from the trailer's metal steps, cringing as his weight pushed the gravel making up the surface of the compound against his bare foot. He then stood by the steps, up against the trailer, so that Nate could lean on his shoulder while he hopped down on one foot. Ed helped ease him down from the last step onto the gravel below.

The two escorts then led them back in the direction they had come, beyond the main door in the center of the sheet metal compound wall, to another sliding metal door on the inner compound wall. As they walked, they looked around, trying to learn as much as they could about their new environment. Both the inner and outer sheet metal walls were approximately ten feet high with razor wire coiled on top. There was a distance of approximately thirty feet between the walls, and in each corner of the outer wall there was a guard shack with what appeared to be a guard armed with some sort of rifle, although it was hard to discern any details, as the guards stood in the shade of the interior of the tower's guard shack.

All of the guards seemed to wear the same solid-color navy blue BDU style uniform, with a plain blue ball cap with no official logo. They had no nametapes sewn onto their uniform tops in the normal position, just a number. Some of the guards had numbers embroidered with white thread, while others were in yellow or gold thread. The men wearing the yellow-threaded numbers seemed to be the ones with authority over the others.

As they approached a sliding metal door on the interior wall, a guard on the ground received a visual signal from the adjacent watchtower and slid the gate open. Ed and Nate were then led inside, where they found a sheet metal building in the center of a large graveled courtyard. The lower floor of the building had a steel entry door with a guard posted next to it, while the upper level of the building seemed to contain an overwatch facility with windows on all sides.

In the very center of the compound, where the inner walls seemed to all come together, was a flagpole with a United Nations flag flying above an American flag. This enraged both Ed and Nate. *Someone is clearly trying to make a point about who is really in charge around here,* they thought.

After the door had slid shut with a noisy cacophony of metallic sheet metal clangs and scrapes, they turned around to see that their escorts were gone. Turning back toward the building in the center of the gravel-covered square, they saw a door open on the upper level of the building, with three men exiting and climbing down a narrow retractable metal staircase.

The three men approached them, one of which was of African descent, while the other two were of European decent. One of the Anglo-looking men stepped out in front of the other two with a scowl on his face. The one difference that both Ed and Nate immediately noticed was that his uniform was embroidered with red stitching instead of yellow or white. The man said in a firm voice, "I'm the quad leader for quad two. You are now residents of quad two. The rules here are simple; do what you're told, when you're told, and everyone will treat you fairly. Step out of line, and you will be treated as a hostile threat and dealt with as such. If you try to escape, you will be shot. There are no blind spots here at Camp Twenty-one. When mealtime approaches, you will be led into the chow hall located in the center of the compound through that door," he said as he pointed to the far right corner of the graveled square, behind the center building.

Quad two will eat together, sleep together, and shit together. There are no individuals here. If you have an altercation with another resident, the most recent addition to the quad of those involved will be relocated to one of the other quads. This, of course, will only happen once. You will be dealt with on another level if problems with discipline and good order persist beyond your relocation. During the day, weather permitting, you will spend the day out here in the courtyard. At night, you and your quad mates will be secured inside the quad barracks behind me," he said gesturing to the lower level of the central building.

"When we open and close the quad door through which you just entered, all quad residents will be secured in the barracks until such time that I deem the quad secure. It's pretty straightforward, really. Am I going to have a problem out of either of you?"

"No, sir," replied Nate quickly before Ed could respond. He knew Ed's penchant for getting under people's skin wouldn't serve them well here, as they had already seen.

"Good," the quad leader said. He then motioned to the guard to his left who had a digital scanning device of some sort in his hand. The guard reached the device out to Ed's left hand and waved it around until it beeped. He read something off of the scanner's display, verified it against a computer printout, and then moved on to Nate, repeating the process. The guard nodded in the affirmative, and satisfied with the results, he turned and walked back toward the building, ascending the stairs to the upper level. Once he was topside, he signaled for the lower-level doors of the inner building to open.

Chapter Eleven: Mutual Acquaintances

As the sunlight shined through a gap in the curtains, Jason awoke to find himself on the sofa in Carl's living room. Looking around, he saw Evan still sound asleep on a sleeping bag on the floor. *He's probably still knocked out from those pain pills Patricia gave him,* he thought to himself. *Oh well, his old butt needs the rest.*

Smelling the mouthwatering scent of fresh eggs, Jason sat up and looked around. Seeing no one else in the living room, he stood up and stretched with a yawn. He walked over to the kitchen to see Patricia cooking up a large breakfast including eggs, some sort of flat bread, and what appeared to be sausage. "Good morning, ma'am," he said, announcing his presence.

"Oh, good morning," she replied. "I hope I didn't wake you."

"Not at all, ma'am. I'm surprised I slept as long as I did."

"Ted is out doing a security sweep of the property. Carl's out in the shed getting some things together. They'll both be back soon and we'll all sit down and eat."

"You have no idea how good that smells. We haven't had fresh eggs since we left home."

Patricia smiled and said, "Yes, I don't know what I would do without our flock of chickens. They are so easy to keep and we always have fresh eggs and meat when we need it. This sausage is venison. It's kind of mild since I am almost out of spices, but it is a protein and that's what really matters. Carl and Ted are quite the hunters. I'm truly blessed to have men like them around in these times."

"Yes, ma'am," Jason replied as he turned to see Ted entering the house through the front door.

"All is clear," he said as he hung his well-worn, brown outback-style hat on the coat rack. "Oh, good morning," he said, noticing Jason standing in the kitchen with Patricia.

"Good morning. No signs of hostiles in the area?" Jason replied.

"No, I didn't see a thing. I heard a helicopter flying off in the distance. I never got a look at it, but it sounded big. How's your friend?"

"He's still asleep."

"Those pain pills like Patricia gave him knock me out cold every time. Lortabs, I think. She had them left over from a tooth extraction that festered up a bit. I avoid pain pills, personally. I hate being out of sorts these days. You never know when something is going to happen, but sometimes you just have to get some rest and let your body heal or you won't be any use to anyone."

"Yeah, he definitely needed it. We've had a rough go of things lately."

"My ears are burning; are you talking about me?" said Evan as he sat up in his sleeping bag.

"Yep. I was just telling them how you keep slowing me down," replied Jason with a nod.

"Whatever you have to tell yourself to boost your own self-esteem," Evan said with a chuckle as he stretched, only to wince in pain from his side with the movements.

"You gonna live?" Jason asked.

"Probably. So what's the plan?" Evan stood up, wobbling back and forth before regaining his balance.

"The plan this morning is to sit down to a wonderful breakfast, compliments of my beautiful wife, here," Ted said, massaging Patricia's shoulders from behind as she cooked. "We can worry about what comes next after we eat and chat for a while."

"Compliments of you and Carl," Patricia replied, blushing at his compliments and affection. "I wouldn't have anything to cook if you two didn't either raise it or hunt it all."

"We've gotta earn our keep, somehow," he said.

"How's your side, Evan?" she asked as he joined the other men in the kitchen.

"It still hurts, but it feels much better. Do you have any more bandages you can spare for our trip home? I think I've pretty much seeped through these already."

"Of course; I'll cut up some old t-shirts or something and change your dressings before you leave."

~~~~

As they sat down for breakfast around the large rectangular dining room table, Carl sat next to his daughter and granddaughter, Ted and Patricia sat opposite them, and Evan and Jason sat at opposing ends. Patricia had prepared the table with a lovely setting as if it was a special occasion.

"Forgive me for the formalities of the meal, gentlemen. I don't get a chance to entertain very often, so I have to put my skills to use whenever I get the chance," Patricia said with blushing cheeks.

"We appreciate every detail, ma'am," replied Evan.

"Yes, we do," added Jason. "We've needed some civility in our lives as of late. You can only sleep on the ground and eat squirrel so many times before you need to be reminded what life is supposed to be like."

Carl took Vanessa's hand, reached out to Evan next to him, and said, "If everyone could indulge me, I would like to say grace." Everyone joined hands, closed their eyes, and bowed their heads. "Our heavenly Father, we thank you for the ability to welcome our new friends into our home and provide them with some much-needed nourishment. Father, please ease the
~~~~

burden on Vanessa's and Audrey's hearts as they cope with the loss of their dear husband and father. May his memory and the example he set continue to guide young Audrey as she faces the many challenges of this world. Guide us all through these trying times and help us persevere; no matter what comes our way, please help us all to keep your love in our hearts. In your name we pray, Amen."

As everyone at the table said, "Amen," Vanessa wiped a tear from her eye and kissed young Audrey on the head. Audrey seemed to be lost in another world as she stared at the table in front of her, barely interacting with her family around her.

"Okay, folks. Let's eat," said Carl, as he patted Vanessa on the leg, giving her a loving and supportive look.

~~~~

Shortly after breakfast, Carl said, "I've got something to show you gentlemen out in the shed. Come on outside and take a look."

"Yes, sir," replied Jason as he and Evan joined Carl and Ted outside.

As they strolled over to the shed, Carl said, "I feel like I can trust you fellas; I hope I'm not mistaken about that."

"As long as you don't side with the occupiers or their masters, you can trust us to the grave," Jason replied sharply.

Carl stopped and faced them, looking them square in the eye. "Good. I have one question for you."

"Go right ahead," said Evan in reply.

"Who was the coward who abandoned you... at the farm? What was his name?"

Glancing at Jason with an intrigued look on his face, Evan replied, "Dustin."
~~~~

Carl looked at Ted with a smile. “Good. That checks out. Who else escaped the barn with you?” he asked, this time looking at Jason alone.

“Kyle and Quentin.”

“I’m sure Q will be pleased to hear you boys are still in one piece,” Carl replied with a satisfied look on his face. “It seems we have a friend or two in common. Q has been a big help to us for quite some time. We met him when the Blue Ridge Militia first started reaching out to folks like us in the outlying areas.”

Surprised by Carl’s announcement, Evan asked, “How did you get in touch with Q so fast?”

“I took a ride this morning on my horse. We’ve got some things in place that allow us to get comms back and forth semi-discretely. Setting up contingency communications plans was why the BRM, uh, the Blue Ridge Militia, reached out to us, in particular. Our location on this mountain gives us access to his COM equipment as well as being a prime location to observe from the ridge behind us. As far as anyone else knows, Ted and I are just hunters milling around in the woods looking for our next meal.”

Evan and Jason shook their heads in amazement at just how small the world had become. Even without social networking and the internet, people were still making the connections that needed to be made. Evan often wondered if that would be the saving grace of America—that patriotic Americans, even those who like to keep to themselves and live on their own terms, still tend to seek out like-minded individuals with whom they share a common cause. Even the founding fathers, who sought a world where individual rights and freedoms would trump the rule of the majority, understood that without standing as one when the times required it, they would all fall to tyranny.

"If it's not too much to ask, how exactly are you able to communicate with Q?" asked Jason, afraid he may be overstepping his bounds by asking the question.

"I'll let Q answer that himself this evening when he comes by. He wants to talk to you two before you head home."

"This evening? We are very grateful for your hospitality and help, but our families are not that far away at this point, and we don't know how things are going there. We've really got to be getting home."

"You'll want to stay until Q gets here. Trust me on that. It will do you both good to talk to him. If the occupiers start to put the screws to people around here, you'll need to be connected to friends you can call for help. I know you've got friends near your homestead, but you'll need more help than that. Fighting off thugs and criminals is one thing, but fighting off an army is another. You really need to stay for Q's visit."

Sharing a mutual concerned, but understanding, facial expression, Evan nodded and Jason replied, "Okay. You're right. We'll stay to hear him out and then be on our way after nightfall."

Chapter Twelve: Incarceration

As the quad leader reached the upper level of the central structure, he signaled to one of the guards below to open the lower level's steel security door. Once the door had slid open, the guard motioned to those inside to exit the building. Slowly, individuals dressed in orange jumpsuits, with bare feet like Ed and Nate, began to exit the building into the courtyard area.

Nate leaned on Ed's shoulder as they both watched their new neighbors file out of the building. "I count thirty-three," whispered Nate.

"Me, too," Ed replied. "They sure are a rough-looking bunch. They don't look like they've shaved or showered in quite some time."

"I imagine that will be us soon, not that we are fresh as daisies now."

"As Josey Wales would say, 'I reckon so,'" replied Ed, attempting to inject humor into their dire situation.

Ed and Nate were immediately approached by four of their fellow prisoners who walked with swagger and determination to greet them. "The name's Tate," the man in front of the other two said firmly. "Let's get something straight around here. If you mess up and piss them off, we all suffer. That being said, going by the quad leader's rules, if either one of you piss us off or cause any trouble, we will beat your asses. You will then be relocated to another quad where your fun will start all over again. And trust me when I say your new quad mates over there won't be thrilled to have troublemakers in their midst and they will deal with you in the same manner. Just stay the hell out of our way and keep us all out of trouble, and you'll get along just fine here. Understood?"

"Sure thing," Ed said, crossing his arms and standing tall.

"Good. Now that we've got that settled, the new guys lie down to sleep last. You wait until everyone else has found the cot of their choosing and take what's left. The same goes for seating in the chow hall. If you don't like it—tough shit—that's how it goes. Then when more fresh meat arrives and someone else is rotated out, you will move up the chain."

"Rotates out? To where?" Nate asked.

"Different places. Release, transfer... or hell—for all we know—execution. Just play things by the rules while you're in here and you can worry about what goes on outside when, and if, you get out."

The men then turned and walked away from Ed and Nate as quickly as they came. "What the hell was that?" Ed asked. "Didn't we just get the same damn speech from the Gestapo boys in blue just a few minutes ago?"

"Yep. If the quad leader is Colonel Klink, I guess that loser has dibs on Sergeant Shultz."

Sharing a chuckle, Ed turned to Nate and said, "Yeah, and if anyone tries to make you drop the soap in the shower, it's gonna be that guy. C'mon, let's find a wall in the shade to lean on."

For the next half hour, Ed and Nate sat silently in the far rear corner of the courtyard. Ed stared blankly at the ground while Nate tossed pebbles aimlessly onto the dirt, one by one. Almost completely fixated on his pebble-throwing task, Nate was startled by a fellow prisoner who was passing by as if he was out for a stroll and then changed course to stop and talk to them.

"Good afternoon. Aaron Lacy; nice to meet you," the man said.

"I'm Ed, and this is Nate," replied Ed, snapping out of his trance-like state.

"I saw that you met our resident rulers earlier."

"Which ones? There seemed to be two sets of them," replied Ed sarcastically.

"Yeah, well, the only ones around here with any real authority are the blue bellies topside. Tate's only authority around here is based on the strict adherence to the camp's policy on dealing with disturbances involving quad mates. Lots of people have rotated in and out, but he and his entourage have been here the longest, basically giving them immunity in the event they get into an altercation with a new guy. It's bull, but it is what it is."

"Well, it sure is good to see a genuinely friendly face around here."

Aaron smiled. "Most of the guys in here are pretty decent individuals. Most seem to be confined for affiliation or political reasons. Outside of these walls, they would have been the guys you teamed up with to get out of a bind, if you know what I mean."

Ed looked up to see Aaron staring him square in the eye as if to drive his last statement home. "I can see that," Ed said looking around at the other residents. "So what's your story?"

"We'll talk more tomorrow," Aaron said as he shuffled off in the direction he was originally headed.

"That was weird," said Nate as he began to throw his pebbles once again.

"Yep. It sure was. I would venture to say we will encounter many more awkward moments over the next few days... or weeks... or hell, months."

As the sun began to set behind the camp's walls, a whistle blew from the upper level of the central building. Ed and Nate looked up to see their fellow prisoners begin to walk toward the steel door on the lower level as if they were a group of mindless zombies.

"They look like trained rats, heading off to get their cheese at the sound of the bell," Nate said, throwing his last pebble.

He looked down to see that he had picked the area directly in front of him clean.

"If our cheese is a good night's sleep, let's fall in behind the other rats. It's been a long day."

~~~~

After a long and sleepless night on wornout cots, Ed and Nate were awakened by the lights in the room being switched on, followed by a metal trash can flying across the room and bouncing off of the opposite wall. "Rise and shine! Up! Up! Up! It's time for roll call," a guard in blue BDUs shouted as he walked into the center of the barracks room.

As the other residents of the camp stood in front of their cots, Ed and Nate quickly followed suit. The guard standing in the center of the room looked around to ensure everyone was standing, and then motioned for two of the other guards to proceed. Each of them had one of the handheld scanner devices and as they approached, each of the residents would hold out their left hand to allow themselves to be scanned. After scanning Ed's hand, one of the guards read the display and said with a chuckle, "Did you enjoy your first night at the Four Seasons?"

"Yes, sir," Ed replied smartly, fighting his natural urge to make a wise crack in response.

Once everyone had been scanned and the two guards with the scanner devices gave the thumbs up to the guard in the center of the room, he shouted, "Chow time. Let's move." Everyone began to file out of the barracks building in a single-file line. Nate fell in behind Ed, reaching forward and placing a hand on the back of Ed's shoulder to allow him to hop forward on his leg while in line without losing his balance.

They entered the chow hall located in the center of the complex, which was accessed from their quad from the right-
~~~~

rear corner. Ed and Nate observed everyone flowing through the chow line and then sitting down to eat in what resembled a military mess hall.

"This reminds me of the aft galley of an aircraft carrier," Nate whispered. "Only with higher ceilings and fewer pipes and valves. I just hope the food doesn't taste like JP-5 like on the boat."

"Huh?"

"Jet fuel... JP-5 is the mil-spec term for jet fuel. Anyway, purple pipes ran all through the ceiling of the aft galley. The purple pipes carried the jet fuel throughout the boat. For some mysterious reason, more often than not, the food had a hint of jet fuel taste and smell."

"Damn, maybe that's why you act the way you do. You've ingested way too many chemicals."

"Yeah, maybe."

After getting what appeared to be a crude form of steel-cut oatmeal plopped hastily onto their trays, Ed and Nate saw several open seats next to Aaron Lacy. Nodding to them as a quiet way to ask them to join him, Ed and Nate sat down for their first meal as residents of Camp Twenty-one.

"Good morning," Aaron said.

"Good morning," they both replied.

"So what do you know about this place?" Aaron asked.

"Not much," replied Ed. "We were yanked off the street while traveling with some friends of ours and were taken to a building on what seemed to be an airfield of some sort. After trying to get us to spill the beans that we didn't even have, they tossed us in here. We're freakin' clueless as to what sort of mess we're in."

"This place is known as Camp Twenty-one," Aaron continued to explain. "It's located near what used to be the Atlanta Hartsfield-Jackson International Airport, which is now a forward operating base for the UN troops in the region.

Camp Twenty-one is operated internally by the federal government under the guise of the NDAA. The blue bellies are all civilians who have taken jobs as guards. They all come from various backgrounds and just sold their souls to the devil in exchange for a more comfortable place in the world... at least that's my opinion. Anyway, the UN troops protect the immediate area outside of the facility and the blue bellies operate the day-to-day operations inside."

Aaron took a bite of oatmeal and then continued, "I think the original plan when they dreamed all this up was to have it operated by our own military, but as you two probably know, their attrition rate is through the roof. Hence the fed's willingness to bring the UN boys in to lend a hand. The problem is they are lending a fist.

"Anyway, back to the camp," Aaron said, getting back on track. "The reason they keep referring to everything as a 'quad' is because if you picture the camp from an aerial view, there is a square outside wall with a guard shack above the walls in each corner. The walls are topped with razor wire. Inside of the first wall, there is a kill zone. That's where you were in-processed at the trailer. It lies between the two walls in the kill zone. Inside of the second wall are the quads. The second wall makes up a second internal square, which is further divided into four units or 'quads.' Each quad is a separate housing unit, identical to ours, with its own guard team that resides above us on the second level. The chow hall that we are in now is in the center of the four quads, accessible by each, but only accessed by one quad at a time. Don't be surprised when they rush you in and out. They've got to feed all four quads separately in the same facility. One of the quads—quad one, I believe—is where they house the women detainees, and two, three, and four are for the men."

"What happens to the people being held here?" asked Nate.

"It depends on what they find out about you. Everyone here is being held for a reason. Generally speaking, it's because you were involved in activities that are deemed a threat to the agenda."

"The agenda?" Nate asked.

"The agenda to tear down the nation in order to rebuild it in a different form," Ed interrupted. "Those attacks and the subsequent actions taken by the powers that be were premeditated and coordinated, in my opinion. Everything that happened over the past ten years led up to the final events that pushed us over the edge. Now that they have succeeded in tearing us down, they won't let those loyal to the Constitution and to the founding principles stand in their way. Hence, NDAA—indefinite detention without due process."

"Exactly," replied Aaron, glad to see that Ed and Nate were on the same page as him.

Ed leaned back in his chair, paused, and asked, "Forgive my rudeness, but how exactly do we know you aren't a fed planted in here to turn on people after you've befriended them and earned their trust, getting them to admit to some sort of insurgent activity?"

"You'd be a fool not to think that is a possibility. I don't have much time so I have to be rather upfront with you guys. Besides, that concern goes both ways. I should be equally concerned that you two are here for the same reason—to flush me out. I just don't have time for that these days."

"Don't have time for what?"

"I just don't. When the time comes—follow your gut."

As Nate began to ask another question to clarify the confusing statement, Aaron stood up, collected his tray, and walked away. "How many times am I gonna have to ask 'what the hell was that about' around here?"

"I just keep waiting to wake up from the bad dream, brother."

Chapter Thirteen: The Meeting

Pushing their way through the thick brush, following closely behind Carl, Evan and Jason made their way through the woods for their meeting with Q at the pre-arranged rendezvous point.

Looking back at Evan and Jason, Carl said, "Sorry it's so far out here, guys, but the golden rule in regards to meetings where there is a potential for aerial surveillance is to not be seen anywhere near your loved ones. If I run into trouble and get taken out, they won't be able to pin down my homebase at a glance, and Ted will still be there to provide security for the women and children. He and I generally alternate who will be making the trek."

"How much further?" asked Evan, trying not to show weakness by acknowledging the fact that the pain was slowing him down.

"Over the next ridge we'll drop down into a wash. At the bottom, there is a shallow cave. It's only about twenty feet deep, but provides excellent cover from visual and sensory detection. We use this place along with a few others on a random, rotational basis to keep them from being able to pattern us like a deer. It's by no means a fool-proof system, but it's what we have."

Reaching the top of the ridge, Carl signaled to Evan and Jason to hold their position lower on the hill. Scanning the sky and the steep terrain below for potential threats, he pulled a deer call from his cargo pocket and made a series of doe bleats, directed at the terrain below. Hearing a similar response, he put the call away and motioned for Evan and Jason to continue.

"Trying to catch some dinner?" asked Jason in jest.

Chuckling, Carl replied, "There's probably not too many UN boys who carry a deer call on their person when setting up an ambush. That's Q down there. His reply lets me know the coast is clear. Given a different response, or no response at all, I'd have known to high-tail it out of here." Pointing down the hill, he said, "You see those rocks where the trickle of a stream flows?"

"Yep," Jason replied.

"About twenty yards to the left of that, back behind the brush, there is a rock overhang. Underneath that overhang is the cave I was talking about. The steep and hostile terrain combined with the fact that once inside, there is a good thirty to forty feet of each over the top of us, we're pretty secure. Using the local mountainous terrain is the only advantage we have over the UN or any other group that may want to put a squeeze on us. Those of us who have lived here all our lives know this place like the backs of our hands. They are just outsiders relying on maps and intel briefings. Our blood runs through this place. That's an advantage that's hard to quantify."

"Just like the Taliban and the Mujahedeen in Afghanistan against the Soviets and us," replied Jason.

"I'd personally rather be compared to the Spartans at the battle of Thermopylae, but whatever gets the point across to ya."

"Sorry."

"Oh, I'm just messin' with ya. Getting back to business, though, the best way down the hill is the rocks following the creek. It makes a natural ladder or staircase and you're a lot less likely to leave tracks on the rocks. I'll cover you while you scurry down to the bottom, then you just head on over to where I said the cave was. Q will be waiting. Then I'll send Evan and take up the rear."

"Roger Roger," said Jason smartly as he slung his AK74 over his back and began working his way down the steep rock and brush-covered hillside. Reaching the bottom, Jason gave Carl the thumbs up and proceeded to meet Q in the cave.

Once both Evan and Carl were safely at the bottom of the rock-strewn hill, they continued into the cave, where they found Jason and Q standing watch at the opening, covering Evan and Carl's entry.

"Long time no see, Evan!" Q said as he gave him a hug and a firm slap on the back.

Evan winced in pain. "Ouch. Sorry, but Jason and I got into a little scrape and they left their mark on me."

"Oh, sorry," Q replied. "Yeah, we heard about your "little scrape" as you put it. We've always got someone listening in on their common frequencies. They weren't too happy about that. It pisses me off to no end what they did to Bill, Vanessa, and poor Audrey though. I'm damn glad you guys took care of that shit on the spot."

Carl nodded in agreement.

"We've been paying a little extra attention to this area," Q added. "We wanted to make sure you two made it home okay—knowing how everything that went down on the farm would force them to step their game up a bit."

"Have you heard anything about our friends who were captured when we were?" asked Evan.

"We haven't heard anything for sure, but we do know that there are detention centers popping up all over the country. There are at least twenty-five that we know of. Our sources tell us that most of the folks taken from this area end up being processed through a camp down by the airport in Atlanta. Our friends with the Southern States Defensive Coalition (SSDC) tell us something big is planned for the airport, which is now just a forward operating base for the UN and its not-so-peaceful peacekeeping forces."

"Something big?" Jason asked.

"Yeah, instead of giving them free reign to hunt us down like dogs, several of the militias that are part of the SSDC plan on hitting it and hitting it hard. The goal is to keep them on the defense instead of the offense. They've got dedicated assets to help in the fight, so don't worry, they won't be too outgunned."

"What about the camp?" Evan asked.

"They've got that covered. Some of their own are there and once the party starts, they're gonna take the place down and get everyone out. From what we know, it's not a hard target. Mostly corrugated sheet metal construction with razor wire and lookout posts. It's strong enough to keep an unarmed man in, but I doubt they can keep us out. Once the Russian UN forces are tied up with the assault, a team specially put together for the mission will hit the camp and try to evacuate all of the detainees."

"Damn," Evan said. "Things are starting to get serious. I guess we always saw something like this coming. It just couldn't go on like it was forever. Someone was bound to show up eventually and try to stake a claim; it just seems like that was more of a distant thought than a reality."

"It's a reality now," added Carl.

"So what do you need us for?" asked Evan.

"The Blue Ridge Militia is gonna stay put during the hit. There is already a strong UN presence in the area and we can't just leave our families to their mercy while we take a road trip to Atlanta. There is already a more than sufficient number of personnel and assets assembled from several of the area militias. The Southern Appalachian Militia, the Smokey Mountain Militia, and the Georgia State Constitutional Militia will all be representing the SSDC during the strike."

"That's good to hear," replied Jason. "I'm glad so many are stepping up to the plate."

"Yes, it is," Q continued. "That being said, we want to put an encrypted radio repeater or two in the hills near your homesteads. We've got this side of Del Rio covered, but we are still blind in regards to what's coming in from your direction."

Jason and Evan shared a concerned look.

"What we have is a number of HiveNet tactical suitcase-sized repeaters that utilize solar charging to be as portable and maintenance-free as possible. They are perfect for our application. The system is fully encrypted so that if a repeater is compromised, the rest of the network remains secure. Also, a radio operator can roam throughout the deployed network without any channel selection or interaction. Your handheld encrypted digital radio will simply jump from repeater to repeater as you travel through the HiveNet network. This makes it easy for the operator of an associated transmitter to move around to various locations within the network, making location triangulation more difficult. The network is also self-healing, which is important for us. If they take out one of the repeaters after homing in on it, the rest of the system continues to function without it, with no corrective action on our part. Repeaters can be added or removed at any time without compromising the network."

"How easy are they to DF?" asked Jason, referring to the UN potential ability to use direction-finding equipment to home in on the repeaters and transmitters.

"Well, that's always a possibility. We've got a few guys on board who are a bit smarter than I am in that regard though; they've developed some strategies for us to use to keep the risk as low as possible. Considering factors such as antenna polarization, using the lay of the land to control wave propagation, using just enough power to transmit to the next repeater and not beyond, and good COMSEC (communications security) procedures such as extremely short bursts of communication, we can mitigate that risk to an acceptable level. Especially considering the current patrol presence they have. If we were facing the best and brightest of the U.S. Army during their peak, that would be another story."

Giving each other a look of mutual understanding, Evan and Jason nodded in agreement, and Evan said, "Okay, just tell us what to do."

"Great!" Q said. "Now here is exactly what we need you to do..."

For the next half hour, Q showed Evan and Jason several locations marked on a topographical map that would best be suited as additions to their secure repeater network. He also explained the COMSEC procedures they were to follow when transmitting on the network, as well as explaining in detail the operation of the units.

"I also recommend that your homesteads keep their own CB and HAM transmissions to a minimum. You don't want to give them any reason to begin snooping around your area. A HAM station these days is a telltale sign of a preparedness-minded individual, and that will get you on their visit list in a hurry."

Jason looked around the small cave, and not seeing any extra equipment, he asked, "So, did you bring them with you?"

"No, we have several caches of equipment prepositioned at various places that users can retrieve on their own. That way, there isn't the extra logistical step of transporting and making face-to-face handoffs, which would increase our exposure significantly. For you guys, the closest cache to your route of travel is here," he said, pointing to the topographical map. A watertight Pelican-style trunk is hidden in a densely wooded and brush-covered area near a large, fallen walnut tree. You will see several football-sized rocks lying in a straight line, extending out from the dead tree. Follow the direction of those rocks until you find yourself in the thick of the brush. At that point, you'll just have to beat around until you find it. Once you do, take two repeaters and two handheld transmitters. Place the repeaters where we discussed, and I would recommend placing the second transmitter in a fallback location. That way, in the event of trouble, you can give us a call for help, even if you can't get to your house. You definitely don't want to make a habit of keeping a transmitter on your person. That would be a dead giveaway of militia involvement if you were stopped for questioning. You'd find yourself in a detention camp in no time."

"That all seems pretty straight forward to us," Evan replied.

"Good. Your daily monitor time will be from 1300 to 1315. If we need to get in touch with you, we'll do it then. And remember, keep a pen and paper handy because the info will be in short bursts and won't be repeated. If you need us, we've always got ears on the air. Now, you two get back to your families. Thanks for taking the time out to meet me today; it's been great seeing you two again so soon."

"You, too, man," Evan said, shaking Q's hand.

"Yeah, man; thanks again for everything you do," added Jason, shaking Q's hand as well.

As Carl turned to lead Evan and Jason out of the cave and back to his home, Q shouted, "And remember, guys, these guys think they're just messin' with a bunch of hillbillies. We'll make 'em afraid of the hills when we're done!"

Chapter Fourteen: Reckoning

As several days passed, the monotonous life inside Camp Twenty-one began to become routine for Ed and Nate. They had begun to make friendships and acquaintances with the other detainees of quad two. Though they had no direct contact with detainees in the other quads, the thin, corrugated sheet metal walls around the camp did not hide the sounds of daily life on the other side. The occasional scuffle that they could assume was between detainees and guards, as well as the opening and closing of the noisy metal sliding doors, made them constantly aware of the activity around them.

Shortly after returning from breakfast, as the sun was making its way across the sky, Ed, Nate, and two men named Matt Wilkes and Tommy Phelps, who they had recently befriended, were relaxing in the shade in the only corner of the quad not already covered by the rays of the pre-noon sun.

"So how old are your kids, Tommy?" Nate asked in an attempt to alleviate his own boredom with conversation.

"Six and four," Tommy replied. "Well, for another week, that is. My six year old turns seven next week... um, I think it's next week. I've sort of lost track of the days."

"Yeah, I hear ya on that one. Neither Ed nor I have wives or kids, so the actual date is meaningless to us with no birthdays or anniversaries to have to remember. I only care what season it is these days."

"Heck, Nate," Ed replied with a chuckle. "You'll have a wife and a kid before long. Nate here has a pretty young thing with a little boy waiting for him back home."

Though Nate appreciated Ed's positive outlook, it was a depressing reminder that the life he had recently dreamed of might be slipping out of his reach. He could not see a positive outcome arising from his present situation. Hanging his head low, he tossed a pebble at the ground and said, “Yeah... I hope.”

“It’s not over ’til it’s over, man,” added Matt. “It’s not like this is a Nazi death camp.”

“Maybe not yet, but it’s off to a good start,” Nate replied, tossing another pebble to the ground, fixating on its short flight through the air.

“Ah, crap,” Ed said with contempt in his voice. “There comes our friend Tate.”

Tommy looked up to see Tate walking toward them with his buddies. “I’m so sick of that bastard. I don’t know what sort of life he lived before they threw him in here, but he sure as hell seems to be enjoying the place.”

“We’ve just got to play the game a little longer, man. Play the game,” added Matt.

Walking up to the group, Tate stood tall with shoulders back and chest extended. “You guys are in our spot.”

“There’s lot’s of room here, man,” answered Tommy in a calm but defiant voice. “Can’t you just find another spot? We’re all on the same team. Remember?”

“Get the hell out of my corner. I’m not telling you again,” Tate demanded as his cohorts took a few steps to each side, expanding their visual presence and giving Tate room to do whatever he needed.

Matt replied before Tommy had a chance, “C’mon, man. You’ve been givin’ us all shit since we’ve been here. We’re tired of it. We’re tired of everything. We’ve got nothing to live for in here and, quite frankly, I’m not sure I have anything to live for out there, either. Why don’t you just sit down and join us and let’s all start over? We don’t have to be enemies. We’ve got the blue bellies for that. We can all just kick back like friends and make fun of them to pass the time.”

Without hesitation, Tate kicked gravel in Matt’s face. “I said move!”

Shielding himself with his arm, Matt exclaimed, “What the hell, man?” He jumped to his feet. “I’m sick of your crap! I’m sick of all this crap! Now get the hell away from us or get your ass beat. I, for one, am not gonna take it anymore!”

Glancing up at the upper level of quad two’s central building, Ed could see the guards watching with interest from above, but taking no action. “Calm down, boys. The blue bellies are watching the show.”

“You know how it works. Last in, first out. I win the game by default,” replied Tate, disregarding Ed’s warning.

“I don’t give a shit about that anymore. Maybe getting kicked out of here would be a good thing if it gets me away from you. Not to mention the satisfaction of watching you bleed.”

“Matt!” Tommy said insistently.

Ignoring the warnings of his friend, Matt stepped forward and came to within inches of Tate, standing face to face. Tate had several inches and about twenty pounds on Matt, but Matt had no intention of backing down, punishment from the guards or not. “Your little reign of terror is over, Tate. Back the hell off,” Matt said through gritted teeth.

Tate spat directly into Matt's eyes and threw an uppercut punch, knocking Matt to the ground. Ed and Tommy immediately jumped to their feet as Tate’s friends squared off on them.

Matt sprinted from the ground and ran shoulder first into Tate’s knees, taking his legs out from under him. Landing firmly on his back with a solid thud, Tate struggled to catch his breath while Matt began punching him like a mad man.

“Matt, stop!” Tommy shouted as he started to run over and stop the fight. Tate’s friend intervened and held him back. Tommy wanted to help, but considering the fact that Matt was holding his own and gaining ground, he momentarily chose to stand down as thoughts of his family and the freedom he so longed for flashed before his eyes. *Just stay out of it,* he said to himself.

As Matt drew his fist back to throw a punch at Tate's face, Tate's other cohort threw dirt in Matt's eyes, giving Tate an opportunity to overpower him and get back to his feet.

"Hey! You stay out of it!" Tommy shouted as his adversary blocked him from running to Matt's aid.

As Matt leaned forward and attempted to clear his eyes with his hands, Tate kicked him square in the jaw, creating an awful cracking sound; blood flew from Matt's mouth with the impact.

"Hey, do something!" Ed shouted to the guards as they sat by patiently watching the fight as if it was for entertainment.

Nate hobbled up to his foot and hopped over to the wall to get out of the way. Without his prosthetic leg, he knew he was in no condition to get involved in a physical altercation like this.

Stumbling backwards, almost falling to the ground, Matt dodged Tate's next roundhouse punch and followed through with a swing of his own, hitting Tate directly behind the ear as his body carried him forward from his missed punch.

Matt's punch sent Tate forward onto the ground, sliding face first in the gravel. In a total fit of rage, Matt raised his right leg as if to stomp on Tate's head.

"Matt, no!" Tommy yelled, knowing Matt was about to cross a line from which he could not return. At the same time, a crack rang out, echoing off of the camp's steel walls. Matt's body jerked violently as a mist of blood erupted from his back, knocking him to the ground.

Ed and Nate turned to see one of the guards in the watchtower in the far corner of the quad holding a rifle, still aimed at Matt.

As Matt writhed in pain on the ground, a second shot rang out, impacting him directly in the center of his chest. All movement stopped, as Matt now lay lifeless. In total shock of what happened, the men felt frozen in time. They were quickly snapped back into reality, though, as the guards on the second floor of the center building ran down the retractable stairs, clubs in hand, screaming, "On the ground! On the ground!"

The detainees all dropped to the ground in compliance with the orders from the guards, knowing there was no course of action they could take that would have a good outcome other than to comply.

Tommy lay facedown on the ground, looking at Tate, repeatedly saying, "You son of a bitch; this ain't over... this ain't over."

A guard kicked Tommy in the side, yelling, "Shut up!"

Everyone lay silently as several of the guards dragged Matt's lifeless body toward the main steel door. They showed him no respect, treating him as if they were simply taking out the trash.

The loudspeaker from the second floor rang out a command. "Quad two detainees, enter the barracks immediately. I repeat, quad two detainees, enter the barracks immediately."

As Tommy slowly got to his feet and began to walk toward the center building in compliance with the order, he mouthed the words to Tate, "This ain't over. You're a dead man." The look on his face sent chills up Tate's spine.

~~~~

For the rest of the evening, the detainees of quad two remained in the barracks. The doors remained closed and locked, and as chow time came and went, they knew they would be on lockdown at least until the next morning. Tate kept mostly to himself; his friends had abandoned him, understanding the risks that his behavior had brought to them.
~~~~

"Why the hell is that bastard still in here with us?" Nate asked, trying to get his frustrations off his chest. Tommy sat next to him, his hands on his face and his elbows on his knees, still in shock and in dismay about what had happened to Matt, who had become his best friend since their mutual detention.

Aaron Darcy walked up and replied, "I'm not sure why he garners favor with the blue bellies. It's been that way as long as I can remember though. There have been a lot of people come and go since then. Perhaps some of them were rotated out because he gave some information to the blue bellies about them. Who knows? Just trust me, guys... stay out of trouble for just a little longer. Trust me," he said again, ensuring they understood the importance of what he was saying.

As Aaron walked off to converse with another group, Ed said, "I want to believe him that something big is on its way for us, but these days, it's hard to let yourself get your hopes up for things that may never come."

"It'll come," Nate said, looking at Ed and Tommy. "It'll come."

Chapter Fifteen: Diversions

"Okay, guys, we came down one at a time, we'll go up one at a time," Carl said, pointing up at the rocky wash they had climbed down from the ridge to join Q at the cave. "Jason, you go first since you'll make it to the top quicker than Evan—being hurt and all. Then we can both cover him, and I'll bring up the rear. Once at the top, just keep your eyes open until we all get joined back up and head back down the other side. The tops of the ridges around here are about as close as the drones and choppers can get to us with the steepness of the terrain. They don't have much room to drop down between the hills."

"Roger Roger," Jason answered sharply as he immediately began to ascend the steep and rocky hill.

"How you hangin' in there, Evan?" Carl asked.

"Oh, I'll be fine. I'll be glad to be home, that's for sure."

"We'll give you a good meal and send you on your way once we get back. By the time we finish with supper, it'll be getting dark and you can travel under the cover of darkness on a full stomach."

"That sounds like a plan," Evan replied as he watched Jason bound from rock to rock like a mountain goat. *Show off,* he thought jokingly.

As Jason crested the top of the hill, he took a moment to scan the area for any potential threats, then motioned for Evan to proceed. Evan slung his AK over his back and began climbing from rock to rock, pausing occasionally to deal with the pain from his wound. *Suck it up, buttercup!* he admonished himself, trying to ignore the pain and not slow the others down.

Reaching the top of the ridge, Jason reached down and grabbed his hand, pulling him on up the last few feet. "Damn, man. I didn't think you were ever gonna make it up here. I thought I was gonna have to come down and carry you up like a pack mule."

"Yeah, yeah... whatever," Evan replied.

As Jason looked back down the hill at Carl, he noticed that Carl had turned around and was looking behind him. Just then, an Mi24 attack helicopter rose above the opposing ridge like an ominous specter with its weapons stations loaded down as if prepared for war.

"Go!" shouted Carl as he pulled something from his daypack and began running laterally across the hillside. He fired a flare in the direction of the helicopter, causing it to swerve momentarily as if taking evasive action from a threat. Carl had disappeared into the woods as quickly as he fired the shot.

Evan and Jason began running downhill, dodging limbs and branches, jumping over brush, using the steep incline of the terrain to their advantage. Keeping their momentum moving, they were able to clear many obstacles they otherwise would not be able to make in a single jump.

Hearing the ominous *thump-thump-thump* of the Mi24 Hind's main rotors, Evan and Jason didn't even slow down to look behind themselves to see if it was in pursuit. They heard the Hind's four-barreled 12.7mm machine gun open fire and they realized they were not its immediate targets; they used the opportunity to change course.

"This way!" Jason shouted, leading Evan off course, away from the route they had used to get there from Carl's cabin.

Running through the woods at a breakneck pace, Evan was having a hard time keeping up with his friend and began to slow and lose ground on him. He simply could not struggle through the pain to keep up the pace as the wound was beginning to take its toll on him. He could feel the wetness seeping down his side and knew Patricia's stitch job was simply not holding up under the intense physical activity.

Coming to a stop and taking a knee, he looked up to see Jason turn his head to check on him, immediately causing him to reverse course to come back for his friend.

"Ev, are you okay?" Jason asked, struggling to catch his breath.

Evan was unable to answer right away; his heavy breathing was exacerbating the pain from the wound, making it almost unbearable. "Gotta... gotta slow up for a bit," he said, struggling to speak between his labored breaths.

"C'mon," Jason said as he reached out and took Evan's hand. He then hunched down and pulled Evan onto his back, and began to make his way slowly through the woods, carrying his dear friend. As they came upon another wash in a heavily wooded and shady area, Jason looked around above and said, "This thick tree cover will help. Let's see if we can get over to that large rock with the downed tree lying across it. We'll look and see if we can make ourselves a blind and lie low for a while."

Evan replied, giving Jason the thumbs up with his left hand as Jason held onto his right arm firmly to keep him on his back. Approaching the fallen tree, Jason said, "Sit tight a sec... but keep your ears and eyes open."

Evan nodded in reply and Jason began scurrying around, dragging any broken tree branch that he could move over to the log. He piled the branches haphazardly to create a natural looking pile of brush and then motioned for Evan to join him. "Slide underneath this one and get in," he said, holding up a branch for Evan.

Once Evan was inside the blind, Jason crawled underneath the branch and joined him. "We just have to hope those guys are running old, low-tech gear. If that were our boys, they would have found and smoked us by now. It's hard to fight a war against those who out-tech you these days."

Evan again replied with only a nod. He laid his head back against a rock and rested for a moment while Jason kept a keen eye on their surroundings. “An Mi-24 Hind has an eight-person troop compartment and they could have very easily had some hunter-killer types rappel down to flush us out,” Jason whispered. “I think we need to just lie low for a while. However long it takes to know they are out of the area.”

“Cool,” Evan said with a nod as he continued to rest with his head on the rock.

~~~~

After several hours of no sounds other than those of birds, insects, and a ticked off squirrel, apparently upset that Evan and Jason were occupying his personal space. Jason whispered, “How are you feeling?”

“Better now,” Evan replied softly. “Well, not completely better. I’m pretty sure I tore my stitches open. I’m just afraid to look. But I’m past the acute pain stage.”

“Let me take a look,” Jason said as he lifted Evan’s shirt. “*Damn.*”

“What?”

“She sure wasted a lot of gauze on you,” Jason said jokingly.

“Yeah, yeah... how does it look?”

“The bandages are soaked with blood, but they’re still taped on pretty well. On second thought, we don’t have anything to cover your wound with, so I don’t think I want to remove them. They’re soaked but still doing their job of keeping dirt and debris out.”

“Sounds fine to me,” replied Evan. “I don’t want you poking around in there, anyway. So, what do you think happened to Carl and Q?”
~~~~

"That depends on whether the threat was airborne only or if they dropped some guys in on foot. If they were airborne only, unless they had a tip-off somehow about the location of the cave itself, Q could have probably ridden out the threat in the cave. On the other hand, if they dropped some guys in on foot, that's a whole different ballgame. From where they got a bead on Carl, they could easily have found the cave from there."

"Yeah. That's what I was thinking, too," Evan said in a concerned voice. "Carl's probably screwed either way. I don't know how the hell you can outrun a Hind on foot in rough terrain. Add to that the fact that they were letting their gun rip like that, and one has to assume they had him in a vulnerable situation."

"Yep," Jason replied, looking down at the ground.

"So now what?" Evan asked.

"We follow the original plan of waiting until nightfall. If we have pursuers on foot, they'll be picked up and bug out by then. This terrain is too rough for that Hind to be working close to the terrain in the dark."

"Unless they expect them to hike out."

"I doubt they would do that with the risk of militia-friendly folks in the area. They only have strength in their numbers and equipment superiority. On foot and alone, they are at a disadvantage around here."

"True. I guess we will be footin' it home now, huh? I mean, we can't risk leading them back to Carl's place to get the horses. That would be a death sentence to Ted, Vanessa, Audrey, and Patricia. If they followed us, that is."

"Yep. Do you think you'll be able to make it that far? With your side in this condition? Not to mention your feet."

"My feet are holding up. The pain in my side actually helps me forget about them at times."

Looking at the map Q gave them, Jason followed a route in his mind with his finger, studying the terrain to find a suitable route back to the Homefront. As he slid his finger across the paper, Evan watched, wondering what was going through his mind. After several moments of silence, Jason spoke up and said, “We can’t take the straight-line route for several reasons.”

“Why is that?” Evan asked.

“Well, the first and most obvious is the terrain. We need to stay low in the valleys between the hills to get the most cover from the possible prying eyes above. Second, the radio equipment we are supposed to pick up is a little off our route to the south. Here’s what I’m thinking—we drop down a little further from where we are that way,” he said, pointing through the woods from where they sat. “Then, we can follow this creek through the lowest points of the terrain until we get here. We will have to cross over the mountain at this point to get to the other side, but at least we will have cover along the way, as well as a source of water. Once we get to the other side, we can drop straight back down into the next valley and follow that to near the radio cache. That will be a good spot for you to take a break while I retrieve the gear and bring it back. There’s no reason to put any extra mileage on you if we can help it.”

“What if you can’t carry it all after hiking to it by yourself?”

“I’ll cross that bridge when I get there. I’ll make two trips if need be. Q said the repeaters were suitcase-sized. The handheld transmitters can’t be too heavy or bulky.”

“I imagine the batteries and solar chargers for those repeaters are gonna be kind of heavy though,” added Evan.

“True. Well… I’ll carry what I can. If I can’t get it all in one trip we—or I, rather—will just have to come back and make a second trip.”

“Heck, Sarah won’t ever let you out of the house again after all this. She won’t be up for you traipsing off into the woods again right away. You’ll be on spousal lockdown.”

They shared a laugh as Jason folded the map and put it in his shirt pocket then they both sat back and thought of home. They felt close, yet far away at the same time. Their journey home from the Blue Ridge Militia's camp had been plagued with setbacks and redirections. They wondered how many more unexpected events would get in their way before they finally reached home.

Chapter Sixteen: Keeping the Faith

The metal trashcan crashed against the sheet metal wall of quad two's barracks, as had become their all too familiar wake-up call. Ed and Nate, along with the others, sprang to their feet. Balancing on his good leg while leaning on Ed's shoulder, Nate noticed one of the guards—apparently the day's quad leader—walking his way with a stern facial expression.

The guard looked down at Nate's missing leg, chuckled, and said, "At least you're easy to identify. Petty Officer Nathan Hoskins, you are hereby notified that you are officially being detained as a deserter from the United States Navy. A DOD representative will be arriving tomorrow to escort you and several other deserters, here at Camp Twenty-one, to a facility where you can be properly processed by your respective service components. Do you have any questions, Petty Officer... or I guess I should say, soon to be Seaman Hoskins? I imagine a demotion will be in your immediate future along with your incarceration. Deserters like you disgust me."

"Traitors like you who put this fraud of a government above their neighbors and fellow citizens disgust me," Nate snapped in reply. "When did you serve? I served my country with honor. I left because of what my government had become. I left because my oath and my loyalties were to the Constitution and the values we used to cherish. You joined them for the very same reason I left them. That says everything about you and me both."

"I'm serving now," the man said through his unclean teeth and foul breath.

Before Nate could take evasive action, he felt the sting of the man's open-palm slap to his face, causing him to lose his balance and fall backwards to the floor, hitting his head on his cot. Ed flinched out of reflex as the two lower-level guards who had accompanied the man squared off on him. Knowing he wouldn't be helping Nate's situation, Ed made the wise choice to stand down from his near escalation of the situation.

"Can I at least help him up?" Ed asked.

"Let the piece of trash get himself up," the quad leader said. He then turned around and announced, "In honor of having a treasonous deserter among you, breakfast will be canceled today for all quad two detainees. If there is one among you, there are probably more, and trash like you do not deserve to eat."

He then turned back to Nate, smiled, and said, "I hope they each thank you personally for the hunger you are forcing them to endure."

As the quad leader exited the barracks room with his fellow guards following closely behind, Ed reached down and helped Nate back up onto his cot. "Holy crap, man," he said with a look of concern on his face.

Nate sat on the edge of his cot silently, his elbows on his thighs and his hands in his face. The sting he still felt from the slap was nothing compared to the anguish he felt inside, knowing that his chances of ever seeing Peggy, Zack, and his family again were slipping away.

How did it come to this? Nate thought. *How did I work so hard to make it from California to Texas, and then on to Tennessee, only to end up dying alone in a prison somewhere? Or even worse, living a long life that way?*

Ed patted him on the shoulder and said softly, "It's not over until it's over."

Grumbling from some of the other detainees could be heard from across the room about their missed meal. Aaron Darcy stood on top of his cot and said in a firm and loud tone, "Shut the hell up! Every damn one of you running your mouths over a missed meal right now, just shut the hell up! You didn't miss breakfast because of what Nate did in his past, which I don't blame him for one bit. In fact, I applaud him for refusing to follow orders contrary to his oath of enlistment. The reason you are missing a meal is because that same government, from which he fled now holds you in the clutches of its hand. They put these cowardly guards, who are only here because they can't take care of themselves without the government's hand to feed them, in charge of you, and they abuse you as well. They are small and insignificant cowards placed in a position of authority simply because they are willing to do the job. Don't let them get into your heads. Don't let the government—or what is masquerading as our government—turn us on each other. We may need each other sooner than we all think. They used the strategy of divide and conquer on us as a nation for years before the collapse. They split us into groups, pitting us against one another to weaken us so that their plans could come to fruition. Don't let them use the same strategy on us here. Let the hunger that is in your stomach be replaced with a hunger to regain your freedom."

Aaron stepped down from his cot and walked across the room to Ed and Nate. "Just hang in there, Nate. Just hang in there," he said with a pat on Nate's back. Giving Ed a nod, Aaron stood up and walked back across the room as the door to the barracks slid open, followed by the order from one of the guards for all detainees to exit the barracks and enter the yard.

~~~~

Later that evening, Ed, Nate, and Tommy were sitting in the same shady corner as they had the day before. Matt's bloodstains still painted the gravel in front of Nate as he mindlessly tossed pebbles on the ground, staring at the stain.

"I'm not going," Nate said, tossing another gravel.

"What?" Ed asked with a confused voice.
~~~~

"I'm not going with them. Whatever happens will happen. I would rather stand up to them like a man and let the chips fall where they may rather than be hauled off as if I am their property. If I die here, at least I'll die by the terms of my choosing."

"Nate," Ed paused, trying to put his words together. "I really don't think that's a good idea. A lot has happened lately. I know you're down. I know it seems hopeless. But you can't... you just can't stop trying to get home to Peggy and Zack. You can't give up now."

"I'm tired, Ed. I'm so damn tired. The last few years have taken the life right out of me. I'm tired of worry. I'm tired of misery. I'm tired of watching the horrors this God-forsaken world inflicts on good people. I'm just tired."

"Well, Peggy's not giving up on you so easy; I can damn well promise you that. Now snap out of it. We'll get through this. You'll get through this."

Nate gazed at a gravel he held between his index finger and thumb, looking it over as if he was trying to find some sort of answer within it. He then tossed it on the ground, in the center of Matt's bloodstain, and lay back with his arms crossed behind his head. "I'm just tired, Ed."

Ed worried about his friend. He had never seen Nate without a fire in his soul. The events of late had taken their toll on all of them, but it seemed Nate had demons in his life that he had yet to deal with properly and they were chipping away at him from within.

~~~~

Later that night, as Nate lay awake in his cot, staring into the darkness of the ceiling, he thought of Peggy and Zack. He thought of the love he felt inside for both of them and had often wondered if the drive he had inside to find his mother
~~~~

and father had been meant to be so that he could find them. He fell for her as soon as he met her, as if he had known her all of his life. *Was it the desperation of the situation? The desperation of the world we lived in that made us want to latch onto the first person we found? Were we just rebounding from the world's biggest breakup? Were we rebounding from our loss of the world as we knew it?* He asked himself. *No! Of course not! I love her. I really love her. I love the smell of her hair. I love the sparkle in her eyes. I love her smile, her touch, her laugh. I love her... I love her completely and with all of my heart and soul. I love Zack. I love my family. I can't go out like this. I can't leave this world without being there to provide for them for a long damn time to come!*

Nate's thoughts were interrupted by a muffled thump off in the distance. His heart skipped a beat, not knowing what it could have been. Then another thump could be heard, followed by several loud cracks. *Shit! That's gunfire!* he thought. "Ed... Ed..." he said as he shook his friend's arm to wake him.

"Wut... uh, what's wrong?" Ed replied as he awoke and looked around the room, confused. Another distant thump immediately told him the story of why Nate was waking him. "What the hell is going on?"

"I don't know. It just started."

As Ed sat up, several other detainees could be heard whispering in the darkness of the room. As more and more began to wake, the whispers turned to louder conversation as the distant noises began to increase in intensity.

There was a scuffle outside the door; then they heard the sound of the large steel beam that was always propped up ominously next to the door sliding into position, filling the two large brackets welded to the door frame.

"They're barricading us in!" one of the men shouted in the darkness.

Chaos ensued in the barracks as the detainees all scrambled to get up and put their orange jumpsuits on, as that was all they had to wear.

"Everybody, listen up!" shouted Aaron. "If you want to make it out of here, follow my lead. Stay away from the walls. Everyone gather in the center of the room. Gather all of the cots together, lay them on their sides, and arrange them in a circle around us."

"Why... what for? What's going on?" one of the men asked in a panic.

"The cavalry is here," Aaron said. "They'll have to breach the walls to get in. They can't take much time to do it, so it'll probably be violent, and they're gonna be relying on us to be prepared. Just do as I say, for now; everyone get in the center of the room and lie on the floor. When they breach the walls, there may be shrapnel and the cots could help protect us. Shove all of the pillows and blankets between the cots for extra protection."

As the sounds of mortar fire, gunfire, and explosions continued to increase in intensity outside, most of the men in quad two followed Aaron's directions and built a circle out of cots and blankets. Several others, including Tate, ignored his pleas for cooperation and ran to the door and began to bang on it violently while screaming at the guards for help.

Tate yelled, "Let me out! Let me out! You owe me! You owe me! Get me the hell out of here!"

As Tate pounded away at the door, Ed attempted to get him to join the others for safety. "Tate, get your ass over here! Get over here!"

Tate ignored him and continued pounding relentlessly at the door. A nearby explosion, with a near-deafening shockwave, rocked the flimsy metal building. Bits of shrapnel tore through the walls, leaving small jagged holes scattered throughout the structure, illuminating the room with small rays of light from the light outside.

After having ducked behind the cots for cover when the explosion hit, Ed looked up to see one of the men limping back towards them with a leg injury and Tate lying on the floor, convulsing; he was covered from head to toe with shrapnel wounds. Ed and one of the other detainees ran over to him and dragged him into the protective circle, closing the gap behind him.

"You stupid son of a bitch," one of the men said as he began assessing the extent of his injuries. With barely enough light to assess him properly, the man, who clearly had past medical training, noticed a bulge on the side of Tate's head. He gently felt around with his fingers and quickly realized that Tate's skull had been ruptured and his exposed brains were partially spilling out onto the floor.

The others noticed that he immediately stopped his assessment and just sat there as if he had given up as soon as he started.

"What? What is it?" one of the others asked.

"There's nothing we can do. Nothing," he said.

Aaron spoke up amidst the chaos and said, "There's nothing you could do, Doc, but thanks for trying. Just look for others who may need you now." He then turned his attention back to the group and said, "I told you to stay down and stay in the center. We don't know which wall will be breached, but I can assure you it's coming. Now, stay the hell down behind the cots and look out for each other. When the time comes, and you'll know when it does, follow my lead or the orders of the militiamen who enter the room. Don't appear to be a threat or they will smoke you. Understood?"

The detainees now seemed to take Aaron's advice and orders seriously and stayed down, clinging tightly to one another in the confined space of their tightly packed circle.

As small-arms fire seemed to be getting closer to their location, they could hear gunfire originating from the observation level just above their barracks. They could hear empty shell casings hitting the metallic ceiling above their heads as they were ejected from the guards' rifles. A barrage of incoming fire both ricocheted off of and penetrated the structure. The sound of each impact was deafening as the detainees struggled to stay together on the floor as tightly as they could, and out of the line of fire.

During the barrage of incoming fire, Nate heard what he assumed was a rifle hitting the ceiling above them, followed by the thump of one of the guard's bodies as he seemed to go down hard during the exchange. That sound was followed by another, and then another until the remaining shots seemed to be incoming, with no more defensive fire originating from the observation floor.

They heard three loud bangs on the north wall of the quad as if someone was striking it with the butt of a rifle.

"Down! Everybody down!" Aaron shouted as a small explosion blew a section of the sheet metal free, exposing a large opening in the wall

Before the smoke even settled, three armed militiamen, all wearing various types of camouflage and gear, entered the quad and yelled, "Darcy!"

"Here," Aaron said as he raised his hand and motioned for the militiamen to proceed. "Over here."

They immediately shoved and kicked the cots out of the way, clearing a path for the barefoot detainees and shouted, "Move! This way! Go! Go! Go!"

Nate threw his arm around Ed's shoulder and the two joined the others in their rapid egress from the building. Once they got outside, they noticed an entire section of the outer wall was missing and three former school buses, painted in flat

OD green, were inside the camp walls with detainees from the other quads already piling inside.

"In the buses!" Aaron shouted, directing his fellow detainees toward the closest bus.

As the last man to climb into the back door of the bus, Aaron gave the militiamen who were still on foot the thumbs up. One of them ran to the driver's side window, banged on it with his open palm, and gave the driver the thumbs up. The bus accelerated through the missing section of the camp's wall. Once on the other side, it joined up with the other two buses, as well as several pickup trucks and two Humvees, making up a convoy away from the facility. The militiamen on foot climbed into the back of a woodland-camouflage-painted '79 Ford Bronco and brought up the rear, maintaining a steady stream of suppressing fire during their escape.

Ed and Nate were tossed around in the back of the crowded bus as the driver made several abrupt turns, changing the route and splitting up from the other two buses. "Where are we going?" asked Nate.

"We're splitting up from the rest," Aaron said in a loud voice, trying to overcome the loud sounds emitted by the speeding truck. "We have several former Air National Guard AH-64 Apache attack helicopters in the area to fend off any pursuit, including putting on a diversion with any of the UN's Mi-24s that may be called in for support. By splitting up the three personnel carriers, we reduce the risk of a total loss if we are pursued. Chances of which aren't too high, as the intel we have on the facility indicates that they were mostly set up as a security and patrol force and not a highly mobile tactical force. They can operate hunt-and-strike patrols, but until now, they didn't have this sort of contact on the forefront of their mission planning or protective posture. I'm sure that will all change now though. We've got to brace for impact from this point forward. We just threw a sucker punch at the bully, but he will get back on his feet soon and will be looking to save face."

As Aaron finished his sentence, two Apaches, in tight formation, flew directly overhead the convoy, traveling in the direction of what remained of Camp Twenty-one. The Apaches broke formation, one bearing off to the right, and one to the left and began to engage targets on the ground off in the distance.

"That'll teach those bastards," Aaron said with a smile on his face.

Chapter Seventeen: A Shared Struggle

"Ev... Ev... wake up, buddy."

Flinching from being startled by Jason's gentle nudge on his shoulder, Evan looked around, regained his senses, and said, "Damn. I didn't realize I was that tired. How long have I been out?" he asked, noticing that the darkness of the night was upon them.

"A few hours. It's around nine o'clock—I think," Jason replied. "How are you feeling? You look pale."

"I'm fine," replied Evan, knowing that he wasn't himself, though he couldn't pinpoint exactly why. "I'll be okay. Just a little hungry and tired, I guess."

"Yeah, we were stupid for not bringing our packs along. I know we planned on returning to Carl's place with him to retrieve our horses, but we've really got to stop setting ourselves up for failure like this."

"I hear ya. Well, at least the first bit of the hike is downhill towards a stream. A good long drink of water will help."

Jason stood and stretched. "If you're up for it, I think we should get a move on. We don't know how long it's gonna take, and moving in the dark will be slow going as it is."

"Yeah, let's get on with it," replied Evan as he struggled to his feet, wincing in pain.

"Are you sure you're up for this?"

"I would rather push on through it and die at my own house than lie around and die out here if I'm worse off than I think. So yeah, let's get on with it."

"Roger Roger." Jason pushed a large, downed tree branch that made up part of their blind out of the way. "So, we're gonna head down the hill to the creek and then turn left and follow it until we reach a small fork. Then, we're gonna have to make it over a ridge and back down the other side."

Jason motioned for Evan to follow as he began slowly working his way through the thick vegetation and low tree limbs. With the moon hidden behind the steep mountain ridge behind them, it was hard to see beyond arm's length. Feeling in front of them as they went, they worked their way down to the stream below, pushing brush out of the way when necessary. As planned, they turned left and followed the stream, working their way alongside its banks.

As the moon worked its way across the night sky, finally illuminating their path, Evan looked at the stream next to him and said, "Hey, man. It's dinner time."

"What?" asked Jason, confused since they hadn't brought any food along.

"Watch and learn, city boy," Evan said jokingly. He stepped out into the stream and positioned himself facing upstream. Allowing the disturbance of the sediment caused by his boots to clear before proceeding, he studied each and every stone and stick in the water.

"What the hell are you doing?" asked Jason.

"I'm getting our dinner."

Jason watched him intently, not sure whether he had finally snapped and lost it, or if he was truly on to something.

Evan then reached into the cold water of the small stream and gently lifted a six-inch long, flat, oval-shaped rock, attempting to limit the disturbance he made with his movements. As soon as the water was once again clear, he removed his hat and gently placed it in the water, downstream of the depression in the soft mud where the rock once lay. He then took his other hand and wiggled his finger in the water in front of the depression. Jason thought Evan had truly lost his mind when he saw Evan lift his hat back out of the water while staring inside. As the water drained from his hat, he carefully passed it over to Jason, who was still standing on the dry creek bank.

"Well, hell," Jason responded with a smile as he saw a crawfish scurrying around inside of Evan's hat.

"It's a piece of cake, man. I grew up catching crawdads—that's what we called them—in the creeks of East Kentucky. If you lift the rock gently and slowly, the crawdad won't run. They're not much more than small freshwater lobsters; they swim backward when threatened and can't see where they're going. You place something behind them to catch them in, pose a threat in front of them, and they swim right into your trap. A fast food soda cup works great, but having a wet hat in exchange for fresh protein isn't that bad of a tradeoff. Now, whack that sucker so he won't get away, and toss me my hat so I can keep it up."

Jason shook his head and laughed.

"What?" Evan asked, wondering if he should be offended by Jason's laughter.

"Oh, nothing. I had just assumed I would be taking care of you this whole time, and here you are feeding me."

"It's called a team, man. Besides, I have to feed you so you'll have the strength to carry me later."

"Ha... deal, then."

For the next half hour, Evan worked every rock in the creek while Jason killed and cleaned their catch. Once he was satisfied that he had harvested every crawfish within reach, Evan waded back to the bank, unrolled his pant legs, and asked, "So, what do we have?"

"Thirty-two of the suckers," Jason replied. "How do we eat them?"

"You killed them, right?"

"I cut their heads off."

"Good." Evan fished around in his pocket for something. "Ah, here we are," he said, pulling a cigarette lighter from his pocket. He then reached into the pile of headless crawfish, pulled one out, ripped the tail from its body, and stuck it on the end of his knife like a kabob. He then flicked his lighter, held his crawfish over the flame for approximately thirty seconds, looked at it, and said, "That'll do."

Peeling the shell from the tail, Evan popped the morsel of meat into his mouth and said, "Oh, yeah. Creekside Bic lighter crawdad just can't be beaten."

After a satisfying meal of fresh crayfish, Jason turned to Evan and said, "I have to hand it to you, Ev. I would have never thought of that. I've never eaten crawfish—or crawdads, as you put it—like that before. Or even thought of where they come from. I've had them in New Orleans on layovers, of course, but that's it."

"That's just the northern boy in you," Evan replied with a chuckle. "You grew up in Massachusetts before moving to Ohio, so you probably had better things to do than play in a creek. See, we didn't. If it was a hot day, we played in the creek to keep cool. We didn't have much else to do. It was tire swings into a pond or crawdad hunting in a creek. Sure, city kids would probably have just called us backward hillbillies, but I wouldn't trade that upbringing for the world."

"Hell, yeah, your hillbilly superpowers just fed us."

"I guess we should be moving on," Evan said. He then began to chuckle. "Along the way, maybe I'll activate my hillbilly superpowers once again, and conjure up a squirrel or a rabbit."

"I wouldn't complain," Jason replied as he stood up and stretched. "Well, let's get to it."

As they reached the fork in the creek, which was their predetermined location to turn up the hill to the left until they crested the ridge, Evan said, "Well, the fun is over, I guess."

"Yes, until we get up there, at least. It'll be a struggle to the top in your condition. We can stop and rest all you need on the way up. Once we get to the top, we can diagonal downhill—terrain and brush allowing—until we get to the bottom. We'll stay in the bottom for a while as we press on toward the Homefront and the radio gear cache. How are you holding up?"

"Better now that I had a chance to rest and got a bite to eat." Evan then looked up at the hill, took a deep breath, and said, "Lead the way, brother."

~~~~

After several more hours of trekking their way through the rugged wilderness in the dark, Evan said, "Hey, man. I need a break. I'm starting to get shaky. I've sucked it up for as long as I can for a while."

"That's okay, man," Jason replied, reaching into his pocket for Q's map. "This is close enough to the radio cache for me to strike out on my own. Let's get you situated where you can rest up comfortably and securely, and I'll get a move on. As slow as the going is, the sun may damn near be up by the time I get back, so you might as well tuck in for a while."

"Sounds good to me," Evan replied as he sat down and leaned back against a tree.

Jason did a quick scan of the immediate area and found a bush of rhododendrons and mountain laurels that would provide natural visual cover from both the air and the ground if Evan were to remain there after sun up. He then cleared a spot out for him to lie down and led him to it. Jason took Evan's AK-74, verified that a cartridge was in the chamber, the safety was on, and was ready to go. He propped the rifle up on a tree branch where Evan could grab it easily and asked, "How many mags do you have?"

"Four. I'll be good."

"Take one of mine; you'll have one hundred and fifty rounds that way. You can hold your own for a while with that if need be."
~~~~

"Hell, no. You might need everything you have," Evan insisted.

"The difference is, I can run. You're not really in any condition to be sprinting through the woods. You've probably pushed yourself over the edge already." Jason felt Evan's side, feeling him twitch with pain from the lightest touch. "You're bleeding again. Just take the damn magazine and do as I say. Molly will kill me if I come back without your dumb ass, so just listen to me on this."

"Alright, man. You take care out there. If you need me to help carry something, come back for me. I'll be rested up and feeling as good as new in no time."

"Just rest up and don't worry about anything else for now. Understand?" Jason said in an insistent tone.

"Yes, Mommy," Evan replied with a crooked smile.

As Jason slipped off into the dark woods, Evan closed his eyes and thought of his beloved wife, Molly, and his wonderful children. *Maybe I can dream about her,* he thought.

Chapter Eighteen: Angels from Below

Ed, Nate, Tommy, Aaron, and twenty-three other detainees on board their bus gazed out the windows, fearing an airborne response to the escape would catch up with them any minute. The camouflaged Ford Bronco still trailed their bus, but the other escort vehicles from the raid had split off with the other two buses.

"Where are we going?" asked Nate.

"Each bus is going to a location that only the driver and his escort know," Aaron explained. "I don't even know. They were locations determined at the last minute before the raid took place and not shared with anyone else. That way, if any one of the buses are captured, or if individual personnel are caught, they can't be forced to share the whereabouts of the others with the feds or the UN. We'll get there when we get there is all I can tell you."

"That's sound thinking," replied Ed.

"What we lack in material support, we have to make up in any way we can," said Aaron, still scanning the sky for threats as he spoke.

"What happens when we get there? To wherever it is we are going, that is," asked Tommy.

"Debrief, medical attention, and aid and support in getting you back to where it is you need to be—within reason, of course. We can't return you to downtown Atlanta, obviously, but if you were taken by the UN from somewhere else that we have freedom of movement, we will do what we can."

Ed looked over at Nate with a smile on his face. "See, never give up hope. There are still good people in this screwed up world."

"Amen to that," shouted Tommy.

For the rest of the ride, Nate gazed out the window, thinking of Peggy. He wondered if she had any idea what had happened to him. He and Ed hadn't seen or heard from Evan and Jason since they were taken, and were not sure if they shared a similar fate. He hoped they had somehow already made it home to the homesteads. If not, he feared for the safety of those who remained without sufficient protection from the ever-encroaching reach of the occupying forces.

Turning his attention back inside the bus, Nate looked around to see some of his fellow detainees with tears of joy rolling down their cheeks. He clearly wasn't alone in assuming he may not see his loved ones again and that his life, as he had known it for the past year, might be lost to him forever. But now, with the selfless acts of these militia volunteers, they might all be able to be reunited with their families and begin to pick up the pieces of what was left of their lives.

"So, what's next for you guys?" Tommy asked, interrupting Nate's thoughts.

"Home..." Nate said with a smile. "And then to propose to my girl. One thing this mess has taught us is that we can't put anything off in the world. If you have something that you know you want for sure, you had better seize the moment and take it while you can. None of us can be confident what will happen from one day to the next anymore."

"I hear you on that one," Tommy replied with a smile.

"What about you?" Nate asked in return.

"Well... I may just be home for my kid's birthday, after all," he said with tears of joy welling up in his eyes. "Damn, I just can't believe it," he said as he fought back the tears. Looking to Aaron, he said, "Thanks, man. I knew there was something about you. Something a little more calculated than the rest of us. Something about the way you carried yourself and were always observing. Thanks. Thank you for putting yourself in that position to be able to help us out like that. The rest of the world could have just forgotten us and left us to rot, but you guys... you risked everything for us. And for that, you have my eternal loyalty."

"So what's next on the agenda for you guys, Aaron?" asked Ed. "I'm sure this isn't the extent of what you have planned in response to the occupation."

"No, not at all," Aaron said as a flash of light behind him illuminated the inside of the bus. The thunderous sound of an explosion followed the flash of light as the Bronco that served as their escort exploded, sending a shockwave through the bus.

The bus swerved, followed by another explosion just to the right of the bus, sending it careening to the left, overturning and rolling over several times before coming to a stop. As it came to rest on its top, Ed shook off his confusion from the violent event and immediately kicked out the shattered remains of the nearest window and squeezed through the opening. He then reached inside, grabbed Nate by the arm, and dragged him free. He threw Nate over his shoulders and ran toward several run-down houses off to the side of the road. Looking back for a moment to check on the others, he saw several of the detainees limp away into the darkness as the whirring sounds of a rapidly approaching turbine-engine-powered aircraft streaked through the sky. A few seconds later, another explosion decimated the bus, sending debris in all directions, the shockwave knocking him to the ground.

Winded from the impact, but undeterred, Ed stood back up with Nate still on his shoulders. He ran toward the houses under a veil of darkness and smoke, which came from the burning remains of the two vehicles.

Ed ran as fast as his bare feet could take him with the extra weight of Nate bearing down on him. A few blocks into the neighborhood from where the attack on the bus took place, the pain of multiple blunt-force trauma injuries suffered during the crash began to replace Ed's adrenaline. He carried Nate into the backyard of one of the suburban neighborhood homes and laid him down behind several overgrown decorative shrubs.

"Nate... Nate... Wake up. C'mon, Nate," he said as he smacked him gently on the cheeks. Getting no response, he checked for a pulse and signs of breathing; he was pleased to find both life signs present. He then gave Nate a cursory look for indications of trauma and found a laceration about two inches long on the top of his head. Ed did not have enough visibility in the darkness of the night to do a thorough evaluation. He decided that, for now, he needed to get Nate inside somewhere to hide, as he knew it was only a matter of time before UN soldiers would be sweeping the streets, looking for survivors.

As Ed took Nate by the arm and started to lift him off the ground and throw him back over his shoulders, he heard the familiar click of a cocking hammer followed by an elderly man's voice. "Don't you move a damn muscle."

Paralyzed with fear, yet desperate to get Nate some help, Ed said, "I'm sorry, sir, but my friend here is in desperate need of medical attention. I just—"

"Shut up. I didn't ask you for your life's story. I told you not to move a muscle. Your jaw muscles included. Now... only speak when answering a direct question. Do you understand?"

"Yes, sir," Ed responded, feeling defeated and fatigued by the night's events.

"Who are you with," the man asked.

"His name is Nate. He's a good friend of mine and—"

"No, dumbass. Who were the people in the vehicles, and who was shooting at who? And what's with the orange jumpsuit? Did you just escape from somewhere?"

"My friend and I were captured by UN peacekeeping forces and were being detained by some federal outfit. I'm not sure who. They wouldn't tell us much. All I know is that they were working in concert with the UN and the Russian troops in the Atlanta area. They called the place Camp Twenty-one."

Ed heard the hammer click back to the safe position as the old man whispered, "Come, give us a hand with this one."

Ed turned around to see an elderly man leaning his old Winchester model 1897 hammer-pump shotgun up against the overgrown shrubbery. Emerging from the shadows behind the man, an elderly woman of around the same age came out of hiding and knelt down next to Nate.

"What's wrong with him?" she asked.

"We were hit pretty hard and the bus rolled over. He hit his head, but I'm not sure what else. He's alive, but that's all I know."

"Let's get him inside," the old man said as he reached for Nate's feet, only to be startled by his missing limb.

"Don't worry. That's a previous injury," Ed said. "He's had a rough few years. I can carry him."

As Ed lifted Nate into his arms, the man retrieved his shotgun and his wife led them into the home through the back door. Once inside, she led Ed through the house to a corner bedroom. The man then opened the bedroom closet and began moving boxes out of the way, revealing a lift-up type door, underneath which were stairs leading down beneath the house.

"Can you carry him down these rickety old stairs or do you need my help?"

"I've got it," replied Ed as he twisted his torso sideways in order to fit down the narrow stairs with Nate in his arms.

The elderly man's wife led Ed down the stairs using a candleholder for a light. Once they were at the bottom, he heard the door shut above them, followed by sounds of the boxes being placed back on top of the door and the closet being closed once again.

"Put him here on the sofa," she said as she directed Ed to lay him on an old sofa that was up against the old, damp brick wall.

Ed did as she asked and then looked around the room to see that they were in a small space of about ten feet by fifteen feet. The space seemed to have been constructed many years ago, as the brick and the construction techniques seemed very old to Ed's reasonably trained eye.

"I'm Meredith," she said, leaning over and checking Nate's pupils by holding the light over him.

Nate moved his head back and forth slightly as if he was struggling to get the bright light away from his eyes. Ed knelt down next to him and asked, "Nate... are you in there, buddy?"

"His resistance to the light is a good sign. Let's just let him rest for a while," she said. "He took a pretty good hit to the head, but his pupils responded well to the light and his heart rate and breathing seem fine."

"Are you a nurse?"

"Oh... many moons ago I was an army nurse. That's been a long time, though. My husband served in the Army from the tail end of Korea to the beginning of Vietnam. He's a retired Sergeant Major. That's where we met. He brought some of his injured soldiers to our field hospital for treatment and the rest is history."

"Is this some sort of bunker?"

"It was a storm cellar for the house that was here previously. My husband bought the lot back when he first retired from the Army after the house that was on it burned to the ground. When he built the new house, the storm cellar didn't really fit into the floor plan so he just worked the closet upstairs into the design so that he could maintain access to it. It has mostly gone unused until recently. We find ourselves hiding down here a lot these days."

"I can imagine so," Ed replied. "Some things almost seem like they were meant to be."

"What do you mean?"

"Well, your husband bought a lot with this old storm cellar on it. He could have easily filled it in and built right on top of it instead of working the floorplan of the house around it. And here you are, all these years later, blessed to have it in these troubled times."

"Yes. I guess you're right. When the attacks first started, we thought it would all just pass like September 11th, 2001. We assumed the government would just go after whoever did it, and we would begin the process of rebuilding. Things just didn't go that way," she said, her reflections of the past few years showing in her eyes as she paused. "Then when people started getting desperate and crime shot through the roof, we would hide out down here until the danger passed. There were times when we barely came up for weeks."

"How have you been surviving? I mean... you're located in a residential area where there really isn't a natural food source readily available."

Meredith stood up and walked to the other side of the room. Pausing for a moment, she drew back a large curtain covering the back wall, revealing that the room was twice the size it had initially appeared to Ed in the low light and the stress of the situation. The other side of the room was filled with old wooden shelving, similar to an old library, with two freestanding shelves and one against the far wall. There was just enough room to walk between the shelves to retrieve the items stored on them.

"One thing my husband learned during his time in the Army, watching people's lives being turned upside down and losing everything they had, was to trust nothing. *The only sure thing in this world is us*, he would often say, to justify hoarding all these supplies all these years."

"I guess you could say he was a prepper before it was a household word," replied Ed.

"Yes," she responded with a chuckle as she looked through the remaining items on the shelf, much of which had already been utilized. "We never thought of it as a doomsday sort of thing. The things he saw over there simply made it so that he could no longer trust the world around him to stay safe, stable, and fair. I don't think he actually thought we would ever use this stuff. I just think it made him feel better to be doing it. It was sort of like therapy for his nerves."

"Like I said, some things just seem meant to be," said Ed with a smile. "Your husband's uneasiness with the world around him was well justified and has kept you two alive all this time. There aren't many people, especially in a residential neighborhood such as this, who have been able to maintain themselves in their own homes without resorting to extreme measures. Most people in urban and suburban areas, at least from my experience, have had a very hard time, to say the least."

"I'm pretty sure Henry has resorted to extreme measures. I'm also pretty sure he will never tell me what he has had to do. He's just that kind of man. No matter what he has to go through for us, he will—and he will bear the burden alone."

As she finished her sentence, they heard the sound of the boxes placed above the hidden entrance to the storm cellar being pushed aside, along with Henry's familiar knock. This was to let her know it was him and that the coast was clear.

Henry walked down the steps, shotgun still in hand and at the ready. As he reached the bottom, he looked deep into Ed's eyes and said, "We don't make a habit of inviting strangers inside. Especially strangers in prison jumpsuits. If I hadn't seen those commie bastards directly attack you, I might have shot you myself. You've got five minutes to convince me not to do that now."

"Henry!" Meredith said with a scowl on her face.

"Well... let's hear it," he said insistently.

"Yes, sir," replied Ed as he began to tell the tale of his former affiliations with the state of Ohio, how both he and Nate ended up at the Homefront with the others, and how they were on a simple supply run when they got caught with weapons that may have implicated them in militia activity, leading to their arrest and detention.

"So you're not militia?" Henry asked.

"No, sir. We met some members of the Blue Ridge Militia early on during our supply run, but we're not affiliated with them. But in the spirit of openness and honesty, I would be glad to call any patriot currently serving in a civil militia, my friend. I'm not sure how many, but militiamen lost their lives tonight rescuing us from Camp Twenty-one. I'll forever owe them a debt, and my service where I can give it."

Gazing into Ed's eyes as if looking deep into his soul, Henry turned and leaned his shotgun against the wall and said, "Damn fine answer. You are both welcome to stay here until you can get back on your feet."

"Speaking of feet," Meredith said, interrupting the intense conversation. "We need to find them some shoes for their feet and some clothes, too. When they are fit to travel, we can't just send them away barefoot and in orange prison jumpsuits."

"I'll see what I can scrounge up tomorrow," Henry replied. "We need to lie low tonight. I'm sure those commie bastards will be on the ground in the area soon to check out their handy work."

Chapter Nineteen: A Weakened State

Hearing his children play in the other room, Molly's arms wrapped around him, Evan smiled and snuggled in next to her, enjoying the moment. Hearing his own stomach growl, he nudged her and asked softly, "Hey baby. What's for breakfast?"

Molly answered, whispering into his ear, "You are. Wake up."

Evan's eyes opened immediately, seeing a coyote standing merely feet in front of him, as if it was sizing him up for a possible meal. He knew that coyotes are pack animals; where there is one, there are more. He slowly reached for his rifle, clicking off the safety lever with his hand before picking it up. "Easy now," he whispered as he sat up ever so slowly, trying not to induce an attack. As he began to raise the weapon, the animal lunged, causing him to flinch, discharging the rifle with a blinding flash of light and a thunderous crack from the high-velocity 5.45x39 round, redirecting the hungry coyote as it darted off into the woods. The bullet whizzed right in front of Evan's own face, as he was not prepared or aimed to fire. Momentarily blinded by the contrast of the bright flash of light on the dark night, Evan panicked, reestablishing his grip on the rifle in preparation for a continued attack. They could come from any direction and he knew that they were surely lingering in the darkness, waiting for an opportunity to take him down as injured prey.

They must have smelled the blood and the wound from a distance, he thought as he squinted and blinked his eyes, trying to recover his night vision. Seeing spots and hearing nothing but the ringing in his ears, Evan stood and turned around, desperately scanning the darkness, hoping his senses would soon return.

After several minutes of watching and waiting, Evan yelled into the darkness, "And stay the hell away from me, you damn filthy dogs!" as if his threat would carry a perceivable warning to the hungry wild animals. Feeling light-headed, Evan leaned against a tree and continued to scan the darkness for any signs of movement.

Ah, I feel like shit, he admitted to himself as aches and pain shot through his body. Shivering and feeling weak, Evan slid himself down the tree with his back dragging against it until he was seated on the ground. *At least they won't be able to jump me directly from behind with me up against the tree,* he reasoned as he struggled to come up with a better plan than simply waiting.

Hearing the eerie howl of a coyote directly in front of him in the darkness, perhaps twenty yards or so, he knew the threat was not gone, but had merely fallen back to regroup. Evan shouted blindly into the darkness, "Jason, if you are there, say something."

After giving his warning, he counted to five, closed his eyes to protect his returning night vision, and fired off three rounds in the direction he thought he heard the howl.

Hearing rustling through the brush off in the distance growing louder, Evan prepared himself for another attack; he gripped his rifle, shouldered it, and heard, "Evan! Evan, are you okay? Evan!"

"Jason! Over here, man. There are goddamn coyotes out there all around me. One nearly had me while I was sleeping."

"Just stop shooting unless you have one in your sights," Jason said as he sprinted towards Evan.

As Jason appeared in the moonlight, Evan said, "Oh, thank God you're back."

"Did you say coyotes?" asked Jason as he bent over and placed his hands on his knees, breathing heavily from his run through the woods.

"Yeah. I wasn't seeing things. The bastard was within five feet of me when I woke up. I'm damn lucky I woke up," he said, remembering that it was Molly who woke him in his dream as chills ran through his spine. "Did you find them... the radios and stuff?"

"Yeah. I was working my way back to you when I heard the gunshots. I dropped them and took off running at the sound of the first shot. I had no idea what was going on."

"Well, screw going back for them in the dark with those bastards running around out there, acting like they are not afraid of man. Coyote attacks on humans are rare, but they happen. With man's presence being reduced these days, those sneaky bastards may be getting braver. If they've come across weak and weary travelers in the recent past, they may have found that humans can make an easy meal. I think we need to just hang tight till the sun comes up and then go back for the radio equipment."

"Damn, man. You're really shook up."

"You would be too, brother. You would be, too. Especially if you smelled like a wounded and sick animal, like I do. They can probably smell this festering mess for miles away. Speaking of which, I think it's getting infected. I don't feel so good. When I stood up earlier, I felt shaky and I feel like I have the chills or something. I suppose it could be the cold air, but I just don't feel right. I know something's not right."

"Okay, man. We'll just sit tight until sunrise. Try to get back to sleep. I'll stay up and keep the critters away," Jason said as he leaned back on a tree, rifle in hand. "If you're starting to get sick on me, you need to get your rest. Tomorrow morning we'll try to push on through after we retrieve the gear. If you feel up to it, of course."

~~~~
~~~~

As the sun came up over the ridge, with rays of light finding their way through the thick vegetation of the woods, Jason leaned over and felt Evan's forehead. "Damn, man. You're burning up," he said quietly, not knowing if Evan was awake.

"I feel like I'm freezing to death," Evan said without even opening his eyes. "I've got to get home quick before things really start to go south."

"Yeah, I agree," Jason replied, pulling the map from his shirt. "Screw the radios and repeaters. I can get one of the other guys to come back with me and get them. I've gotta get you home and get you to Doc Rachel for some of those cow antibiotics she gives people, before you get much worse. We're ditching one of the rifles, too. I can't carry everything and you can't even carry yourself. Here, take a drink of water," Jason said as he put his water bottle up to Evan's lips.

Taking a sip of water, Evan said, "Thanks, man."

"You're gonna have to drink more than that," Jason said, shoving the bottle back in his face.

Getting another drink and pushing the bottle away, Evan asked, "So what's the plan?"

"On the steep stuff, I'm gonna have to have you hoof it. In the fast moving terrain, I'll carry you on my back."

"You can't carry me all the way home. That just won't work," Evan insisted.

"Hey, listen to me," Jason insisted. "We've not got that far to go. We can move better now that the sun is up. We just have to make sure we don't expose ourselves more than necessary as we make our way through the woods. We will stop when we need to stop, but at this point, you need to shut the hell up and get yourself up and about. If you have to piss, do it now so that we can get moving."

Jason tossed Evan's rifle and pack into a thick mass of vegetation for concealment. "I'll get this stuff when I come back for the radios."

Evan stood up and leaned against a tree, looking down at the ground and shivering. Jason noticed how pale he looked and was concerned for his injured friend. Turning around and getting down on one knee, Jason said, "Hop up."

Evan reluctantly put his arms around Jason's neck as Jason stood up, grabbing his legs, and Jason immediately started walking in their planned direction of travel. "I guess pedaling those bikes all this time was a good thing. Building up my leg muscles to carry your broke ass, that is."

"Yep. I sure did whip you into shape," Evan said, attempting to keep up his sense of humor during the bleak situation. Unable to maintain his jovial mood, Evan closed his eyes and laid his head on Jason's back as Jason marched steadily on.

With Evan on his back in place of his pack, Jason had his rifle slung around his neck, hanging in front of himself. He took two of the loaded magazines, placing one in each of his side cargo pockets, leaving the rest behind with Evan's gear in order to lighten the load. *I sure as hell hope I don't need that stuff along the way,* he thought, knowing that he could not sustain a firefight for long with three magazines total. One in the rifle and the two in his pockets. He knew the tradeoff in firepower was necessary, though, as he was already operating at his maximum capacity and had a long way yet to go.

Chapter Twenty: Wisdom

Ed awoke beside his friend Nate, lying on the floor, wrapped up in several blankets in front of the sofa. With no access to outside light from the cellar, he had no idea how long he had been asleep. A candle placed on the small table in the middle of the room flickered as the wick floated in the pool of melted wax, with very little of the candle remaining in solid form.

"Hello," Ed said quietly, unsure if Henry or Meredith were in the room. He sat up as his eyes adjusted to the low light and looked around the best he could. As he began to stand, he flinched with pain as his back and his right hip tightened up, causing him to momentarily drop back to his knees to recover. "Damn it. Damn it. Damn it," he whispered. "Oh, I took a beating last night."

Taking it slowly, Ed stood up fully erect and stretched as best he could in an attempt to work out the stiffness and the pain. "Mr. and Mrs... um... Henry and Meredith?" he asked again, wondering if they were in the cellar with him, still unable to see as the faint light of the candle finally extinguished itself in the puddle of wax. "Damn," he said aloud.

Not having another light source readily available, Ed wondered how he could possibly get some light so he could check on Nate's condition.

Just then, the door to the closet overhead opened, casting light down the stairs. Ed's heart felt as if it skipped a beat as he wondered who was walking down the stairs to join them in the cellar. Seeing Meredith's legs appear, he breathed a sigh of relief and said, "Meredith... is that you?"

"Yes. Yes, it's me. How is your friend?"

"I was just about to try and figure that out, when the candle went out," he replied.

"Oh, I'm so sorry about that. I didn't think I would be gone that long. Here, I made you some breakfast," she said as she handed him a towel wrapped around a glass bowl.

Opening it to look inside, Ed was elated to see homemade biscuits, some sort of potted meat, and grape jelly on the side. "Thank you so much, ma'am. This is amazing."

"I'm sorry there aren't any acceptable breakfast meats to give you. We are down to canned meats at this point, so that's the best I could do."

"No need for apologies, ma'am. None at all," Ed said as he picked up one of the hot, freshly baked biscuits and took a bite, savoring the flavor as he chewed.

"It's nice to have someone to cook for. Henry and I don't get to see many people on a friendly basis these days."

"Where is he?" Ed asked.

"He's shopping."

Looking at her with a confused expression, Ed said, "Shopping?"

"Oh, that's what we call it when we scavenge from the other homes in the area. There isn't any food left, but it's still possible to find clothes and things of that nature here and there."

"Oh, okay," Ed replied, now realizing what she meant. "So what time is it? How long did I sleep?"

"We don't keep track of time these days. There's not much need for it. I would guess the sun has been up for several hours," she said as she walked over to Nate with a handheld oil lamp lighting her way. "Pull that table over here next to him," she said.

As Ed moved the table next to the sofa, Meredith set the small oil lamp on the table and began to look Nate over. "I cleaned him up last night after you fell asleep. The cut on his head seems to be clotted nicely under the bandage. It hasn't bled any more from what I can see. Has he moved or made any sounds?"

"I'm sorry. I don't know. I just woke up myself. I was out of it," Ed said while rubbing his hands over his face and yawning.

"Well, that's understandable, all things considered."

Hearing footsteps through the house above, Meredith said, "It sounds like he's back."

"How can you tell that's him without his signal?" Ed asked.

"When you've been together as long as we have—you just know," she replied with a look of confidence.

Henry knocked and then came down the stairs to the cellar with a sack full of clothes. "Is he still not awake?" Henry asked, referring to Nate.

"Not yet. I'm gonna start an IV on him. It's been too long since he would have drunk anything at this point and he's gonna need some fluids. I'll give him some anti-inflammatories as well. From the looks of it, he took a pretty good hit to the head, and my guess is he has had a pretty rough go of things lately."

"Whatever you think. You're the boss," said Henry as he kissed her on the forehead.

Handing the bag to Ed, Henry said, "You should be able to find something that fits in here. There are two pairs of shoes in there. A ten and a half and a twelve."

"I'm an eleven and a half, so the twelve will probably work just fine," Ed replied, happy to finally have shoes to put on his feet for the first time since their detainment.

Henry looked at Nate, then turned to Ed and said, "I'm not a medical person, but Meredith will take good care of your friend. She was a trauma nurse when things couldn't get any uglier. I've seen her work miracles. It's been a few years, but she's still the best you could hope for."

"Sir, we are truly blessed to be here with you and your wife. We will be eternally grateful."

"Don't bother thanking us. We're pretty blessed ourselves, so it's the least we can do. Back to the other business at hand, though; I scouted the area this morning. There were several signs of human remains with the wreckage of the bus. There was another fellow in an orange jumpsuit who looks like he made it a little ways on foot before being shot in the back. My guess is you got out of there in the nick of time. They must have had ground troops in the area ready to secure the scene as soon as the airstrike went down. I really can't tell you if anyone else got away. Let's just hope they did."

Looking down at the floor in dismay, Ed said, "Thank you, sir. Tommy, one of the other guys on the bus, was so happy that he might actually make it home for his kid's birthday. Damn it; what the hell is wrong with this world?"

"I've been asking myself that question since 1953, son. I used to think the evils of the world was all the same crap, just on a different day. There was always some sort of tyrannical madman terrorizing his people somewhere on Earth. These days, though, it's a whole lot of shit and it's been a whole lot of days. These are the end times, if you ask me. I'm just gonna do the best I can until the Lord decides to take me, at which point I'll know deep down inside that I did the best I could for my wife. I just stay focused on that and let this screwed-up world worry about itself."

"That's about as healthy of an attitude as I've heard since this whole mess started. I tried to stay out of everyone else's business and just keep myself going up in Ohio. I had a small farm just outside of the Columbus area. I thought I had enough room and resources to let the world tear itself apart without my direct involvement. Unfortunately, that's not how the world saw things. As the outside forces expanded their grip, my little oasis turned out to be just a little too close to the city to stay under the radar. Once the powers-that-be began injecting themselves into the people's daily lives, confiscating firearms, food, and other resources, I knew it was time to head south to meet up with my friends who put themselves a good little situation together. They also had the manpower to defend it—where I didn't. Unless you're a backpacker in the Rocky Mountains or Alaska, staying on the move and out of civilization's way, it will catch up with you eventually."

"If I had it to do over," Henry said, "I would have moved Meredith into a cabin in the mountains a long time ago. The human mind is an interesting thing. On the one hand, we can convince ourselves that our current situation is fragile and that we must prepare for a not-so-positive eventuality. Then we turn right around and convince ourselves that it's okay to put it off because we have plenty of time."

"A lot of people were guilty of that, sir. Myself included."

"Well, that shouldn't have happened with me. I've seen and done some things that should make no man trust any government. I firmly believe that deep down inside, government is the root of all evil. As individuals, humanity is a wonderful thing. As soon as a group of individuals form a tribal or local government, however, it all goes to hell. Take, for example, if a man was living in a cabin deep in the woods, minding his own business, not bothering a soul, then one day while out hunting, he stumbles across another man doing the same thing on the other side of the mountain. His first reaction may be cautionary, but once he figures the new man out, his instinct would not be to enslave the man and force him to do his work back on his own homestead, regardless of the other man's skin color or ethnicity. His instinct would either be to avoid the man and remain autonomous, or befriend the man for possible barter, trade, and mutual protection. Now, fast forward a decade where more and more cabins and homesteads have popped up in the same woods. These new homesteads could be occupied by people with the same goals and values where everyone gets along just fine. Then someday, some asshole would say, 'We need a leader' and it would all start to unravel. As soon as one man or a committee of men see themselves above others, the inevitable oppression of mankind would begin. Wherever a majority has control over a minority, whether it's real or perceived, mankind will suffer. An individual does not enslave another individual; it takes a ruling majority to make it okay for that to happen."

"Wiser words have never been spoken, sir," replied Ed, giving deep thought to what Henry had said.

"If I were wise, I would be in that cabin in the woods today, instead of hiding down here in a hole in the middle of it all," Henry said with a chuckle. "It's easy to be wise after the fact. The truly wise ones among us take the steps they need to take before it needs to be done."

Chapter Twenty-One: Steps of Desperation

Stepping out onto the trail, Jason dropped to his knees and laid Evan flat on his back. Jason lay down next to him, looking up at the sky and trying to catch his breath. With his eyes closed, he could hear his own heart pounding in his chest. "Damn, Evan. You're heavy. How long do you think we've been going since our last break?"

Hearing no reply, he opened his eyes. Squinting from the sun shining directly into his eyes through the trees above, he looked over at Evan. "Ev... You okay, man?" he asked, shaking him. Jason sat up in panic at the realization that Evan was no longer conscious. "Evan... Evan... Wake up!" he shouted, but still no answer. He checked Evan's pulse and felt his forehead. "You're on fire, man. Damn it!" he said, looking around frantically. "Hang in there, buddy. We're on a four-wheeler trail. We'll make good time from here. We'll be there in no time. Just hang in there. Don't make me carry you all this way for nothing!"

Struggling back to his feet, Jason threw his rifle into the bushes, emptied his cargo pockets of the loaded magazines, and said, "Home stretch, man!" as he grabbed Evan by the arm, pulling him onto his back once again. "Come on!" he said as he started to jog with Evan. The absence of the extra weight of the rifle and ammunition was noticeable at his level of fatigue. *Focus Jason. Focus,* he chanted to himself keeping his steps in rhythm. *Almost there... A few miles... Little miles... Short miles... Almost there... Almost home... Gonna make it... Hooah!... Goin' all the way... In no time... Almost there... Hooah!... Little run... Short run... Get it done... Not so fun... Gettin' home... Anyway... There today... All the way... Hooah!... Oh, yeah. Gettin' there...*

In an instant, Jason's face slid to an abrupt stop on the dirt as he tripped violently on a root spanning the width of the trail. Holding on tight to Evan, he was unable to catch his fall. "Son of a...!" he yelled with rage-filled emotion. Crawling out from underneath Evan, he felt his face to find his lower lip was lacerated and bleeding heavily, and his lower front teeth felt loose to the touch. "Damn it!" he again yelled, in an attempt to vent his frustrations. "Sorry, man. Sorry. Here we go," he said as he heaved Evan onto his shoulders once again, continuing his jog for home. *Goin home... Almost there... Even though... The stupid ground... Tripped me... Gonna cut... That stupid root... With a saw... When I come back... Screw you... Dumb ass trail... Hooah!*

~~~~

As the ATV trail wound down a steep hill, Jason slowed his pace to avoid another fall. His legs were cramping and shaking as if he was on the final mile of a marathon. Through the thick trees below, Jason could see light as if the trail was opening into a clearing. Keeping his steady pace down the hill, his quadriceps were burning in a way he had never felt before. He felt he would lose control of his legs at any moment, as all valid and usable inputs from them had left his body long ago. He was now operating solely on pain and devotion to his friend.

As he reached the bottom, he nearly fell from the simple change in the slope of the terrain. Pressing on, he found himself in a pasture filled with grazing sheep on the other side of a barbed wire fence. His extreme exhaustion clouded his mind. He now knew where he was. They were on the outer edges of the Homefront. He dropped to his knees, laying Evan gently on the ground next to him. Evan was soaked with sweat and shaking. His skin was hot and clammy to the touch. Jason patted Evan on the shoulder and said, "Almost home, buddy."
~~~~

Trying to stand once again, Jason's legs felt as if they were being squeezed in a vice as severe cramps ran through his calves and thighs. He shook from extreme fatigue and dehydration. He had pushed his body to the breaking point, carrying his friend for miles and miles over the rugged mountainous terrain. "Come on!" he said aloud, punching the ground. He knew there was no way he could keep up the trek any longer, no matter how close they were.

Looking up at the sheep, Jason picked up a rock and hurled it at the center of the flock, barely missing a grazing ewe. "Damn it!" he said, frustrated by the situation. He then picked up another rock, throwing it again at the center of the flock. This time his rock struck a ewe directly in the side, causing her to run, triggering an instinct in the others to follow suit.

~~~~

Sitting in a tree stand overlooking the pasture, Jake sketched a caricature of one of his former childhood video game heroes. He found himself flashing back to such things often these days. His mother, Molly, often worried that he was in search of his childhood, which was taken from him too early. She didn't say anything to him about it, though, as reflecting back to a simpler time might not be such bad thing.

As Jake shaded in the character's hair and contemplated the position he would hold his sword of fire, he heard the sheep *baaaah* off in the distance and reflexively looked up to see what was going on. Initially, looking through his binoculars, he saw them running away from the tree line alongside the fence. "Dang coyotes," he said as he lifted his rifle, scanning the area through his rifle scope. "Don't those stupid mongrels know I have more important stuff to do while I sit up here—besides shooting at them, that is?"
~~~~

As he placed the reticle of his scope on the fence and panned slowly from left to right, he saw movement and prepared to pull the trigger. Focusing on his target, Jake said, "Wait... what the...?" He twisted the zoom dial on his scope, reducing his field of view, but bringing the image in closer for a better look. "Is that? Holy crap! That's Jason!" Jason was on his knees, waving his hands in the air, with Jake's father lying on the ground next to him.

Being too far away to communicate with Jason, Jake frantically called out over the radio, "They're back! They're back!"

"Who's back?" Molly answered from the radio base station in the house. "What's going on, Jake? Who's back?"

"It's Dad and Jason. In the south pasture. Something's wrong. I'm getting out of the tree," he said, laying the radio down frantically. Clipping the emergency egress rope to the harness he wore, he rappelled down the tree, landed on the ground, and took off running for the fence.

"Jake! What did you say?" asked Molly repeatedly over Jake's now unattended radio.

~~~~

Shivering, he pulled the covers tight around himself, attempting to fend off the cold. Feeling a hand dab a wet washcloth on his forehead, Evan opened his eyes to see Molly staring down at him. Wiping a tear from her cheek, she sniffled and said, "Welcome home, baby. Now don't you dare ever leave me again." She broke down into an uncontrollable sob as she hugged him and held him tight. "I thought I had lost you forever. We were starting to feel like a group of widows around here."

"Where's Jason?" he asked softly, his throat sore and dry.

"He's fine. He's with Sarah and the boys."
~~~~

"How... how did I get home? I was in the woods. There were coyotes all around us and... Now I'm here. Is this just another dream?" he said as he touched her face.

"No. It's not a dream. Jason carried you home."

"Carried me?" Evan asked, confused.

Wiping another tear from her cheek and smiling, she laughed. "He literally carried you all the way home. He'll probably be sore for quite some time."

"On foot?" Evan asked, still confused by the feat she described.

"Yes, silly. He carried you here, on his back, on foot."

"Wow," Evan said as he reflected on the events of the recent past.

"Yeah, 'wow' is right," Molly replied. "He said just buy him a beer someday when the world returns to normal, and you'll be even."

Smiling and squeezing her hand, Evan said, "I guess that would be fair."

"Oh," he asked, his memories returning to him. "Did Charlie and Jimmy make it back? Did they get the girl to the church? And what about Ed and Nate? Did they make it back?"

Evan could tell by the change in Molly's facial expression that something was wrong. She broke eye contact and looked away for a moment. "Charlie and Jimmy did make it back. And yes, they got the girl to the church. We've not seen or heard from Ed and Nate. We hoped they were still with you. Jason told us what happened and how you got separated. Peggy and Judith are both wrecks now."

"What's wrong?" he asked, attempting to look her in the eye as she evaded his gaze.

"We can talk about all of that stuff later," she said as she stood up and adjusted the blinds.

"What stuff? Why later?"

Just then, Rachel walked into the room. “It’s good to see my patient is awake and responsive,” she said with a smile. “Like I said, if an antibiotic is strong enough for a cow, it’s strong enough for a bull-headed man,” she said jokingly as she felt his forehead. “Still a little warm, but much better than how you looked when Jason got you here.”

“So what happened with Charlie and Jimmy?” Evan asked Rachel insistently.

Rachel looked to Molly, only to have Evan restate the question. “What happened? I already asked her. She didn’t want to tell me.”

Rachel turned back to Evan and said, “Charlie is fine. Beth... Beth was killed by someone she caught stealing from her while you were gone. Daryl got them. They aren’t a threat anymore. But when Jimmy got home—”

“Oh, God. Beth was pregnant,” Evan said, interrupting her.

Molly sat down on the bed beside him, her eyes welling up with tears. “Jimmy couldn’t handle it. He was devastated. He didn’t want to go on.”

Evan closed his eyes as his thoughts raced back to every moment leading up to the supply run. How many opportunities he had to shut it down based on their security concerns, yet he pressed on with it and now their once rock-solid homesteading community had suffered devastating losses. He felt guilty for his part in taking her husband away from her when she needed him at home.

Molly squeezed his hand. “Everyone else is okay. Griff got banged up pursuing the murderer. He fell off his horse and was hurt pretty bad, but he’s up and about now. He’s not back up to his full strength, but he’s fine. Everyone else is fine.”

She then turned to the door and motioned for Griff’s wife, Judy, to come on in. Evan looked at Judy to see that she was bringing young Lilly and Sammy into the room.

Upon seeing their father awake and alert, their eyes opened wide; they ran to him, yelling, "Daddy! Daddy! Daddy!"

They both climbed up on the bed as Molly said, "Be careful, girls. Daddy is hurting."

"Nonsense. Come here, my angels," Evan said as he reached out his arms, hugging both of the girls and kissing them on the head. His heart was overfilled with joy. He was on an emotional roller coaster ride—anguish and heartache over the loss of Beth and Jimmy, yet love and happiness to be reunited with his dear little girls. "Where is Jake?" he asked.

"He's on watch. He'll be in here as soon as he can. I'll let him tell you the story of how he found you and Jason," Molly said with a smile, her eyes welling up with tears of joy.

Chapter Twenty-Two: Happiness, Worry, and Regrets

Early the next morning, Evan awoke to the smell of a fresh, home-cooked breakfast. He looked around the room and thought, *Yep, still here. It must be real this time,* as Molly walked into the room with his breakfast on a bedside tray.

"Oh, good. I'm starving," he said, anxious to see what she had brought. Looking at the meal, he saw one fried egg and one piece of toast from Molly's homemade bread. "Are we having trouble getting the chickens to lay again?"

"No, silly. Rachel said to give you small meals until we see how you hold it down. If you do well with breakfast and lunch, I'll get you a more suitable dinner. She said that due to the location and the severity of your wound, she doesn't want you to go through the convulsions associated with vomiting, which the meds she has you on may contribute to."

"Orders are orders, I guess," he said, accepting Molly's explanation.

"There's my sandbag," Jason said from the doorway as he entered the room.

"Sandbag?" Evan replied.

"That's what you felt like. Just a big ol' heavy bag of sand."

"I don't know how to thank you for getting me home, man. That must have been quite the hump."

"Ah, don't sweat it. Like I told Molly—you can just buy me a beer someday."

"Deal," Evan replied sharply. "As long as it's not a craft beer or an import. That's like five bucks, and with the new economy—whatever that's going to be like—it could be fifty, for all we know. A three-dollar domestic should settle the debt just fine."

"Good to see you didn't lose your attitude like you lost your left testicle," Jason said with a smirk.

Evan felt under the sheets in a panic to verify if what Jason said was true. "Good one, man. You got me. Now I may have a heart problem in addition to an infected bullet wound."

Jason couldn't help but snicker out loud at the success of his joke.

"So, you know about everything that happened here while we were gone, I take it." Jason replaced their jovial mood with the cold, hard facts of their new reality.

With the smile leaving Evan's face, he said, "Yeah. I know."

"Other than that, Daryl is gonna take a packhorse and look for the radio gear I left behind. I gave him the map and details of its location. If he has room, he said he will look for the gear we left behind as well. He should be back later tonight; then maybe tomorrow we can talk about getting it up and running. He gave me a full debrief last night. In addition to what you already know, they've seen drones in the area. Several times, they have loitered overhead some of the homesteads, including yours. One time they saw a helicopter, too. I asked them if it was an Mi-24, but they weren't sure. They just saw the silhouette in the distance. Either way, things are changing around here, and fast. The shootout at the farm seems to have forced their hand."

"So, nothing on Ed and Nate?" Evan asked, hoping Jason had heard something from Daryl.

"No. Nothing yet."

"Damn," Evan said, disappointed with the answer.

"Once we get the radio links up and running, maybe we'll be able to get some more info from Q and the militia guys. Until then, though, we can't give up hope. I mean... we just got back ourselves. They could be working their way back here as we speak," Jason said, trying to remain positive and hopeful.

"Yeah. They're both tough as nails. They've got to be doing fine."

"Hey, man, I hate to run," Jason said, changing the subject. "But Sarah doesn't want me out of her sight for more than a few minutes at a time. You were right about the shorter leash," Jason said with a smirk. "I'll let you get back to your breakfast. I'm sure Daryl will want to see you when he gets back from his run. We can all have a pow-wow then."

Evan turned back to Molly as Jason left the room and said, "Can I at least get some of your amazing homemade hot sauce for my lonely little egg?"

~~~~

"Honey... honey... wake up," Molly said gently as she nudged Evan's shoulder.

Yawning loudly, Evan shook his head in an attempt to wake up and said, "Oh, man... that's why I hate pain pills. They zonk me out. I hate that feeling. I hate not being myself."

"Maybe that's a good thing. It keeps you in bed recovering, where you belong. Otherwise, you would probably be out there working already, hurting yourself again."

"Not this time," he replied with a serious look on his face. "I just about cashed in all my chips this time. I need the down time."

"Well, good. Anyway, you've got visitors," she said gesturing toward the door.

Evan was overjoyed to see Daryl and Griff, along with Jason, entering the room. "Well, look at this rag-tag bunch," he said with a smile from ear to ear.

"Evan Baird, it sure is good to have you home and mostly in one piece," Daryl said as he walked over to Evan's bedside.

"It's good to see you, too, my friend," Evan replied, reaching out to shake his hand. "I'm sorry about what you had to go through back here without us. I've been haunted by all of
~~~~

the *could haves, should haves* since we left. If I had any idea things would have—"

"Evan," Daryl said, interrupting him. "It's not your fault. We were all in on this. We all knew there were risks involved with splitting our group up like that in the name of barter and trade. We all had things we wanted, leading us to the decision to make the supply run happen, and we all share the blame. Some of the things were tragic, yes, but we are all learning to navigate this messed up new world together. It's no one person's burden to bear."

Evan faked a smile as his eyes welled up with tears, unable to reply in words.

Standing there with his arm in a sling, Griff added, "Heck, my injuries are my own damn fault for being such a lousy horseman."

"Hey, before we get off on another subject, which I'm sure will take us down a totally different conversational path, did Charlie and Jimmy get Sabrina back to the Gibbs family? How did that go? Where are they all now?"

Griff spoke up and said, "Yes, they got her to them safe and sound. Tyrone works security for the church now in exchange for room and board for his family. From what Pastor Wallace says, he's a real class act and has been a huge help to them. Hopefully, someday they can find something more permanent, but at least they have a safe place for now."

"Excellent. At least we have one happy ending around here. Tyrone really seemed like he had his head on straight. I'd love to see the Gibbs family, along with Sabrina, of course, as permanent residents around here someday."

"Amen to that," replied Jason. "I feel better about the church with another permanent security guy on staff with them, too. If you're gonna have an open-door policy at a place like that these days, you've got to be able to deal with what shouldn't be walking in the door."

"Now, back to business; I'm assuming we have some things to discuss," said Evan, redirecting the conversation.

"We sure do," replied Jason. "First off, Daryl successfully made it to the radio gear and back with his packhorse. He stashed everything underneath that rock overhang on the hill behind his house for now. It's far enough away from him for plausible deniability if need be. Before we venture out into the woods to set up the repeaters, we want to observe for at least the rest of the day and maybe tomorrow to make sure there aren't any prying eyes above us. Speaking of which, I'll let Daryl explain."

"Last week, I was over at Linda's place... just checking in to see how she was doing. We sat on the porch, sipping some of her delicious homemade herbal tea—"

Evan, Jason, and Griff all shared a grin.

"—when we saw a large bird high above the ridge directly in front of her place. She grabbed her binoculars, and low and behold, we had a drone buzzing around the skies."

"Armed?" Evan asked.

"No. At least, I don't think so. I'm a primitive weapons guy, so I'm not all up on that stuff like you guys, but the wings looked slick with nothing hanging beneath it," Daryl replied. "Anyway, Luke said they saw something similar in the skies over the Thomas farm over the course of the next few days. It looks like someone is curious about the area."

"Has there been any helicopter traffic?" Evan asked.

"Nothing like that here," answered Griff. "Pastor Wallace said some of the remaining Del Rio residents have seen a large single-rotor helicopter come in and out, landing down by the river near the bridge. And as Carl said, there have been UN patrols driving through town, asking if anyone has any information on insurgent domestic terrorist groups like the Blue Ridge Militia. Of course, everyone is being tight-lipped about it, but we're afraid the right pressure will be placed on the right person to start tipping them off. It's only human nature that you'll have a worm in the apple, eventually."

"Domestic terror..." Evan said, shaking his head. "The only terror being perpetrated around here wears a big UN logo on the side. Any word about Q? Ted? Carl and family? What about fallout from Vanessa's place?"

"We aren't sure about Q and Carl's folks. We are hoping to raise them on the radio once we get the repeaters in place and online. As far as Vanessa's place, yes, the UN patrol that cleaned up the scene burned her house and barn to the ground. They also threatened the surrounding neighbors with the same thing if any information regarding the perpetrators was withheld. In this case though, I doubt anyone beyond us and those involved know anything other than there was a shootout in the middle of the night."

"That's good."

"Yep, the last thing we want is a Waco or Ruby Ridge style assault on this place or any of the other homesteads as they try to root us out," added Griff.

Daryl spoke up and said, "Speaking of which, we need to put together a contingency plan to evacuate the women and children if it comes to something like that, or if things get too hot and heavy anywhere in the local area. I think we need to meet with the other homesteads and possibly have two or three fallback locations where our non-combatant family members can hide out until things blow over."

"I never thought I would see the day when we could consider our family members non-combatants," Evan said, looking out the window as the children played on their swing set.

"I know, but just look at what happened at Vanessa's place with her little girl present," Jason said in a serious tone. "It was by the grace of God that we happened along when we did."

Griff walked over to the window, looked outside at the children, and said, "Unfortunately, all throughout human history, children have not been sheltered from the evils of tyranny. Here in America, we were lucky to have been sheltered from it for as long as we were. The rest of the world, or rather the ugliness of humanity and the evils of corruption and power-hungry collectivism, have violently knocked down the walls of our once stable and free society. As Thomas Paine said, 'If there must be trouble, let it be in my day, that my child may have peace.'"

Chapter Twenty-Three: Building Faith

As Ed continued his bedside vigil beside his friend Nate, he read from a tattered old Bible given to him by Meredith. As the candlelight flickered and danced across the page, he sensed movement on Nate's bed. Startled, Ed placed his hand on Nate's and said, "Nate, buddy. Can you hear me?

Nate's hand flinched, followed by the batting of his eyes and a deep breath. "My head hurts," Nate said softly as he began to shift around restlessly on the bed.

"Nate. Oh, I'm so glad you're back with us," Ed said as he wiped a tear from his eye.

"What the heck happened? Where are we?"

"We are safe with friends. We're free, buddy. No more Camp Twenty-one. No more worry of you getting shipped back to the feds. I'm gonna get you back to Peggy, where you belong."

"Where is Tommy and everyone else? Are they okay?"

"The Bronco and our bus were hit by an aircraft of some sort. Not everyone got out. I'm not sure who did," Ed explained sorrowfully. "After the Bronco was hit and we crashed, people started to scramble. It was dark and chaotic. I kicked out a window and dragged you away as whatever hit us came in for the deathblow. We barely made it out. I did see others get out, but I honestly don't know who. I just saw orange jumpsuits, no faces."

After a moment of silence, Nate said, "Thanks, man. You've been dragging me around for a long time now. I owe you everything."

"You don't owe me anything. If it weren't for you guys, I would be alone in this world now. You are my family, blood or not."

"Same here, brother," Nate said. "I really need some water. My head is pounding, and I feel like I haven't had a drink in days."

"You haven't... except for this bag, that is." Ed held the candle so Nate could see the IV drip that Meredith had set up for him.

"Where are we?" Nate said, looking around.

"An old shelter of some sort under a suburban neighborhood home. The couple that lives here is awesome. I'd love to have them as neighbors back at the homesteads," Ed said with a smile.

Just then, he heard the door to the stairs creak open as Meredith said, "It's just me."

"He's awake, Meredith! He's awake!" Ed said with joy in his voice.

Meredith hurried down the stairs and said, "Well, hello, there. It's nice to finally meet you."

"Thank you, ma'am. Thank you so much for taking care of me and hiding us away, wherever we are."

"Oh, you don't need to thank us. We were getting pretty bored around here with nothing to do, anyway. We consider it a welcome break in the monotony."

"Where's Henry?" asked Ed.

"He's upstairs. Why don't you go and tell him the good news while I check out your friend here. Light that oil lamp and hand it to me before you go, if you could be so kind."

"Of course, ma'am." Ed lit the oil lamp with his reading candle. "Here you go," he said, handing it to her. "I'll be right back."

Hurrying up the stairs, Ed realized it was his first time out of the basement since they had brought them in. Looking around the home, he noticed what used to be a nice leather sofa in the corner of the room, which looked like it had been hacked to bits. Looking at its proximity to the fireplace, he immediately understood why.

"Welcome to the surface," said Henry from the adjacent kitchen, startling Ed. "It's good to see you in real clothes instead of that jumpsuit, as well. How do the shoes fit?"

"Oh, hi," Ed replied. "Nate is finally awake." He could barely contain the excitement in his voice. "And the shoes fit just fine. They are a little loose, but when you've been stripped of your shoes and forced to walk around on hot gravel and concrete, loose shoes are good shoes. We can't thank you two enough for everything you've done."

"See, son, prayers do work. Say, do you want to go on a run with me tonight? I might as well take advantage of the backup while I've got it. I've got someone I'd like you to meet, as well. Meredith will take good care of Nate while we're gone. You won't have to worry about that."

"I'd be honored, sir."

"Great," Henry replied. "After we eat tonight, we'll head out."

"What are we looking for tonight? Food? Supplies?"

"Sure, those things are always on the radar. Most importantly though, to use a phrase from the modern corporate world, human resources can be one of your most valuable resources."

~~~~

Later that evening, as Ed continued to read from Meredith's Bible while sitting alongside Nate's bed, Nate remarked, "You seem to be really getting into that."

"Yeah... I guess so," Ed replied. "I always considered myself a worldly fellow. Being born and raised in the New York City area of Long Island, I saw the rest of the country as 'flyover states' that were there to merely link New York with
~~~~

California. After moving to the Midwest and then ultimately Ohio for work, I started to see things in a different light. I slowly began to see that the great infrastructure of modern-day collectivism was a sham. None of it will ever truly be mine, although they say it belongs to the people. That, combined with the social engineering of governments and a culture that puts modern day humanism on a pedestal above all else, regardless of the damage we do all around us, really started pushing me back to basics. And now, with this all around us," Ed said, making an all-encompassing gesture with his hands, "I'm really starting to think that, like my mother always said, the 'Bible is the operator's manual for life.' We, as modern humans, had drifted too far away from the basics of life. Prior to the attacks that caused the collapse, people may have lived in the same house their entire life, yet they had no idea if there was anything they could eat in the woods behind them. As a society as a whole, we had completely forgotten how to live on our own planet without a vast infrastructure to support us. And now look what our high and mighty modern society has become without that infrastructure firmly in place. So, yes, I'm taking a new interest in this book in my pursuit of the true basics of life."

Nate smiled and sat up in bed. "Damn, my head hurts."

"Still the same?" Ed asked.

"No, it's truly getting better. I just feel like I lost a championship fight against Mike Tyson. It's sort of a ghost of a headache at this point that reminds me it's there when I move or something."

"Well, don't push yourself."

"I need to get the hell out of this bed. Speaking of which, where's the bathroom?"

"Ha. Bathroom..." Ed said with a chuckle. "You're in the city now, boy. Or, well, the suburbs. Same thing though. They were all on city water and sewer, which hasn't worked for quite some time. Living on the Homefront and the Thomas farm with their own well water and septic systems has gotten you spoiled."

"Yes, that it has. So... what do we do?"

"Oh, sorry," replied Ed, still chuckling under his breath. "They have a bucket upstairs converted to a toilet with some sort of homemade treatment in it to keep the stink down. They dump it in a hole in the backyard when it's full. They keep it up there because it would stink things up down here without adequate ventilation, but I can go get it and bring it down here to you."

"I'd be forever in your debt. Those old stone stairs look like a bitch for a guy on one leg."

"No problem, brother. I'll be right back," said Ed as he set the Bible on Nate's bed and headed upstairs.

~~~~

After Nate had taken care of his business and Ed dealt with the bucket, Meredith came down the stairs and said, "Ed, Henry is ready for you."

"Ready for you?" queried Nate.

"Oh, he wants me to accompany him on a supply run this evening. I figure it's the least I can do."

Looking concerned, Nate said, "Well, don't go and get yourself killed. It's a long way back to Tennessee to have to hop the whole way there on one leg."

"Don't worry, man. I'll be back. I've got as much faith in Henry as I do just about anyone."

With that being said, Ed smiled and proceeded up the stairs to join Henry for their supply run. "Hello, Henry," Ed said, closing the hidden stairwell door behind him.

"Hello, Ed. I've got something for you," Henry said, opening an old leather saddlebag. "This was my grandfather's
~~~~

revolver. It's an old Colt Single-Army, chambered in .45 Colt—or .45 Long Colt as some people call it today. It's older than I am, so do your best to hang onto it. It's the last family heirloom I have left. At one time, I had an extensive gun collection, including the Garand I carried in Korea. Unfortunately, during the early stages of the collapse, Meredith and I had to head downstairs unexpectedly to avoid a gang of looters. They cleaned us out. It took everything I had to stay down in the basement and not come up and fight them for it. I'd have killed every last one of those sons of bitches for even touching my prized family possessions. I just couldn't risk something happening and leaving Meredith all alone in what was the most uncertain of times."

"That showed some real restraint," replied Ed.

"It still eats me up to this day." Henry stared at the remains of his decorative wooden gun cabinet that was now just a pile of potential firewood. "But anyway, back to business here. You can carry this tonight. You won't do me any good unarmed. But I need it back."

"Understood, sir," Ed replied with sincerity.

Henry handed Ed the pistol along with an old-fashioned leather holster with cartridge loops going all the way around to hold the .45 Colt cartridges that any good Western-genre film star would be proud to carry. As Ed admired it for its quality and craftsmanship, Henry said, "My grandfather had that holster rig custom made by an old saddlemaker when he was based at the old Camp Travis in San Antonio, Texas, right after World War I. It cost him a month's salary on what was then a corporal's pay, but he knew it would be a prize possession for generations to come, and he sure was right. That pistol and this old shotgun are all I have left from the looters. Thank God I had this old Winchester Model '97 and that Colt pistol squirreled away in a chest down there for safekeeping."

"Well, let's get moving," he said, ending his stroll down memory lane. Getting back to the business at hand, Henry led Ed out the back door and through the backyards of some of the surrounding houses that had since been abandoned by people who had either passed away with no local relatives, or from people who fled the outskirts of Atlanta, looking for a safer and less populated area to wait things out. Henry knew exactly which fence boards were not nailed securely in place, making a known-only-to-him quick and easy way to transit through the neighborhood with little effort, while remaining off the main streets. Pointing to a large white house with a screened-in back porch, Henry said, "That old son of a bitch there should die off anytime and stop being such a headache to me. He's got all kinds of issues and no way to get what he needs. I've tried and tried to be nice to him, but he threatens my life every time I've gone to offer him help. You can only let a dog bite you so many times before you have to just give up and stop trying to feed it."

Henry then led Ed out onto Willow Park Lane and said, "We've got to cross this street and then slip in the back door of that old brick house. That's where we are meeting everyone."

"Everyone?" Ed asked with a curious tone.

"Yes, my human resources I was referring to earlier."

Ed merely nodded in reply as Henry hurried across the street and into the back door of the old abandoned house. Once inside, Ed noticed there was another door that separated the back porch, which had been converted into a room, from the rest of the house. Henry knocked on the door and took a step back, waiting silently for a reply.

"Who's that?" answered a voice from inside the room.

"He's one of the survivors I was telling you about."

"Why is he armed?" the voice inside asked.

"Why wouldn't he be?" answered Henry in an agitated tone.

After a brief pause, they heard the sound of several locks being actuated, followed by the door opening only a few inches, and then the rest of the way. “Come on in,” the man inside said.

Chapter Twenty-Four: A Community's Plan

After several bed-ridden days being cared for by Molly back on the Homefront, Evan was finally up and on his feet again. Although Molly had put him on an austere "light-duty" restriction, he was just glad to be out and about on his own property again.

Walking the fence line of one of his sheep pastures, Evan came upon Jake, standing watch in a tree stand. He noticed that Jake's attention wasn't on his task at hand, as he had slipped in undetected. "What are you working on so intently up there, son?"

"Oh... uh..." Jake said as he shuffled his drawing papers and pencils into his bag, embarrassed that he was caught off guard by his dad's arrival. "Oh, hey, Dad. Sorry, I was just drawing. I let my mind wander off. It won't happen again."

Evan looked up into the tree from the ground and said, "Don't worry about it, son. To be honest, I'm glad you have that as an escape. We all need to live in our own little world every now and then. So... what were you working on?"

"Just a character."

"A character. What kind of character?"

"Just something from one of the games I used to play."

"I didn't mean to disturb you," Evan said. "I just had to get out of the house and go for a walk. I finally talked your mom into letting me out of her sight for a few minutes, and had to take advantage of the beautiful day. So how are the sheep?"

"Good, I guess."

"You guess?"

"I mean, they're good."

"Well, I'll leave you to your work. Just try and remember to look up every so often. You're lucky it was me who snuck up on you."

"Yeah, I know. Sorry, Dad."

"It's okay, son. I just want you to be safe out here. And, by the way, thanks for picking up the slack while I was gone. Your mom said you were quite the man of the house. That makes me feel good to hear."

Jake just smiled down at him in response.

"I love you, son," Evan said as he continued his stroll.

"I love you, too, Dad," Jake replied.

As Evan continued his walk around the property, he reflected on all of the things that had happened to them since the attacks. He looked around and felt truly blessed to be in their situation and to have their resources, while simultaneously feeling cursed from all of the bad that had happened to their friends and loved ones. The harsh reality of it all, though, was eating away at him. All it would take would be a UN convoy to roll up their driveway to make it all go away. They were no longer dealing with looters, criminals, and desperate people who wanted to take what they had; they were dealing with the might of a huge global force that had chosen to insert itself in their world. And to add insult to injury, it was at the invitation of their own government.

Returning his thoughts to reality, Evan knew that Daryl was right. They needed to put a contingency plan together, and they needed to do it soon. The only certainty seemed to be that things were going to get worse before they got better.

~~~~

Arriving back at the house, Lilly and Sammy greeted Evan at the door with their usual exuberance and excitement. "Daddy, Daddy, Daddy," they said, running to his arms.

"Yes, my little angels, Daddy is still here."

"How was your walk?" Molly asked as she put the eggs away that she had just brought in from the chicken coop.
~~~~

"It felt good to be out. I'm still not myself, but I'm getting there. I found Jake standing watch in one of the tree stands... well, sort of."

Looking at him with a confused expression, Molly asked, "Sort of? What do you mean 'sort of'?"

"He was so preoccupied with his drawing that he didn't even notice me walk right up to the tree he was in. I wasn't sneaking around, either."

"Did you get on to him about it?"

"No. I started to reiterate the importance of maintaining vigilance while on watch, but I thought I would talk to you about it first. I know it's got to be hard for a kid his age going through all of this. The little ones don't know any better, but teens, especially, were living in the electronic lap of luxury here in America, with every device known to man within their reach, along with a world that's never gone without air conditioning and heat. They know what they are missing, whereas the little ones don't."

"Yes, he does seem to drift off here and there these days, like he is in his own little world. I was thinking of seeing if Mildred would want to get him and Haley together to hang out sometime. They need some interaction with others their age."

Just as Evan started to mention the future possibility of getting Haley in contact with Sabrina and Rhonda Gibbs, Griff walked into the room and said, "Daryl and Charlie are here."

"Great!" replied Evan, excited to see Charlie for the first time since their return.

Meeting the two men on the front porch, Evan walked right up to Charlie and gave him a hug. "I'm so glad to see you, Charlie." He pulled back and looked him in the eye. "I'm also so sorry how things went when you got back here. I can't imagine what you went through."

“It is what it is, Evan,” Charlie replied. “There’s nothing hindsight will do to fix anything. We just need to learn from our mistakes as we move forward.”

Nodding in reply, Evan said, “So, gentlemen, what brings you out this way? Other than my wife’s fabulous cooking, that is.” He winked at Molly as she stood by the front door listening to the conversation.

Charlie and Daryl grinned at each other as Charlie said, “Yes, Evan, you busted us on that one. But the second reason we came by is that we’ve discussed the contingency plans that Daryl mentioned to you before, and we think we have, at a minimum, something to start with.”

“Okay, great. What do you have?”

Daryl spoke up. “Well, there are several potential safe places, as we see it, for the time being. Back behind Linda’s property, there is an old ATV trail that leads over the ridge and down into the bottom of a valley that’s pretty steep on both sides. If you keep following the natural flow of the terrain, you come up on what used to be an old hunting camp—*used to be* being the key term. The cabin is long gone, but the remnant of an outhouse remains as well as there being the year-round creek in the bottom. The natural layout of the terrain and the thick trees and vegetation give it almost an enclosed canopy feel, helping to hide from potential prying eyes above. Though not a long-term option, it could be a quick hide-and-wait camp with the basics of hygiene already in place. The next one would be the old mine, back behind the Muncie place... uh, I mean the Vandergriff place. Have you ever been there?”

“No, I can’t say that I have,” replied Evan.

“That’s the beauty; I doubt many people have. It’s a failed mine from the early 1900s. It never produced anything—I think they were looking for coal seams—but it never paid off, so they abandoned the place before roads and stuff were put in. It’s really low key. I played there as a kid and visited it just the other day with this in mind. The brush in the area is so overgrown you can't even see the entrance. You sort of have to know it's there. It's big enough on the inside to house everyone, and deep down inside, there is a spring water pool. It's ideal in my opinion—for those who can make it there, that is. And lastly, although not a physical shelter, I think we should hide caches of camping supplies and food at several strategic points away from the primary bug out locations in the event some or all cannot make it to the aforementioned locations, or if changing conditions dictate that we be frequently on the move."

"Daryl, I'm sure glad you're on our team," Evan said with a smile. "I like it. I like it all."

"Good, I've already spoken with most of the other homesteads and everyone is onboard with the idea. I'm gonna take a few folks on a tour to the sites I mentioned above so that everyone is familiar. I don't want to draw maps or write anything down for obvious reasons. Griff here is gonna go with me to represent you folks."

"What's the plan for having the repeaters up and running?" Evan asked.

Jason replied, "Charlie and I are gonna go on a 'hunting trip' in the morning to set them up. Hopefully, we can get in touch with the Blue Ridge folks soon. The way things are going, we don't want to stay in the dark for too much longer. The last thing we need is surprises."

Chapter Twenty-Five: The Rats and the Cheese

As Ed stepped into the dark and musty room of the old, abandoned house, he glanced around to see several men looking at him with uncertainty. He counted five total, including Henry, trying to gather as much information on his situation as he could in his typical analytical style. Each of the men were armed with various weapons, ranging from an A2-style AR-15, a bolt-action Ruger M77, an Israeli Galil, a lever-action Henry Big Boy, and of course, Henry with his shotgun.

"This is Ed," Henry said breaking the silence. "He's the fugitive from Camp Twenty-one I was telling you about."

"I thought you said there were two?" said one of the men, who appeared to Ed to be in his mid-fifties and seemed to be a fairly gruff and sturdy fellow.

"There are two; the other is still banged up. He's back with Meredith right now."

"You trust someone you just met to be alone with your wife?" another man asked as if he was chastising Henry for the decision.

"Damn straight!" Henry responded firmly. "And that should be all you need to know to trust these guys like I do."

A few of the men looked at each other as if they were looking for some sort of unspoken agreement to accept what Henry was saying. After a moment of silence, one of the men reached out his hand to Ed and said, "Any friend of Henry's is a friend of mine. My name is Gary Sobolewski. Nice to meet you, Ed."

"Nice to meet you, too, sir... and thanks," Ed responded with a firm handshake and a smile.

Now that the ice had been broken, the other men each introduced themselves to Ed as the tension left the room. "So where are you headed?" asked Gary.

"My friend Nate and I need to make our way back to East Tennessee. We were on our way with some other friends of ours to Hot Springs, North Carolina, in an attempt to do some trade and barter at the swap meet we heard they had there. A UN helicopter and several Humvees with Russian soldiers apprehended us and split us up from the others. We aren't sure what happened to the other two guys who were with us. They took us to Camp Twenty-one and tried to get any info they could out of us about the militia groups in the area."

"Were they successful?" asked one of the men who had introduced himself as Paul Welch.

"No, sir. Not at all. Which is why they were less than friendly with us."

"Regardless of whether you spilled the beans or not, they would have ultimately been unfriendly with you. They kiss your ass to get you to talk, then after you do and are expecting to win their favor, in the tin shack you go."

"How do you know so much about Camp Twenty-one?" Ed asked.

"Because my treasonous brother-in-law became a 'blue belly.' I believe that's how you guys referred to them. That son of a bitch never was much of a man in my eyes. It killed me when my sister married him. He just wasn't a fit for the family. He likes to brag about the authority he wields there. I just let him run his mouth and make mental notes of it all."

"Was he... was he there during the rescue? Not a lot of those guys made it out, from what I saw," Ed said hesitantly.

"Nope, as usual I couldn't be that lucky. He was off that day. They've got him on some kind of cleanup detail out there now. He hates it. He thinks that's a job for his prisoners. Serves that turncoat right. Actually, he deserves a hell of a lot worse than that. They all do," Paul said with contempt as he spat on the floor. "Just talking about him puts a bad taste in my mouth. If the militias don't get him someday, I have a feeling I'm gonna end up killing him myself."

"Back to business," Henry said, interrupting Paul's tirade. "This group of grumpy, socially maladjusted old men are sort of the neighborhood watch around here. We take care of things that need to be taken care of, and tonight is one of those nights. We thought you might be interested in a little payback."

Ed smiled and said, "What did you gentlemen have in mind?"

"Ever since your bus incident, the UN has stepped up its patrols of the area. We assume they are looking for the few that got away. We would like to put a little dent in their operation. They've come through every day and every night, at varying times, and on varying routes, consistently patrolling the area, but especially on a nightly basis. If you're willing to be the cheese, we can catch the rats."

"Cheese, huh?" Ed said inquisitively.

"Yep, a big ol' slice of American cheese," Henry said, pulling Ed's old orange jumpsuit out of the bag he carried over his shoulder.

At first, Ed was taken back by the suggestion and had mixed feelings about being used as bait. After a few moments of thought, he looked at Henry and said, "Sure thing. Anything for the man who's kept me and Nate alive, and anything to get back at those bastards."

"Outstanding," Henry said with a smile. "Now, go ahead and change into the jumpsuit. You can keep your shoes on though. I suppose it's plausible that during this time you've managed to scavenge a pair of shoes. I'll explain more once we get to the rat trap."

Taking the jumpsuit from Henry, Ed looked at him and said, "Just don't let the rat eat the cheese, if you can help it."

"We'll do what we can," Henry said with a crooked smile.

~~~~

Reaching Henry's pre-planned location for their ruse, he, Ed, and the others slipped into one of the abandoned houses just across the street from where they wanted to position Ed. As Henry led them through the house, clearing it as they went from room to room, he looked at Ed and said, "Just because it was empty last time we were here, doesn't mean it is now."

Ed nodded in agreement and looked around the room, taking it all in. The house had clearly been empty for quite some time and had been stripped bare of anything of use. Even the wiring looked as if it had been torn from the walls.

As they crept into the living room and Henry signaled that the room was clear, he knelt down by the window to avoid exposing himself to anyone outside. Although it was well into the night, the bright moon provided ample illumination that could be both a benefit and liability.

Motioning for Ed to kneel down beside him, he said, "They have a common entry point into the neighborhood before they start randomly patrolling the streets. They come in from that direction," he said, pointing down the street to their right. "Once they enter the neighborhood, they tend to take random routes through the surrounding streets. With that in mind, and as long as they follow that general pattern, if you hide out between those two houses across the street there..." he said, pointing directly across the street.

"You mean in between the brick house and the one with wood siding?" Ed asked to clarify.

"Yep, exactly," Henry confirmed. "You hide over there and when you see them coming, dart across the street as if you are busted, and run back toward us. Paul and I will be in here, and Gary and Joe will be in the blue house next door. Once you run between the houses, we'll take them out as they attempt a pursuit."
~~~~

“Seems fairly straight forward,” Ed said.

“You don’t really have anywhere to keep that pistol in that orange jumpsuit, do you?” asked Henry, looking Ed over, reconsidering the sidearm for their ruse. “Those bastards will shoot you on sight if they see that you’re armed. We want them to chase you.”

Ed considered Henry’s concern for a moment and said, “Maybe in here,” as he unzipped his jumpsuit down to his waist. He placed the holster securely around his waist against his bare skin and zipped the suit back up to his neck. “There, it will be a pain to get to, but it will be there if I need it,” he said.

“That’ll do,” Henry replied. “Okay, Gary, you and Joe head on over to your stations, and Ed, scoot on across the street. Once in position, everyone lie low until the fun begins.”

“Roger that,” replied Gary. He patted Joe on the back, and the two men headed out the back door.

“Stay safe,” Henry said to Ed as he turned to leave as well.

“You, too, sir.”

“Stop calling me “sir,” damn it. I was enlisted. I worked for a living,” Henry said in a grumpy and commanding voice.

Ed just smiled in reply, seeing Henry’s days of hard-fought battles in the lines on his face and the crackle of his voice

~~~~

Several hours passed and the men hadn’t seen anything other than a feral stray cat and a squirrel. Ed’s eyelids grew heavy from the late hours, as well as the boredom of sitting in an overgrown bush growing against the front of the abandoned house. The only thing that kept him awake was the occasional need to swat an ant or some other pest off of himself, as he had become a fixture in their small world.

Nearly dozing off, Ed was startled awake by the sound of an approaching diesel engine. His heart raced as he feared
~~~~

what would become of him if things didn't go as planned. An escaped prisoner probably wouldn't fare well with the Russian soldiers, who were probably looking for revenge.

He watched as the vehicle approached. At first, he couldn't make out the type of vehicle due to its blinding headlights, but once it neared, he confirmed that it was indeed a UN-marked Humvee. As it reached what he felt was the right point in the road to get their attention, while giving himself adequate time to make it across the street without being caught, Ed took a deep breath and sprinted out of the bush as fast as he could for the gap between the houses.

Unfortunately for Ed, he did not hear the commands to stop that he expected. Instead, he was startled by impacts on the pavement directly in front of him, from the rapid-fire shots of the turret-mounted machine gun on the Humvee as the soldiers opened fire.

Crap! Ed thought as he reversed course, running back toward the house from which he came. As the gun trained on him with bullets impacting the ground behind him as he ran, Ed made it between the houses just before the rounds merged with his path, narrowly avoiding being killed. Hearing the Humvee slam on its brakes and soldiers dismount behind him, Ed ran as hard as he could, never looking back. Jumping over a four-foot-tall wooden fence in the backyard, he heard small arms fire behind him, along with the sounds of high-velocity 5.45x39mm rounds whizzing by his head.

Taking a sharp left turn, Ed jumped across another fence, tripping, and falling on a child's backyard toys upon landing. The soldiers gained ground on him as he struggled to regain his forward momentum. Ed heard other small-arms fire behind him and looked back to see several of the soldiers turning to return fire behind them. *Must be the guys,* he thought as he resumed his sprint through the backyard, jumping yet another fence.

As Ed made a sharp turn to the right, running in between two other houses, he heard the pursuing soldier's footsteps gaining on him from behind as the soldier began shouting at him in Russian. Ed wasn't sure what he was trying to say, but he knew the soldier was not simply trying to get him to stop running. He was out for vengeance and sought to get it tonight at Ed's expense.

Unable to outrun the soldier, Ed reached for his zipper, hoping to be able to get to his revolver as he felt the hands of the soldier grab him from behind, tackling him to the ground. Sliding to a stop on his face in the tall uncut grass of the mostly abandoned neighborhood, Ed felt the soldier take him by the hair and begin to slam his face repeatedly into the ground.

Unable to get his hand into his jumpsuit to retrieve his weapon due to the overwhelming weight of the soldier who was now sitting on his back, Ed felt he had only moments to survive. Thoughts of Nate and his potential struggle home to Tennessee, alone, with no prosthetic or even a suitable crutch flashed through his mind as he felt his face become soaked with blood from both his nose and mouth as the soldier relentlessly pounded him into the ground.

The soldier then placed his hand on Ed's shoulder, rolling him violently over onto his back. Ed could see the rage in the man's eyes as he pulled his knife from the sheath on his belt, placing his free hand on Ed's throat as he began to raise the blade high above his head.

Feeling himself losing consciousness from the tight grip the soldier had on his throat, Ed used his last ounce of energy to continue the fight. He reached into his jumpsuit, pulled the old Colt revolver from its holster, and while still inside his suit, he cocked the hammer and sent the 250-grain lead bullet crashing into the soldier's abdomen.

Feeling the soldier's grip around his neck begin to loosen, Ed could see the look in the soldier's eyes change from unrelenting rage to fear as he felt the man's warm blood spill from his gut. As Ed watched the man's life seemingly leave his eyes, the soldier fell onto his back, freeing Ed from his hold.

Ed immediately rolled away from the soldier, got on his knees and drew the Colt clear of his jumpsuit, aiming it at the man. He watched as he convulsed and shook violently, and then nothing. What one moment was uncontrollable rage and violence, had now become calm and silence.

Getting back to his feet, Ed turned his attention back to the direction from which his attackers came. He heard the sounds of footsteps rapidly moving toward him. He raised the old Colt and aimed it at the corner of the house, preparing to fire the remaining five shots at his pursuers as they rounded the corner.

As his target came into view, Ed immediately recognized Henry as he slid to a stop and shouted, "Whoa! Whoa, Ed. It's just us. We took the others out from behind." Looking over at the dead soldier, knife still in hand, Henry said, "The old Colt saved another life, I see."

"Yes... yes, sir. It did," Ed said as he de-cocked the pistol and slid it back into its holster.

"Take a cartridge out of your belt and top that cylinder off," Henry said, pointing at the gun. "You never know when you'll need all six."

Chapter Twenty-Six: Link in the Chain

Walking into the kitchen for breakfast, Evan yawned and said, "That smells so good." He walked up behind Molly, wrapped his arms around her from behind, and gave her a kiss on the cheek.

"Good morning, love," she said, smiling and thankful to have him home. "How did you sleep?"

"Great." He poured himself a cup of the ladies' homemade herbal tea. "I'm feeling a lot better. I think it's high time I drop the light-duty routine and start helping out around here again."

Molly looked gave him a disapproving look. "In my professional opinion as a former nurse, I think it's too soon... but I guess I have to be thankful you took it easy this long. Okay, you have my permission."

Evan chuckled and gave her another kiss on the cheek. "Thank you, ma'am."

"Good morning, Sarah," he said, taking a sip of tea as she walked into the room.

"Good morning," she replied.

"Did Jason get off to an early start with his hunting trip this morning?" Evan asked.

"Yes, he did, and you don't need to use code speak, Evan. I know what he's really doing. I'm not happy about him being out there right now, but I understand it's necessary."

"I'm just sorry I'm not with him," Evan replied.

"By the way," she added. "Mildred and the others at the Thomas farm sent you a get-well-soon radio message this morning. They said they hope to see you soon."

"Oh, how nice. Thank you. I would love to get over that way when conditions permit. I kind of feel like I owe Judith a personal explanation of why we came back without Nate," he said, looking out the window and losing himself for a moment in his own thoughts. "God, I hope they make it home soon. I feel... ah, never mind."

Understanding the internal conflicts Evan and Jason both felt about the situation, Sarah patted Evan on the back and got on with the business of helping Molly with breakfast.

"Where are the kids?" he asked.

"They are studying their school work with Peggy. She's really stepped up with the homeschooling. It helps Zack associate with the other children that way, too. He's starting to make progress toward coming out of his shell."

"Does he still have nightmares?" Evan asked, taking another sip.

"Yes, but not like before. He wakes up crying for Peggy, but he's not in a total panic like before. He asks about Nate a lot, too," Sarah said. "He doesn't understand the extent of Nate's relationship with his mother. I think he just feels that Nate is filling a void in his life."

Feeling the guilt of returning without Nate build in his heart, Evan quickly changed the subject. "I'm gonna go check on some things," he said and quickly left the room.

"Oh, I'm sorry," Sarah said to Molly. "I didn't mean to..."

"It's okay," Molly replied. "I know."

~~~~

Sitting quietly on top of a ridge, providing overwatch for Charlie down below as he positioned and enabled the encrypted radio repeater, Jason scanned the skies around them, looking for signs of prying eyes from above. He brought with him an AR-10 in .308 Winchester from the Homefront's arsenal, as his beloved Remington was no longer in his possession.
~~~~

Once Charlie gave Jason the thumbs up, Jason returned the signal to let him know the coast was clear. Slipping off the ridge, Jason met back up with Charlie further down the trail, in the direction of home. “Is it online?” he asked.

“So far as I can tell,” Charlie replied. “There’s only one way to know though. How do you want to test it?”

“I’m not a communications expert, but from what I gathered from Q, when we transmit from one of the handheld units, the repeaters bounce the signal around in the network, making it difficult to DF the sender’s location. I imagine it’s possible, though, if someone is actively engaging in electronic intelligence and is close enough to pick up the signal directly from the handset.”

“But wouldn’t the relay from the repeaters throw it off?”

“Probably. Like I said, I’m no expert, but that makes sense. Unless, of course, the timing of the signals could be locked down in order to track the initial transmission, while ignoring the relays. I dunno,” Jason said, shrugging his shoulders. “There’s only one way to find out if it works, though, and that’s to give it a shot.”

Using the call sign given to him by Q that identified the Homefront to the Blue Ridge Militia radio operators, Jason switched on the handset, pressed the talk key, and said, “Fox Three Two,” and released the key.

Waiting a moment, Jason began to press the talk key again to transmit a second time when he heard, “Fox One Two, bravo.” Looking at Charlie with a smile on his face, Jason then said, “Kilo India Lima Lima Echo Romeo.”

“Killer?” Charlie asked with curiosity.

Jason shrugged his shoulders. “I didn’t make up the verification codes; they did.”

A reply came over the radio saying, “Copy Fox Three Two. Fox Three sends regards.”

“Sweet,” Jason said to Charlie with excitement.

"What?" Charlie asked, not being privy to the lingo.

"Quentin must have made it out of the cave that day!" Jason said in an elated voice. "He is Fox Three."

"You need to share this info with me and the others. What if you got—you know—if something happened to you? How would the rest of us use the radios?"

"You're right, Charlie. I'll brief you up on the walk home."

"Excellent," Jason replied over the radio. "Updates?"

"Light activity."

"Copy. Fox Three Two out."

Receiving a double click of carrier only, with no voice, Jason understood their reply and switched off his radio to conserve the battery.

"That was the shortest conversation I've ever heard," said Charlie.

"That's the idea. Short and sweet. The longer you key up, the more time they have to DF your location and smoke you from above."

"Oh, yeah. I see that now. So you... or we, are Fox Three Two?"

"Yeah, each group gets a mutual call sign. It would be too complicated to try to assign each individual their own. Quentin, or Q as he likes to be called, is Fox Three because he is the area field commander for Area Three of the militia's areas of operation. Fox is the term for those out in the field or away from any type of HQ position that the militia can consider an asset or an ally."

"What exactly is his role as a field commander?" asked Charlie.

"The Blue Ridge Militia are big on keeping themselves separate from a governmental force in any sense. Being firm believers in the concept of individuals standing together, rather than a group simply following orders, they don't use traditional rank structures.

"Also, they don't have permanent ranks. For example, in their field components, they have team members, team leaders, strike leaders, and field commanders. A team member is just that, a member of the team. He or she is not subservient to the person above them in position; they are simply there as a voluntary member of the team.

"A team leader is the person assigned to call the shots and to be the point of contact for a specific movement or operation of a team. It's not a permanent rank or appointment. You only carry the title while carrying out the movement.

"A strike leader is the same thing, but they are in charge of, or rather represent, more than one team working in coordination for the accomplishment of a common goal. Again, it's not a permanent position; you only wear the title while fulfilling the role. A specific operation can last a long period of time; however, so you may be in that position for the duration, but you aren't seen as a superior to any individual like you would be in a traditional military sense.

"The field commander is responsible for the ongoing operations of an area. That position is held for more than one movement or operation for the sake of continuity. Again, there is no superiority of one man over another man; it's simply a role that's being filled. No permanent rank appointments and no social hierarchy.

"The only position above the local field commander is the militia commander, which is an elected position chosen by all of the militia members. Every man or woman is just another link in the chain. Their organizational structure basically looks like a circle, where all links in the chain form the unbroken circle, unlike the straight-line structure of the governmental military units."

"Are we militia members, then, since we have a call sign?" Charlie asked, confused about the depth of the situation.

"I think Evan and I pretty much are. We've pledged to help hold down the fort here on this end of Area Three as well as be the eyes and ears out this way. They know you guys are all a part of us, though—that we all stand together as one out here."

"Damn straight about that," Charlie replied. "Based on their organizational structure, I like the way those guys think. Everyone on the same team, voluntarily, with no man having power over the other. Leading by mutual interest alone and not based on a superiority established by law."

"Yeah, that's how Evan and I felt when they explained it all to us back at the cave where Carl took us to meet up with Q."

"As much as I like to think of us being up here in our own little world—as self-reliant as we are—it sure is nice to know we aren't alone in the grand scheme of things."

Jason nodded in agreement. "Yep. As long as people band together to do wrong, other people will have to band together to do right. Even if it's just in a time of emergency or extreme hardship. In a perfect world, we wouldn't need to. But this world, as well as any society the world has ever known, has been far from perfect."

Chapter Twenty-Seven: New Beginnings

As the night passed, Nate feared for the safety of his dear friend, Ed. "So, how long do these runs usually take?" he asked Meredith.

"Henry is usually not in any sort of hurry. He always says rushing gets you killed. He prefers to take things slow. I try not to sit up and worry while waiting for him, but it never gets any easier knowing he's out there alone. I do feel better knowing your friend is out there with him tonight, though," she said, placing her hand on Nate's shoulder with a smile.

"Yes, ma'am. Ed's made it through a lot. He's got me through a lot. I'm sure the two of them will be just fine. If something happened to Ed, I would be all alone again. I had quite the solo trip in the not-too-distant past, trying to make my way to Tennessee, and that was hard enough with both legs."

"You lost your leg after the collapse?" she asked with a confused look.

"Yes, ma'am."

"Well, how on Earth did you manage to survive that? I mean... without our healthcare system being intact? Lots of people have died from much less lately."

"I was blessed to be with the right people," he said. "My brother was a medical student and the first stop on my journey was to find him. He was dating a doctor and working with an outstanding group of patriots back in Texas. He was—" Nate stopped as they both heard the back door to the house above them open.

"That's not them," she whispered.

"What? How... how do you know that?" Nate asked in a soft voice.

"I just do. I've sat down here many a night, analyzing every little sound while Henry has been away on his runs. I know every move that man makes, and I know how he makes them."

"Do you have any other guns down here with us?" Nate asked, trying to get himself prepared for a fight.

Shaking her head no, she whispered, "No. They took the only two. I usually have the pistol, but Henry wanted Ed to be armed. All we have is an old Civil War replica sword he found while on a run one night, and a bat." She then slipped behind the curtain and returned with both items.

The footsteps grew louder as the intruders were now directly above them in the bedroom. She and Nate stopped to listen. Nate reached out, took the sword, and said, "They must be looking around for stuff to steal."

"Everybody around here knows there isn't anything left in these houses. I don't know who they hell they are, but I don't have a good feeling about this," she said, visibly shaking from fear.

"Go. Hide behind the curtain with the bat. I'll hack their damn feet off if they try to get down here," Nate said as he got down on his hands and knee to quietly work his way to the stairs, hiding alongside the wall. He then motioned for her to turn out the light and go.

Doing as he asked, she extinguished the candle and disappeared into the total darkness of the room.

Nate waited silently as he strained to hear every footstep and sound from the room above. Clutching the sword, he tried to imagine exactly what he would do with it if such a thing came to pass. When the footsteps moved into the closet, Nate's pulse raced as he prepared for what now seemed to be an inevitability; then he heard the boxes that Henry placed over the door being dragged out of the way. *Damn it to hell,* he thought. *Why... why... why did they have to leave?*

Hearing some faint mumbling above, unable to make out what they were saying, Nate could tell that they had found something of interest in the closet. Just then, the trap door was pulled from above, being stopped by the sliding bolt Henry had installed for Meredith to lock when he was away. The sound of Nate's pounding heartbeat, which was nearly drowning out the faint sounds from above, was interrupted by an explosion of wood debris as fully automatic fire erupted, nearly disintegrating the old wooden trapdoor. Ricocheting bullets and bits of wood and brick bounced all over the room as the gunfire from above deflected off the old brick wall at the base of the steps.

Nearly as soon as the gunfire began, it ended with the sounds of two bodies falling to the floor like sacks of potatoes. After a moment of silence, Nate heard the terrified screams from Henry as he called out, "Meredith! Meredith! Are you okay?" followed by the sound of footsteps racing down to the basement below.

"Yes. Yes. Oh, my God, yes," she shouted with tears in her eyes, running to his open arms as he reached the bottom of the stairs. "What the hell is going on? What happened?" she asked him through the tears and panic in her voice.

"No time to explain. Get your bug-out bag," he said as he began tossing the remaining canned food into a sack.

"Where's Ed?" Nate asked, fearing for his friend.

"He's keeping a lookout upstairs. Here," Henry said, handing Nate a crutch. "Can you use this to get around?"

"Yeah. Yeah, no problem," Nate replied, still confused, but understanding of the urgency of the situation and the need to simply comply and ask questions later.

As Meredith donned her backpack and handed Henry his, he took her by the hand. "Come on. We've got to get the hell out of here and right now," he said as he nearly pulled her up the steps.

Nate struggled with the crutch to the top of the stairs, where Ed was waiting with a hand out, pulling him up the last few steps with one hard tug. Stepping over the bodies of two UN soldiers, Ed said, "This way. Follow him." He handed Nate one of the downed soldier's rifles while he carried the other over his shoulder via the sling. Nate slung the rifle on his back, positioned his crutch, and followed Ed's direction.

Leading them out of the house, Henry looked around, listened, and then said, "This way. Let's go this way to get the hell away from here."

As they proceeded through the yard of the abandoned house next door, Nate looked back and noticed a UN-marked Humvee sitting in front of the home. "Hey, what about their truck?" he asked.

"No way, they'll spot us too easily," Henry replied.

"No... I mean how about we move it to another house. It may stall them while they look for their comrades inside the wrong house—giving us more time and distance."

Looking back at Nate, Henry said," Damn good idea."

"I'm on it. Go with them, Nate. I'll catch up," Ed said as he ran back toward the Humvee. Climbing inside, Ed looked around for anything of use. He found a load-bearing magazine vest containing four fully loaded AK-74 magazines, a flashlight, and a handheld radio. *Outstanding,* he thought as he started the truck and began driving it across the street, behind the next block of houses. Grabbing the found items, Ed donned the vest, pocketed the light and magazines, and left the Hummer running with the lights on, pointing at the front door of one of the homes. He wanted whoever came looking for the two soldiers to find the Humvee right away, leading them into the decoy house.

Running back toward the location where he had last seen the others. Ed couldn't help but frantically scan the sky as well as his surroundings on the ground, expecting more pursuers at any moment. "Ed," he heard from behind an overgrown line of shrubbery on a neighboring street. He immediately altered his course for the sound and saw Nate stand, waving to him from around the side, near the ground.

Reaching the others, Ed ducked behind the shrubs and said, "I got us a few extra items."

"Great. What?" asked Henry.

"Ammo, a light, and a radio."

"Outstanding," Henry replied. "Let's get some more distance and then lie low. We can use the radio to listen in to any possible activity in the area. It would obviously pose a threat for us to transmit in any way, but if they are on the same frequency, we should be able to tell if they are getting close from the chatter and signal strength alone, even if we can't tell what the Commies are saying. But for now, let's just get the hell out of here."

~~~~

After several hours of trekking through the suburban area in the dark, the group, now consisting of Henry, Meredith, Ed, and Nate, came to the edge of an old abandoned lawn mower dealership with an overgrown field on the other side of the road in front of them. "I hate to keep being the boat anchor, but I need a break," Nate said, becoming sore from the use of the crutch to which he was not accustomed.

"Oh, it's not just you, son. My old bones need to call it a night. I don't think I can keep going, either," added Meredith, agreeing with Nate.

"I think we've gotten far enough away for now," said Henry as he looked around.

Ed noticed Henry attempting to look off into the brush of the field in the darkness. "I'll go check it out. You all stay put," he said as he slipped off into the night.
~~~~

Returning after only about ten minutes, Ed said, "There is a tree line on the other side of this field. There is a small creek with a little bit of running water. It looks like this used to be farmed, and they left the trees around the creek. On the other side, there is maybe another ten feet of trees and then what appears to be what was once a farmer's field. It looks clear to me. It's a reasonable place to get some water and wash up, as well as take a nap. I'll get the first watch while you all catch some rest."

Agreeing with Ed's suggestion, they all made their way across the field in the darkness. Reaching the other side, Ed flicked the flashlight on momentarily to show the others the terrain they would be working their way down to get to the creek below. After slipping into the trees, they had to creep down a slight incline to the creek. Henry started down, holding Meredith's hand, leading her safely to the bottom. Ed stood watch while Nate started into the woods.

"Damn it!" Nate yelled as he hit the ground, having had his crutch slip out from underneath him on the slick grass-covered slope.

Ed shone the light to see what was wrong; Nate was on the ground, covering his eyes. "I'm fine. Turn it off," said Nate in a frustrated voice.

"Oh, sorry, man," Ed replied. He then went to Nate's side and offered him a hand.

Brushing him away, Nate replied, "I've got it. I'm fine. I still can't believe those bastards took my leg. I felt nearly one hundred percent with it. But now... back to being the boat anchor."

"Oh, stop it," Ed said, dismissing Nate's negativity.

Once they all settled in at the side of the creek, they washed up and Ed and Nate both began to drink water directly from the small stream with the cupped palms of their hands.

Henry pulled two plastic tubes from his and Meredith's packs, handed one to her, and they both leaned over and began to drink, sipping water through the tubes.

"What's that?" asked Nate.

"LifeStraws," Henry replied.

Ed and Nate both just looked at him, trying to get a better idea of what he had with the limited moonlight in the confines of the trees.

"It's a water filter and a straw combined," Henry explained. "They're really great. We tested them after we bought them, but this is the first time we've had to use them for real. Back at the house, we just used a filtration pitcher and purification tablets."

"This is much better," Meredith added. "Those tablets make the water taste horrible to me. Would you like to try?" she said, gesturing toward Ed and Nate with her LifeStraw.

"No, thanks," Ed replied. "My body is accustomed to drinking straight out of the creek. It hasn't killed me yet."

"Yet," Henry replied with a chuckle.

"By the way, Henry," Ed said, removing the old cowboy holster and Colt Peacemaker. "Now that I've got this AK, I'll give you this back before something happens to it. I'd hate for you to part with another heirloom."

Reaching out to take it, Henry said, "Thanks. Yes... I imagine what few things we have are all we are gonna have from here on out. We can't go back to the house now. They'll be crawling all over that neighborhood." Looking at Meredith, he said, "But at least I finally got her out of there. I don't know where we will end up, but I was getting tired of the love of my life living like a rat in a hole."

Meredith smiled. "I'd prefer to be referred to as a mouse, my dear. Besides, I was very thankful for that hole. It kept us alive. But the house was just a house. Nothing was ever going to be the same there again, anyway. I'm happy as long as I'm with you. This will just be our new beginning."

They shared a sweet and gentle kiss, seeming to get lost in each other's eyes, and in that moment. Ed took the opportunity to give them some privacy and began to work his way back to the edge of the field, facing the road for his watch. He looked up at the bright, full moon and wondered how everyone back at the Homefront was doing. Having no family of his own, they were all he had in the world. Nate had become like his brother, and getting Nate safely home to Peggy and Zack had become his number-one priority in what was now his life.

As Nate got comfortable, he looked at Henry and said, "Thanks for the crutch. I'd have had an impossible time without it. Where did you get it?"

"One of the other gentlemen in the neighborhood came across it a while back. We had put it back with some other healthcare items in the event one of us needed it someday. When Ed and I were on our way back, we picked it up."

Meredith interrupted the casual conversation and steered them back toward a more serious note by saying, "So what happened out there tonight? And don't give me your sugarcoated B.S. that you usually tell me. I've always wondered what was going on, and I have a feeling our visitors tonight weren't random."

Henry looked down at the ground, took a deep breath, and said, "The boys and I knew they would be looking for Ed and Nate. We knew it would be an opportunity to catch them off guard and send a little payback their way. We used Ed as a guinea pig. He put his orange jumpsuit on for us, and when the initial patrol rolled into town, he caught their attention and started a chase. They were so focused on him, they didn't even know we were there. On our way back—"

"So you killed them," she said with an icy stare.

"Yes. Yes, we killed them. In our defense though, they were trying to kill Ed, not capture him. He took one of them out with the Colt hidden inside of his jumpsuit. Anyway, afterward, we worked our way back to the rally point—"

"The *what*?"

"A house on Fourth that we were using to meet up away from anyone's actual residence. Anyway, we worked our way back there, being careful to make sure we weren't being followed. Ed changed out of his jumpsuit, we grabbed the crutch, and just as we started to leave, we saw another Humvee go by one street over, heading in the direction of our house. Ed and I went straight there, while the others went back to their homes just in case any of us had been seen leaving our own residences, or in case someone had tipped them off to where we might be. I have a feeling some son of a bitch around here rolled over on us. They seemed pretty intent on searching our house with a fine-toothed comb.

"As Ed and I arrived, we heard the shooting begin. I almost died of a heart attack right there on the spot. If anything had happened to you..." Henry paused to maintain his composure. "Anyway, we rushed straight in. The bastards didn't hear us running through the house because of their own irresponsible gunfire. We dropped them both on the spot and that's when I came running down to the basement."

"How long has this little neighborhood war of yours been going on?" she asked.

"War? There hasn't been a war. Oh, no, nothing like that. The boys and I just had to take care of things every once in a while. Tonight, I'll admit, we took things a little too far. Our overzealous attitude has brought those foreign bastards down on our homes. Before that, we just did what we had to do to keep the looters and criminals away."

"So you killed others before this? When you were out supposedly searching for supplies, you were out killing anyone you didn't want in our neighborhood."

Henry stared at the ground then raised his head, looked her in the eye, and said, "I did what had to be done. Nothing more. Nothing less."

Meredith took a deep breath and placed her hand on his. "I know you're a good man, Henry. I trust your judgment. Please don't ever doubt that. Just, please, please don't hide anything from me ever again. I'm not a child. I don't need or want you to shelter me from what's really going on around us. Promise me."

Henry smiled and said, "I promise, my love. Never again."

Chapter Twenty-Eight: The Imminent Threat

Back on the Homefront, several days had passed since Charlie and Jason had gotten the encrypted radio relays set up and connected to the HiveNet network. Jason had been the point man in regards to network communications. He dutifully monitored the radio a safe distance from the Homefront and the other homesteads each day at his assigned time. Each day, he had received a routine update of light activity in the area. Jason would respond in kind and then return to his hectic daily life, trying to keep up with all of the things that made the homesteads function as a quaint and civil little society. Additionally, the moves to the new properties for the Jones and Vandergriff families had been put on hold, given the outcome of the supply run and the current security situation.

After the days of relative calm, as Jason listened in at his assigned monitor time, he received a slightly different message than usual. "Fox Three Two... Fox Three Two. Fox Three One. JADAM. JADAM. Fox Three One. JADAM. JADAM."

Jason's heart skipped a beat as he realized JADAM was their call for Joint Area Distress Message, meaning something was underway that was affecting all of their area of concern. Gathering his thoughts, he replied, "Fox Three Two Copies."

"Confirm."

Jason then replied with the day's confirmation code to let the sender know it was indeed him on the other end of the transmission. "Kilo Echo November Oscar."

"Fast movers over Fox Three. Report contact."

Fast movers? Jason thought, wracking his brain to try and remember all of the lingo he had been so diligently studying. Unable to carry a notepad with any such radio coding and lingo on it for security reasons, he had to rely on memory alone, and this was still all new to him. *Damn, that's an aircraft. I think.* "Copy all and WILCO. Contact negative at this time."

"Fox Three Three and Three Five both report soft contact. Go hot air."

"Wilco," Jason replied.

"Fox Three One out."

"Fox Three Two out," Jason replied, signing off. *Damn it!* he thought as he began to jog through the woods for home, scanning the sky as he went.

As he neared the Homefront, Jason ran toward the most recent tree stand on the outer perimeter that he knew to be occupied by a watch stander. "Greg!" he shouted as he approached the stand.

"Yeah? What's up?" Greg shouted from the tree.

Pausing to catch his breath, Jason said, "Eyes up! There may be aircraft in the area. If they spot you, just hang tight. Don't leave the tree. You're just a deer hunter in a stand. No radio calls while it's in the area. Got it?"

"Um... yeah. I guess. What's going on, Jason?" Greg asked, unsure of the extent of the situation.

"It may be something, or it may be nothing. Either way, step up your game and keep OPSEC and COMSEC at the top of your priority list. Travel smart and communicate smart. Someone has an interest in the area, and we want them to think we are just simple mountain folk. Got it?

"Yeah. I've got it," Greg replied.

Jason then turned and continued his jog back to the Homefront. Over the next hill, he could see the house off in the distance as he heard the dreaded sound of the *thump, thump, thump* of helicopter rotors. Without even looking up, he knew it to be the sound of a Hind. He had learned to fear that sound, and from his Army days, knew it wasn't a Blackhawk or other helicopter types in the U.S. Army's inventory. The Hind, to him, had a unique sound that he would not soon forget.

Halting his movement, Jason stepped up next to a tree, sharing its form as the ominous beast flew overhead toward the house, followed closely by a second Hind.

A flight of two? They must mean business, he thought as stress surged through his body. Sarah and his children, as well as the others, were in that house. From the deeds he had personally witnessed the UN soldiers do, he was not confident that this was merely a routine flyover patrol.

~~~~

After placing her eggs in the basket to carry back into the house, Molly started to step out of the chicken coop as she heard the helicopters approaching in the distance. *The girls!* She dropped her basket, cracking the eggs, and ran for the house, not knowing what was about to happen. Swinging the back door open wildly, Molly yelled, "Everybody in the basement! Now! In the basement!"

Peggy ran into the room carrying little Zack and said, "What? What's going on?"

Molly replied frantically and in broken thought, "I don't know. Helicopters. Where's Evan, Griff, and Jason?"

Seeing the fear in Molly's face, Peggy replied, "Jason went to do his thing, Evan's taking a nap—I think he's a little tipsy from his meds—and Griff is—"

"I'm right here!" Griff said, running into the room. "What's going on?"

Before Molly could answer, they all heard the sound of the helicopter rotors fly over the top of the house at near rooftop level. They ran to the window only to see both of them arc around as if to make another pass over the house.

"Downstairs!" she yelled, not knowing if they were going to open fire on the house. After Evan and Jason's experiences
~~~~

with them up to this point, she knew it was smart to expect the worst.

Griff looked at Molly. "You go and get Evan. Peggy, get Zack downstairs like she said. Judy is watching Lilly and Sammy. I'll round up the rest and meet you all down there."

Running into their bedroom, Molly ran over to Evan, who was still sound asleep, and began vigorously shaking him, yelling, "Evan! Wake up! Wake up!"

"What the...?"

"Just get up!"

"What's going on? How long was I out?"

"There are big helicopters circling the house. Everyone is going down to the basement."

Snapping to his senses, Evan threw his legs out of the bed, put his pants on, and ran barefoot across the room, stopping to grab his VZ-58 and magazine-laden load-bearing vest.

As he and Molly joined the others in the basement, Lilly and Sammy ran from Judy's care to the open arms of their parents crying and saying, "Mommy! Daddy! Mommy! Daddy!" They were too young to understand what was going on, but they knew the adults were worried and anxious about something.

"It's okay, girls. It's okay," he said, trying to calm them.

Sarah, Kevin, and Michael came running down the stairs next. Sarah looked at everyone and frantically asked, "What's going on? Griff shouted and told me to get downstairs, but didn't say why."

Before anyone could answer, they all went silent as they heard the ominous pulsing of the Hind's massive main rotor directly overhead. Fear gripped the adults and children alike. They knew they had fared well in the past when faced with hostile intruders, but a well-equipped and trained government force would be a different story.

Evan made a quick headcount and said, "Okay, we're missing Griff, Jason, Jake, and Greg."

"Jason's on his daily comms run, Greg is on watch, and I think Jake was out checking on the sheep," Molly replied.

Sarah spoke up and said, "Griff said he's staying upstairs to keep an eye on things."

Evan's face was serious as he looked at Molly and said quietly, "Unlock the basement gun safe. Don't start breaking everything out just yet and scare the kids to death, but be prepared. We know these bastards aren't here for anything good. We've seen nothing but hostility and oppressive behavior from them everywhere we've seen them. I love you." He kissed her on the cheek, turned, and ran upstairs.

Reaching the upper level, Evan saw Griff looking with binoculars out of the window at the end of the hallway on the south end of the house. "What's going on?" he asked.

"One of the helicopters is lying low off in the distance, while the other is doing a slow orbit around the house. They're both armed up—S-8 rockets on their hard points. They could obliterate this house with the mere twitch of a finger; we don't have a leg to stand on in a fight with them. If they choose to make a move—I don't know what we could do. We can't get away. They could track us and mow us down any direction we run. We would have to have a damn underground tunnel to get away if it comes to blows."

Evan gestured to borrow the binoculars. Taking them from Griff, he watched the orbiting Mi-24 Hind as it made its way back around the house. The Hind turned and faced them, almost seeming to stare Evan directly in the face, as if they knew he was watching. "What are you up to, you bastard?" he mumbled.

"Dude, we could hit the pilot with the fifty from here," Griff said. "We could take that bastard down."

"The other one would smoke us though," Evan said, handing the binoculars back to Griff. "Hence the overwatch position. I have a feeling this guy is up close in order to use thermal imaging or penetrating radar to scan the house for threats. They're probably watching us watching them right now."

Just as Evan finished his sentence, the Hind turned and flew away toward the east, with the other helicopter rejoining it in their formation, disappearing across the ridgeline and over the horizon.

With the stress of the moment leaving his body, his heart still pounding through his chest, Evan said, "Looks like they are heading over toward the Thomas farm now."

"I wonder what they are looking for?"

"Us. Well, maybe not us exactly, but those like us. But then again, considering what Jason and I got caught up in, I guess it really could be us. If they had any real intel at this point, though, they would have been kicking—or blowing—our door off its hinges by now. No, I think they are still gathering intel on the area before they make a move."

"Man, I feel like we should be on the radio by now sending word to the other homesteads."

"Yeah, I know. But if they are taking this sort of interest, employing two helicopters in the manner with which they are, they more than likely are already monitoring all radio traffic in the area. Our house-to-house gear being unencrypted in any way would be wide open to them and would just give them a clue as to our associations and intentions. I think we should just let things play out for the moment. They'll keep their heads on straight over there and at the other homesteads too. Nobody would be stupid enough to make a move on those damn flying tanks unless it was a matter of last resort."

"Yeah, you're probably right. Still, it feels wrong just sitting here, waiting for something bad to happen."

"We'll get with everyone very soon. We need to get our bug out plans that you, Jason, and Daryl spoke about the other day up and running. As individual homesteads, avoidance is our best defense. The militia may have a better way to actually deal with the problem."

Chapter Twenty-Nine: Provocation

At the Thomas farm, Mildred was sitting on the hill beneath the majestic magnolia under which Ollie was buried. She was enjoying the peaceful and beautiful view, talking with him as she did every day, as if he was still right there with her. As she was wrapping up her very personal and private conversation, she heard the faint sound of helicopter rotors off in the distance. Almost immediately, they began to appear over the opposing ridgeline at treetop level, traveling at a high rate of speed.

Crossing the ridge, the two helicopters swooped down into the valley and split up, one heading directly for the house while the other flew up the valley and toward Mildred's herd of grazing cattle. Her heart sank in her chest at the sight of the two helicopters, knowing what had happened in the recent past when citizens encountered them.

~~~~

Closing the gate to the pasture after having counted the cattle as they entered, Luke heard the sound of the rapidly approaching helicopter that was flying up the valley, and immediately turned and ran for the cover of the woods. Entering the trees for cover, he looked back in horror to see the helicopter open fire with its 12.7mm four-barreled machine gun while heading directly for the herd.

Ignoring the urge to keep running, Luke took cover behind a large tree and watched in horror as the cattle, trapped in the confines of the fence, were torn to shreds. As the animals virtually exploded from the high powered 12.7x108mm armor-piercing rounds, the survivors ran in all directions in a total
~~~~

panic, attempting to flee from the helicopter as it continued to make pass after pass until every last cow was dead.

Luke was in shock at the gruesome scene and instantly feared for those at the house. He began to run through the woods toward home with his AR-15 on his back that he always carried along with him when out on the farm, performing his chores.

As he reached Mildred on her special hill, he saw that she was standing out in the open with her hands over her face, crying and screaming. Grabbing her by the arm, Luke pulled her into the woods. "Come on! Get away from there before they see you. Into the woods!"

She didn't respond to his commands and nearly fell from his forceful tug on her arm. Realizing her mental state, Luke picked her up off her feet, threw her over his shoulder, and began running through the woods while she wailed and screamed, "Why? Why? Why, God? Why?"

Getting far enough into the woods to feel reasonably concealed, Luke stopped, put Mildred back on her feet, and guided her by the hand to sit down. "Mildred... shhhhh... Mildred. Please. Please hold it together. Listen to me..."

"They killed them. They killed them all. Why? Why would they do such a thing?" she said, sobbing heavily in a state of disbelief and heartbreak.

"We'll figure that out later. For now, you just sit tight. Don't go anywhere. I'll run to the house to check on the others and possibly get them out of there. Please... just don't go out there. It won't help anything."

Unable to speak due to her emotions, Mildred nodded *yes* to Luke's request.

Luke leapt over downed logs and ran right through bushes, scratching himself on briars, brush, and branches as he continued his run toward the house. Abeam the house, he dropped down through the woods to the tree line, stopping to observe. The helicopter that had been orbiting around the house had just peeled away and was rejoining the other as they disappeared over the ridge as quickly as they had arrived. In just a few moments, the Mi-24 Hinds had managed to decimate Mildred's cattle herd. The food source and livelihood that she and Ollie had worked to build for years had been taken away in an instant.

Once the helicopter was gone, Luke ran into the house, yelling, "Rachel? Haley? Mom? Where are you?" He ran from room to room searching frantically until he finally heard Rachel shout, "We're down here!"

Hearing her voice come from the basement, Luke ran downstairs to find the three women huddled in the corner in tears.

"What the hell happened?" Rachel asked frantically. "Why were they shooting? What were they shooting at?"

"The cows... they killed all of the cows."

"What? All of them? What... I mean, why would they do that?"

"I don't know. Control? Provocation? Maybe they're trying to starve people out of the mountains and force us into food lines in the cities? I don't know, but they're gone—for now, at least."

"Where's Mildred?" Judith asked with fear in her trembling voice.

"She's fine. Shook up, but fine. She saw the entire thing. I'll go and get her and bring her back. While I'm gone, get on the radio with the Homefront. Let them know what happened and to keep their flock hidden."

As Luke ran out the door to get Mildred, his mother, Judith, did as he instructed and hailed the Homefront on the CB radio. "Homefront! Is anyone there? We've been attacked!"

~~~~
~~~~

Back at the Homefront, Judy was dutifully monitoring the radio for any word from the other homesteads in regards to their aerial visitors when she heard Judith's distressed-filled voice cry out over the radio. "Evan! Evan!" she shouted.

As Evan ran into the room, he said, "What? What is it?"

"Something bad happened at the Thomas farm."

"What?" he asked.

"I don't know. Judith only said that they've been attacked. I haven't replied because I knew you wanted us to stay off the radio."

"Attacked? Oh, my God. Go ahead. Respond!"

"We're here!" she said. "What happened? Is anyone hurt?"

"They just started shooting and wouldn't stop! They killed them all! Every single one of them!"

Grabbing the microphone, Evan replied, "What? They killed everyone? What the hell?"

"The cows... I mean, they killed all the cows."

"Oh, thank God!" Evan said aloud, realizing what she had meant. "Is anyone hurt? How are you, Rachel, Haley, Mildred, and Luke?"

"We're okay. Luke went back to get Mildred just now. She was out on Ollie's hill when it happened. She must have seen the whole thing. Luke said they killed the entire herd. We heard one of the helicopters start shooting while the other just hovered over the house as if it was keeping us from intervening. What are we going to do? We're wiped out. The cows are all we had."

Before Evan could answer, Jason entered the room, out of breath from his run to the home. "Hinds!" he said. "Where did they go?"

Evan looked at him and said, "The Thomas farm, apparently. They hit the herd. They wiped it out." Before Jason could respond, Evan said, "Just a sec," as he gestured for him to wait. Getting back on the radio, he transmitted, "Copy all. We will send someone over. Stay safe."

Judith replied with a trembling voice, "Okay."

"Let's take a stroll," Evan said to Jason as the two men stepped outside.

Scanning the sky as he walked, Jason said, "Okay, things are getting serious fast. You know as well as I do why they hit the cattle."

"Yep," Evan replied. "The most effective way to control the population is to control their food. If the government controls the food, they control the people. Looking at the size of Mildred's herd, they probably realized it was providing beef for a lot more than just one household. With the herd wiped out, people will be more desperate and they may have to turn to government assistance out of sheer desperation."

"But how they hell would people trust a government food line after seeing what they just did?"

Jason stopped and turned to look at Evan. "Most people would never see that, though. They would only know that the supply level changed. They could be trying to provoke us, too. Commit some heinous atrocity to flush out the militia when they mount a response."

"Probably a combination of the two. One; flush out the pissed off patriots. Two; destabilize the fortunate. Then there is no one left to help the unfortunate, thereby increasing the number of those in need of assistance and, subsequently, the ability to influence and control."

"There are two things I see that we need to do right away," Jason proposed.

"What's that?"

"We need to contact Q and the Blue Ridge Militia via the HiveNet, and we need to get someone over to the Thomas farm."

“Agreed. You’ve been the comms guy, so you should hit the radios while Griff or I head over to the Thomas farm to see what we can do for them.”

“Are you up to traveling?” Jason asked, concerned about Evan’s recovery from his wound.

“I think so. Besides, Griff got banged up pretty bad not long ago, himself. His clavicle hasn’t had time to completely heal, and I know his chest still has some rib bones that give him trouble.”

“Damn, we’re a mess.”

“It’s been a rough ride for the past year and a half,” replied Evan. “It kind of reminds you why people didn’t live so long back in the day. They were beaten down and worn out.”

“Okay, then. After nightfall, I’ll head up over the ridge to make contact with the militia via the HiveNet, and you ride on over to the Thomas farm. I’ll get back here as quick as I can so that Griff and the boys aren’t standing the watches all by themselves—just in case.”

“Sounds good. Now I just have to convince Molly to let me out of her sight again,” Evan said with a chuckle.

Chapter Thirty: A Helping Hand

Later that night, Evan and Jason went their separate ways to complete their agreed upon tasks... after some convincing of Sarah and Molly. As Evan pedaled his bicycle through the hilly terrain of the homesteads, he began to miss the horse that he had been in possession of for the short time after their escape from the UN detention farm. *I've got to get another horse,* he thought as he pedaled up the last hill, straining his side and bringing back the dull and deep pain he had just started to shake off. *This bike stuff is for the younger, less beat-up generation.*

As he crested the last hill, he hid his bike in the woods alongside the road. He then slipped into the brush to continue toward the house with less chance of any unwanted observation. Slipping up to the edge of the home's front pasture, he retrieved his handheld CB radio from his daypack and clicked the mic four times in rapid succession. Waiting a moment for a response, he began to click it again as he heard, "Go," whispered over the air.

"Clear?" Evan asked quietly.

"Roger," the voice whispered in reply.

"Moving. Don't shoot," Evan then said softly over the radio.

He heard two mic clicks in reply and began to slip quietly into the field, crouching down and traveling low and slow to the house. As he approached, he saw a flashlight illuminate briefly letting him know that they had seen him and that the coast was clear. Reaching the house, Evan looked around one more time, and then proceeded onto the porch, where Luke was waiting to greet him with the door held open.

"Where's Mildred?" he asked, looking around the room and seeing only Rachel with Luke.

"She went to bed early," Luke replied. "Judith and Haley are asleep as well. Mildred is taking this pretty hard. For several reasons, of course. First of which is the herd was basically the legacy that she had inherited from Ollie. She looked at them as more than simply a bunch of animals. They represented a culmination of Ollie's hard work and were a way for him to provide for her, even after he was gone. Also, just as she was beginning to feel secure in her own home again, all that was shattered by being attacked from the sky. That's something we can't just fend off ourselves. It reminded her just how vulnerable we are and how our security is only partially in our own hands. What if they attack the house next time? There's nothing we could do but run into the woods and hope they don't pursue us as the house is destroyed. It's like nothing is really yours anymore in this world. There is always someone there trying to take it every time you turn around."

"Unfortunately, I think you're dead on with every word," Evan replied. He then turned to Rachel. "Oh, and thanks for patching me up, doc. You really saved my bacon."

"Jason saved your bacon. My contribution was tiny compared to his," she replied.

"Yeah. I don't know how I could ever repay him for that one."

"Be careful what you wish for," replied Luke. "You don't really want an opportunity like that these days."

"So... what can I do for you ladies and gentlemen? How bad is the mess?"

"It's awful," Luke replied with a grimace. "Have you ever seen a cow get hit with a barrage of heavy armor-piercing rounds? They evaporate like a ground squirrel shot with a .308. Let's just say there aren't many intact cows lying around. It's a mess."

"When's the last time you fired up Ollie's excavator and that spare tractor he had? The one we got running after the Muncie gang shot his old Massey Ferguson to pieces."

"That old Allis Chalmers? We use it to pull the wood wagon around every now and then. It should start," replied Luke.

"Well, we could put that old rusty rock rake on the back of the tractor. You could drag that through the field, collecting the parts while I dig a hole way out in the back corner with the excavator. Once we've got a pretty good pile of cow parts, we can push them in with the little push blade on the front of the excavator. I've never thought those things were good for much, but in this case, it will fit the bill just fine. That way we don't have to swap out the grader blade with the rake on the tractor. You can just keep raking, and I can keep digging, pushing, and covering the holes. If we don't, it'll get pretty dang ripe around here sometime soon, and the way the breeze blows through the valley, you won't be able to stand it in the house."

"That sounds good to me," replied Luke.

"Let's start at sun-up. I had a good nap today. I'll stand watch for a while. You two go get some sleep. The stress around here has been a lot for everyone to have to deal with lately."

"I can stay up with you."

"No, Luke. I insist. Seriously. After that ride, I'm all pumped up, anyway. Just get yourself some sleep, and at sun up, we'll get on with it. I'll catch up on sleep again when I get home tomorrow evening."

"Thanks, man," replied Luke as he put his arm around Rachel and led her down the hall.

"Goodnight, Evan," Rachel said.

"Goodnight to you, too, ma'am," replied Evan as he tipped his hat.

~~~~
~~~~

Early the next morning as the sun came up, Evan looked out across the property and saw a horse appear out of the tree line with Daryl in the saddle, rifle in hand. Holding the rifle up to ensure he was noticed by Evan, Daryl waved it back and forth over his head.

Evan stepped out onto the porch and waved him on in. As Daryl reached the porch, Evan stepped off and took the reins, tying the horse to the railing. "Good morning, Mr. Moses. What brings you out here?"

"The same thing that brought you, I guess. I was checking on Linda yesterday evening when we heard Judith's frantic transmission about an attack."

"Checking in on Linda yesterday, huh?" Evan said with a crooked smile. "Seems she's been well looked after lately."

"Hey, now," Daryl said. "Linda is a real lady. There's no funny business going on there."

"I was just trying to ruffle your feathers. Relax," Evan replied with a chuckle. "Besides, I think she's a fine woman and you two would make a fine couple."

Changing the subject, Daryl asked what had happened; Evan explained everything in detail, including catching him up on the day's cleanup plan. Daryl offered to stand watch over the ladies at the main house while Evan and Luke were in the back pasture working on the cleanup project, and Evan graciously accepted.

Once everyone in the house was awake, they all shared a home-cooked breakfast prepared by Judith, and the men got down to work.

As the day progressed, one by one, each of the neighboring homesteads sent a representative by to check on Mildred, Haley, and the Hoskins family, as well as to offer their help and support. The outpouring of kindness and devotion to Mildred was heartwarming and indicative of her ongoing benefit to the community.

Back in the far corner of the back pasture, Evan toiled away on the old excavator, digging a large hole to dispose of the remains. His hole finally being of suitable size, he lifted the boom and positioned himself behind a pile of cow remains that Luke had piled with the old tractor and rake. He then lowered the small push blade on the front of the excavator and pushed the cow parts into the hole. Flies were already swarming, making the job even less enjoyable than it already was. As he watched the remains tumble and flop into the hole, Evan pulled his shirt up over his nose and pulled his hat down tight to reduce the constant swatting at flies required to keep his sanity. Before backing the excavator up, he looked over to see where Luke was, and noticed him talking to Lloyd Smith. *Well, well. Look who's here,* Evan thought as he shut down the excavator and climbed down to join them.

Evan began walking toward Luke and Lloyd; they stopped their conversation as Lloyd waved and said, "Long time, no see, Evan! We were so glad to hear you made it back. Like I was just telling Lucas here, we are praying every day for Nate and Ed's safe return."

"Yes," Evan replied. "We're glad to be home, but we won't be whole again until they make it back. Every day I hope and pray to hear something of them—anything at all to give us a place to look. I feel so helpless just sitting and waiting."

"Yeah, that's how we all felt, waiting for all of you guys to get back," answered Lloyd. "So, back to the reason I came by. We're so sorry to see what happened to Mildred's herd. If there is anything at all we can do to help, just let us know. What do you make of all this?"

"Take away a man's ability to feed himself and you've got a subject," Evan replied. "I'm sure it's part of their bigger plan to roust the troublemakers out of the hills. For now, we just have to work on a plan to get our families to safety if the need arises. This just proves we aren't safe from them in our own homes. A man's home may be his castle, but these days, your castle only protects you from the elements and the common criminal."

Lloyd nodded in agreement. "So I was talking to Daryl the other day, and he mentioned the potential bug-out locations that you guys were talking about. I really like his choices, especially the old mine. I went up there yesterday evening. I hiked around until I found the entrance. It's hard to see with all the trees and brush that's grown up around it over the past hundred years. I ventured inside for a bit—as far as I could without having any sort of real light with me—and I think it's ideal. Charlie and I are gonna get together and start positioning some provisions in there. We've got some excess canned goods and stored water we can place inside for now. We've got to make room for this year's garden harvest, anyway."

"Glad to hear you're getting a head start on that. Especially considering all of this," Evan replied, happy with the project already becoming a community venture.

"And don't worry, we'll be very careful to not leave tracks and we'll make sure we're not being observed. In addition to food though, I think we need to place some weapons and ammunition inside. Whenever we have to bug out, we may not be in a position to take what we need for any sort of sustained event. We have to assume our homes may be destroyed or, at a minimum, emptied out in our absence."

"Damn good idea, Lloyd," replied Evan. "I've got some extra weapons and ammunition I can easily contribute to the cache. As you said, I no longer see my own home as a safe place to store everything. A squirrel can put away all the nuts in the world, but they'll do him no good if he's run out of his tree."

"If you want," Lloyd offered, "I can come by and pick a load up from you tomorrow, if you're gonna be around. I know you've got a lot going on with comms and stuff. Not to mention the fact that you and Griff are both banged up."

"That would be great, Lloyd. Thank you so much. Let us know when you're coming, and we'll treat you to a nice lamb chop while you're there. We don't get company very often these days. You know, with the economy and all."

The two shared a laugh as Lloyd said, "Will do, Evan. Will do."

Chapter Thirty-One: The Escalating Threat

Over the next several days, the residents of the homesteads began to prepare for a potential bug out from their homes. Lloyd made good on his offer to transport Evan's weapons and ammunition to the old mine, while the residents of the homefront relocated their livestock to aid in hiding them from the overhead surveillance that led to the destruction of Mildred's herd.

Utilizing their existing materials, they took down hundreds of feet of metal woven-wire field fence and relocated it deep into the woods under the canopy provided by the treetops above. Although there was lots of vegetation in the animals' new temporary home, there simply wasn't enough grass forage to maintain the sheep for long. With that in mind, they supplemented by leaving several five-by-six foot round hay bales that they had produced from their own land the previous year in various places in the animals' new enclosure.

With Mildred's entire cattle herd having been decimated, all of the residents of the confederacy of homesteads knew it was critical that every animal survive what may come in their near future, in order to see them through the next winter. Evan was concerned about the threat of predators in the animals' new and out-of-the-way environment, but considered losses to predators acceptable in comparison to losses from an aerial slaughter.

While those with animals were getting them prepared the best they could, the other homesteaders contributed by stocking and preparing the mine with provisions, should an extended stay become necessary. Some had more to give than others did, but everyone contributed. Though they stood as individuals in their daily lives, in crisis, they stood as one.

~~~~

As the late afternoon sun shone down through the trees, Evan looked at his sheep. "Well, ladies, and you, too, Rambo," he added, referring to their breeding ram, "you all be careful tonight. I'm sorry we won't be around to lend a hand if the coyotes come. Take care." He said this as if they could understand him.

As he turned to walk out of the woods toward the house, his handheld radio transmitted, "Ev... you there?"

"Yep. Go," he replied.

"The dogs are loose."

"I'll be right there," he said in reply. *The dogs are loose, huh? That can't be good,* he thought, referring to Jason's choice of words. Although "turn the dogs loose" was used to signal those at the house to set up the guard and go into lockdown, he knew that was the case. Clearly, Jason had a threat to mention that he couldn't talk about over the air.

Evan picked up his pace and hurried back to the house. As he stepped out into the pasture with the house off in the distance, he saw Jason heading his way.

"It must be bad if you couldn't wait for me," Evan said, anxious to hear the news.

"Yeah. It is. Q passed on some disturbing info. He said their sources have confirmed that the UN troops are moving in a convoy on Highway 70 in the direction of Hot Springs and then on to Del Rio. They expect a house-to-house sweep. They've already hit a few of the other small towns along the way."

"What do you mean—hit?"

"Door kickers. They've gone from house to house confiscating all weapons and taking some men into custody. They seem to have a list of people associated with the militias, but all weapons and ammunition are to be taken."
~~~~

"What's the plan? With Q and the Blue Ridge Militia, that is."

"There's an all-hands-on-deck meeting at midnight tonight."

"Where?"

"He gave me the digits. I've still got to plot it out."

"Hmmm," Evan said with his hands on his hips, staring at the ground. "So what are you thinking?"

"We need to go. You and I can borrow a couple of Mildred's horses to make it easier on you in your condition."

"Ah, man. I'm really starting to feel okay. The infection is gone and the wound is healing up just fine. Don't worry about me."

"No offense, but I've heard that before," Jason said with his crooked smile.

"Either way, yes, let's borrow some horses. As a matter of fact, I think we should go get them fairly soon. We can make our rounds through the homesteads this evening, giving them the heads up in person. Especially knowing they're headed this way, we need to stay off of our radios as much as possible. I seriously doubt they would head out on a roundup without advanced signals intelligence in the area."

"Agreed," Jason replied. "Well, let's get on with it."

~~~~

After explaining the situation to their families and the others at the Homefront, Evan and Jason paid a surprise visit to the Thomas farm. Mildred graciously accommodated their request and fitted them out with two horses and saddles for their journey throughout the homesteads and on toward Del Rio for their meeting.

They visited the Blanchard and Smith homes, then made their way to Linda Cox's place to brief her on the situation. As
~~~~

they approached her home, they stopped to scan the area from a safe distance with their binoculars.

"Well, surprise, surprise," Jason said, scanning the area.

"What?" asked Evan impatiently.

"Looks like Daryl is paying her a visit as well."

"Well, good," Evan replied. "They're both wonderful people and alone. They'd make a beautiful couple."

"Absolutely. It's only funny because of how socially awkward Daryl is anytime someone jokes or asks him about it."

"I hate to crash their party, but we're running low on time. Let's get to it," Evan said as he nudged his horse forward.

Jason grinned and followed along.

As they approached the house, Linda's donkey, Jack, immediately began his dreadfully loud *he-haw* as if to sound the alarm. Evan pulled back on the reins of his horse, bringing him to a stop, and motioned for Jason to stop as well.

"Daryl's liable to want to shoot us just for interrupting. Let's not give him an excuse. Let's wait till he waves us in," said Evan as Jason rode up alongside him and came to a stop.

"That, sir, would be the prudent course of action," replied Jason.

After a moment of patiently waiting, Evan and Jason saw Daryl step out onto Linda's front porch. He waved to them to proceed, making it known that they were recognized.

"I hope this doesn't get too awkward. We don't get much social drama around here these days."

"Well, at least he doesn't have to worry about us making a social media post about it. His personal life is safe with us."

With that, the two shared a chuckle and continued toward the house. Arriving at Linda's front porch, Evan and Jason dismounted as Daryl anxiously rushed out to meet them and help them tie up their horses. "Good evening, gents. I was just stopping by for a few to see how Linda was doing. It's not safe around here for a woman to live alone these days, you know."

“Yes, Daryl; that’s mighty neighborly of you,” Evan replied. “I’m sure she appreciates it.”

“So what brings you fellas out here?” Daryl asked. “I’m glad to see you, but these days it half worries me to get a visitor.”

“We know what you mean. No news is good news these days,” replied Evan. “I’ll let Jason explain.”

“Do you mind if we head inside? We would like to explain this to Linda as well,” asked Jason.

“Oh, yes, of course. Where are my manners? Come on in, fellas,” Daryl replied, fumbling over himself as if he was nervous or embarrassed. Evan and Jason shared a smile and followed him onto the porch and into the house.

“Evan, Jason, it’s so nice to see you,” Linda said as she gave each one of them a hug.

“Likewise, ma’am,” Evan replied while taking off his hat.

“Oh, don’t say ‘ma’am.’ You’re starting to make me feel old,” she replied, swatting her hand in the air at Evan.

“‘Ma’am’ has nothing to do with age; it’s simply a gentleman showing respect to a lady.”

Daryl looked at Evan and shook his head. “Don’t waste your time, Evan. I’ve explained that till I’m blue in the face. Just save yourself the trouble and call her Linda.”

Evan chuckled and said with a smile, “Anything the lady wants.”

“So, anyway,” Linda said, giving Daryl an awkward look, “what brings you two by this late in the evening?”

Jason spoke up. “You know how I’ve been keeping in touch with the militia about the goings on in the area via a secure radio network, right?”

“Yes. Daryl explained the gist of it to me.”

“Well, we received some troubling news this evening that a UN convoy is on its way to Hot Springs. So far, their intentions have been to sweep entire neighborhoods, going door to door, confiscating weapons and ammunition, as well as arresting some individuals on sight, as if they have reason to believe they are involved with one of the area militias. The Blue Ridge Militia has reason to believe they are planning to make their way toward the Del Rio area after Hot Springs."

Daryl and Linda shared a look of concern. "Oh, my goodness," she said. "So what is going to happen here?"

"Evan and I are going to ride to a rally point later tonight to meet up with the local militia guys to get more information. Regardless of what they say, we can assume that things are going to change around here, and soon. No longer can we consider ourselves safely off the beaten path and living on our own terms. The extent of that, we have yet to find out, but we may as well start getting our minds wrapped fully around our contingency plans."

"I'll go with you," Daryl said. "Is it only you two going?"

"That's what we had planned, so far. We didn't want to take too much manpower away from the homesteads just for the meeting."

"That leaves plenty. I'm going," Daryl said forcefully.

"Roger that," Jason replied. "Grab your stuff and you can make the last few rounds with us; we'll head out from there. We've still got to find the place, so we planned on getting on the road fairly soon after we let everyone know to be prepared for what's coming our way."

"Okay, I'll be right out if you guys want to be getting your horses," Daryl said, as if he was trying to get a moment alone with Linda before they left.

"Roger that. We'll see you out front," Jason replied.

Evan and Jason both nodded goodbye to Linda and stepped out onto the porch and into the front yard. As they started untying their horses, Evan quietly said, "That's a couple if I've ever seen one."

“I know,” chuckled Jason. “Did you see the iron stare he got when he said he was going?”

“Yep. That was a little obvious,” Evan replied.

“Okay, guys, let’s get going,” Daryl said, stepping out onto the porch, rifle in hand.

Chapter Thirty-Two: Rally Point

As Evan, Jason, and Daryl rode through the darkness of the cloudy night—occasionally getting a break in the sky for the moonlight to shine through—they stopped periodically for Jason to check his map and his coordinates. Q had transmitted the location to him in code, and he deciphered it the best he could with the information he had. He was, however, unsure if he had gotten it right.

"Guys, I hope I'm not leading us on a wild goose chase, causing us to miss the meeting."

"Why did he have to make it so complicated?" asked Daryl.

"Just remember, the occupiers have stepped up their game. Keep in mind what they did to Mildred's cattle. Imagine if they caught wind of our meeting and knew where it was going to be. Our entire local militia force could be wiped out in one strike."

"Yeah, that's true," Daryl replied. "So how much further do you think it is?"

"From what I've worked up, it should be just a half mile more due east from our current position. It looks like it's gonna take us alongside the river. It's about a half mile or more outside of Del Rio to the west, around the river's bend."

"That would make sense. They would probably want the ease of travel down in the valley. The river is the lowest point in the bottom and there is lots of good tree cover along the banks. Not to mention the railroad tracks and Old River Road for folks to get in and out on," added Evan.

"There are a few old houses along the river, too," said Daryl as he thought about the area. "Some of which weren't really occupied even before the collapse. I know of a few fishermen who kept up old, run-down houses or shacks along the riverbank to keep their boats and fishing supplies in. Sort of a deer camp for fishermen. They weren't fit to live in, but were suitable for their intended purpose. They could slip their little johnboats into the river directly behind the house and wouldn't even have to worry about hauling them anywhere. One of those places would be perfect. Most of them were hidden well into the trees, as they didn't keep up a lawn or anything."

"That makes sense." Jason studied the map. "Let's keep going this way just a bit further," he said, comparing his compass to their estimated position on the map."

They proceeded down a thickly forested hillside, using caution and taking it slow, as visibility was poor, to say the least. As they reached the bottom of the hill, Daryl said, "That's the river up ahead. We just have to cross this clearing, the railroad tracks, and then the clearing on the other side that goes up to the edge of Old River Road. Right on the other side of Old River Road is the tree line. If we're assuming it's gonna be in a wooded area, it'll be over there."

"That's got to be it," Jason said. "Unless, of course, I got it all wrong."

"Well, there's only one way to find out," Evan said as he nudged his horse forward, with Jason and Daryl following closely behind.

As they crossed the first clearing, Daryl said softly, "I'm sure glad it's a cloudy night. The moon would light us up out here, otherwise."

"Yeah, I just hope it doesn't rain," Evan replied. "It would be a long ride back in those dark woods in the middle of a rain storm. It's kind of lookin' like it might just do that," he said, looking up at the sky while holding his hand out in search of raindrops.

As they crossed the tracks and approached the tree line that followed the contour of the river, a voice in the darkness said, "Identify," in a firm manner, followed by the sound of a metallic click.

"We're here to see a friend," Jason quickly replied.

"Who's your friend?" the voice then asked.

"Ignatius Johnson," Jason replied.

"What?" Evan asked.

"Hey, I told you before; I don't make this stuff up. They do."

"You'll find him just up ahead. Good to see you guys," the voice said in a much more welcoming tone.

"Same to you, brother," Jason replied as they continued into the woods.

Just up ahead, they came upon an old run-down house hidden amidst the trees and brush, just as Daryl had described, with several men standing around chatting. "Well, hello, there," one of them said. "I'm Sam Jones. Nice to meet you."

"Hello, Sam," Evan answered as he, Daryl, and Jason dismounted their horses. "I'm Evan Baird," he said as he reached out to shake Sam's hand. "And these two gentlemen are Daryl Moses and Jason Jones. We heard our presence was requested."

Before Sam could answer, they heard a familiar voice call out, "Thank God, you boys made it!"

"Quentin!" Evan said, giving him a hug as he walked up to them. "Man, we sure were glad to hear you made it out of the cave that day. What about Carl? Is he..."

"Carl's fine," Q answered quickly. "He's inside, actually. A few of the gentlemen out here are gonna stand watch while we have our meeting. We've also got a few fellas posted a mile in each direction for early warning. They're watching the roads and the skies."

As the men began to walk inside the house, Evan said, "Oh, and, by the way, this is Daryl Moses. He's one of our fellow homesteaders, and to be honest, none of us would be alive without him."

"Oh, I don't know about that," Daryl said out of modesty.

"I know it to be a fact," added Jason. "On more than one occasion, to boot."

"Pleasure to meet you, Daryl," Q said, reaching out his hand. "Please, call me Q."

"The pleasure is all mine," Daryl responded, returning Quentin's handshake.

"Come on in, gentlemen. We're just about to get started," Quentin said as he led them inside.

Entering the room, Evan looked around to see at least twenty other men, representing every age group, from their early twenties to their late sixties. He recognized several of them as the guards to the entrance to town; Evan's group had been temporarily stopped by them on their way to see Pastor Wallace during their failed supply run. Then across the room, he saw Tyrone Gibbs. Tyrone's face lit up when he saw Evan and Jason, and he hurried across the room to meet them.

Evan reached out his hand, but Tyrone smacked it away and gave him a hug, lifting him off the ground. He then grabbed Jason in the same manner, and said, "I thought I would never see you guys again. Thank you. Thank you so much for everything you did. We had no idea you would actually go after and rescue Sabrina like you did. That was... well, I have no words. You guys..." He paused to wipe the tears from his eyes.

"I feel like I'm missing out on one hell of a story here," Quentin said.

"Yes, sir. You are," Tyrone replied, regaining his composure.

"It's nothing, really," Evan said, trying to downplay the situation.

"That's nonsense. You guys risked your lives for a total stranger. I owe you more than I will ever be able to repay. Where are the others? Where are Ed and Nate?"

"A lot more happened after you saw Charlie and Jimmy, when they dropped off Sabrina at the church. We had a run-in with the UN troops and were separated. We've not seen them since. Every day we wake up hoping to hear any news to give us something to go on. But if we can make it back, they can too, so we haven't lost faith."

"I'm sorry to hear that," Tyrone replied in a defeated tone. "I'll keep them in my prayers. So far, or at least lately, God has been good to me. Maybe he'll grant me one more favor."

"Where's Pastor Wallace?" asked Jason.

"He's back at the church standing watch. He's one of our early warning posts for the meeting. He has a radio to let us know if trouble rolls into town while we're all here," Tyrone explained.

"Time to get down to business, I guess," said Quentin as he walked to the front of the room. "Gentlemen, I'd like to thank you all for coming. If any one of your trusted friends or family members couldn't make it here tonight, please pass along the basics of the meeting, but not the specifics of any particular plan or idea unless they are going to be involved personally. Is that understood by everyone? We can't risk compromising the rest of the group if someone who stays behind is taken and interrogated." Pausing for a moment, Quentin looked around the room to see that everyone was in agreement, and then continued.

"As you already know from the JADAM we sent out, UN forces are moving up Highway 70, towards Hot Springs. Our intelligence folks tell us they aim to continue on to Del Rio once they've secured Hot Springs and its outlying areas. They appear to be in possession of some sort of intelligence as to who may be affiliated with a militia group, as several of our own were taken from their homes, a few of whom were killed when they attempted to resist. Needless to say, if you're taken, don't expect your wives and children to be treated in a respectable manner. Several of us around here can already attest to what can be expected after a run-in with them," he said as he looked at Carl. Carl nodded in affirmation of what he had said.

"How they got this information, we don't know, but each and every one of us here tonight has to play it safe and assume we're on the list, which means you and your families are not safe. You may have already noticed an increased level of airborne surveillance in the area, as well."

One of the men in the back of the room stood up and said, "Damn straight! They buzzed my place just yesterday with two big helicopters. It took everything I had in me not to try and shoot them out of the sky."

"I would highly recommend against that," Quentin replied. "None of us would stand a chance against a Hind. As tempting as it may be, you had better have respect for the capabilities of those things, or you'll find out the hard way."

Evan raised his hand and added, "For those of you who don't already know, Mildred Thomas's farm was attacked by the very same Hinds. They flew over the farm in formation and then split up, one seeming to provide cover for the other while it did its dirty business. The lead helicopter opened fire with its machine gun on her herd of cattle, completely wiping it out. It was a total slaughter. Not one cow that was in the pasture was spared. Luckily for her, she had several milk cows in the milking parlor, but they are now all she has left. Those cattle were feeding a lot more than her household, and those bastards knew it. They intentionally hit our food supply, and hit it hard, to shut down our independent way of life. Don't think for one moment that will be the last time such a thing happens, either."

After a moment of distress-filled conversation in the room, Quentin regained control of the meeting and said, "Gentlemen, that's exactly what we are here to talk about. Since the attacks that brought our country to its knees first occurred, most of us, and rightly so, have hidden ourselves away in the hills to provide for and protect our families, only coming out to hunt or fish to get what we need, but mostly, we've kept to ourselves.

"We can't do that anymore. We can't just hide out and wait for them to pass. It's not going to simply pass. The Blue Ridge Militia, along with the other militia groups that make up the Southern States Defensive Alliance don't intend on allowing our way of life to be steamrolled by the UN, or any government or organization that thinks we are ripe for the picking. Militia groups and guard units in the constitutionally loyal states have been stepping up their resistance. There have been several major operations in Texas, Arizona, Idaho, and Kansas that have knocked the occupying forces on their butts."

"Unfortunately," he continued after a few cheers went through the room, "this isn't something that's going to be won with one decisive battle or one grand achievement. They have the upper hand in equipment and organizational might, but we have what the soldiers who fought under Washington had; we have the fire in our hearts, and souls of men who were born free and for damn sure aren't going to just roll over and let that freedom be taken away.

"The soldiers they bring with them are nothing more than mercenaries working for a paycheck. We, however, are fighting for our homes, our families, our country, and our American way of life, which has been the shining beacon of hope for so many people since the nation's inception. We will out-will them. We will out-fight them. We will out-smart them. We will wear them down, we will beat them, and we push them into the ocean if we have to, in order to get them off of our lands."

Looking around the room, seeing the fire in the eyes of the men who were present, Quentin said, "This is going to be dirty and ugly. Many of us, if not all of us, will lose everything that we have, including our lives. There's never been a war, no matter how just, where the good and the innocent didn't suffer. Many, if not most, of the original patriots who fought to secure our independence during the Revolution, lost their lives or nearly everything they had for the cause.

"But my friends, my brothers, this isn't just a political cause. This isn't a national cause. If we stand up and fight to keep the tyranny that is sweeping the nation from taking over, we are fighting for our children's future. I, for one, don't want my grandkids to look back on this time in history as the time that America—once the Land of the Free and the Home of the Brave—simply gave in to the powers that be.

"I want them to look at this time in our history as the time that we reaffirmed our place in this world as a country of free men and women, who no matter what your race, ethnicity, or background, stood together, and not only said no, but shouted 'HELL NO!' to the tyranny of big government collectivism, and stood up for the freedoms and liberty of our unalienable, God-given, individual rights.

"I want them to be reminded by this time in history, that as Americans, we shall not be ruled by anyone! We are free! We will only allow ourselves to be governed by those we choose freely and by the laws that we accept. Should our grandchildren or great-grandchildren ever face such a foe, I want them to look back on us and be able to take strength and confidence from our actions—that no matter how great the odds are stacked against them, we, as Americans, shall always stand together and prevail against tyranny. Let our actions be a warning to any who may wish to try, that they will not win, but will die on our soil.

"We must resolve, as Americans, all across this nation, to stand up in every single city and town, and show them that the world's largest and most powerful army does not need a uniform or equipment; it only needs the fire of freedom that burns within our hearts to prevail. We, the people of the

United States of America, are our own army and are a force that simply cannot be overcome, so long as we stand together in the name of freedom!

"Let this be our common resolution, to stand side by side and face whatever may come so that our children can live free!"

The room immediately exploded with the applause and cheers of every man present as emotion swept the room. Evan looked over and watched Daryl wiping a tear from his eye. Evan smiled at him and nodded, as they completely agreed without having to say a word.

Quentin cleared his throat and then motioned to the crowd to let him continue. "I'm going to go ahead and assume that means most of you are onboard," he said with a smile, causing cheers to erupt once more. "Okay, okay, so here is the plan that we have so far. You all know that the Blue Ridge Militia is separated into different operating areas. We are designated as Area Three. Counting the people in this room tonight, we have around forty fighting-aged individuals in our area. Each area has been tasked by retired Marine Corps Colonel Tucker Johnson, who is currently our militia commander, with a specific role to play over the next week.

"It is our understanding that the other militia groups, as well as the constitutionally loyal guard units throughout the Southeast and the Mid-south will be doing so as well. This coordinated effort will overwhelm the occupiers in our region, as they do not have the manpower or equipment to take us all on in all areas at the same time, putting them on the defensive and preventing them from being able to respond to each of our actions."

He then pointed to a large map of the local area that he had hung on the wall behind him prior to the meeting. "The convoy heading our way is expected to hit Hot Springs by tomorrow. The town has been evacuated in anticipation of this, with most of the residents bugging out to the mountains in the surrounding area. With this in mind, they should pass through Hot Springs fairly quickly, as the resistance will be virtually non-existent."

One of the men stood up and asked, "Why aren't the militia personnel in the Hot Springs area putting up a resistance?"

Quentin answered, "Good question. First of all, they didn't get the lead time that we did as to the UN's arrival in their town. They had just enough time to get their families out of harm's way, and really didn't have time to mount a formal counter-assault or ambush. They are, however, going to be working in concert with us, as I will get to here in just a moment.

"So, anyway, as our intelligence has stated, their plan is to continue to work their way up Highway 70 toward us, possibly making their way as far as Newport, where they may potentially link up with another UN operational unit moving toward the Knoxville area, that has been working its way up Interstate 75 from Atlanta. That force is said to be much larger.

"The Volunteer Militia out of Middle Tennessee, as well as the remainder of the Tennessee National Guard, are slated to pay them a visit on their way through, the specifics of which, I am not privy to for OPSEC reasons."

Quentin pointed back at the map. "Most of the remaining residents in the Del Rio area live on the south side of the river. Highway 9, on the north side, has been a hostile area, with it being the main thoroughfare for people transiting the region from Tennessee to North Carolina and vice-versa. Our plan is to pinch them in once they get across the French Broad River via the Wolf Creek Bridge and onto Highway 9, attacking them where they are most geographically vulnerable, as well as keeping the ensuing battle on the unpopulated side of the river. The terrain will be to our advantage, giving us the position of elevation to rain down fire upon them from the hill, as well as limiting their escape route to the bridge itself."

"What's to keep them from just turning around and heading back across the bridge once we engage?" one of the men asked.

"We've gotten our hands on several former U.S. Army M136 AT-4 anti-tank weapons. With one positioned on the south side of the bridge, and two on the north, as soon as any attempt to reverse course is made, we will use the M136s to turn several of their own vehicles into roadblocks on the bridge."

"What about if they just hammer down and blast on by us, continuing toward Del Rio? How will we stop them from going that way?" the man asked.

Another man shouted, "Why don't we block the road with a big Caterpillar dozer or something? They couldn't shove past that."

"First to answer that question, we considered pre-positioned physical roadblocks, but we have to assume there will be some sort of aerial reconnaissance available to them that would see such a thing and recognize it as a trap. The last thing we want them to do is to divert down Fugate Road and avoid Highway 9. We will have several M136s just west of the bridge along Highway 9, as well as the IEDs we plan to place on the south edge of the road. Since the terrain immediately falls away to the river from the edge of the road, we should be able to conceal our explosives quite well."

Daryl asked, "Pardon my ignorance. I know I'm new to many of you here, but how did you get your hands on anti-tank weapons?"

"Like I said before, this is a region-wide event. Our role may be small, but the overall operation on the grand scheme of things is not. We've got assets outside of our own militia available to us from both under-the-table weapons deals from friendly foreign interests, to state guard units and defecting military personnel. Your average citizen may not see the size and scope of the resistance that is about to rise up against those who have perpetrated this on our nation, but trust me, it's much larger than us."

Daryl nodded in agreement, satisfied with Quentin's answer.

"Lastly, once the UN convoy is beyond Hot Springs and the families there are safe, half of the militiamen from that operations area will pursue the prisoner transport vehicles that generally do not remain with the assault force. From what we have seen so far, once they take a town, a small convoy is dispatched from the main unit to transport captured prisoners, weapons, and ammunition back to their main body, generally backtracking their route, as it is their most secure area. The other half will form up and pursue the group moving toward us, hopefully undetected, as they advance toward Del Rio."

Pausing to give the men an opportunity to ask any questions they might have, Quentin continued. "In the event we are unable to prevent their retreat, the militiamen from Hot Springs will engage them via a hasty ambush. The effectiveness of that ambush will, of course, be determined by how successfully we can degrade their capabilities during the initial stages of our attack, as well as during their retreat. The best-case scenario, of course, will be that we completely knock them out. If the militiamen do not encounter them during a retreat, they will continue toward our position and join us in our efforts to finish them off."

"Now, before we continue with specifics," Quentin said, pausing, and then taking a more serious tone, "I need a show of hands of who I can count on to be a part of this operation."

Nearly every hand in the room went up in unison. The men who were hesitant quickly raised their hands once they realized the overwhelming support for the operation by the others. With a large smile on his face, Quentin simply said, "Outstanding!"

Chapter Thirty-Three: Preparing for War

After the group presentation at the meeting, individual roles, duties, and responsibilities were assigned based on individual skills and experience. Militiamen were assigned to various duties ranging from IED positioning and detonation, M136 AT-4 operator, battlefield observer and communications, ridgeline machine-gun operators, and sharpshooters. Evan, Jason, and Daryl were all asked to man the .50 caliber Barrett M107s and .50 caliber M2A1 machine guns that would be located with Quentin at the top of the ridge overlooking Highway 9 from the higher terrain above.

In addition, Quentin asked Tyrone and several other men to remain at the church with Pastor Wallace to protect the women and children being sheltered there, in the event things didn't go as planned and the UN forces made it into Del Rio. Tyrone was disappointed that he was not able to join the others in the ambush, but he understood the importance of what Quentin was asking him to do.

The next morning, as the remaining residents all around the town of Del Rio prepared for what seemed to be the inevitable conflict, they cleared their homes of any weapons, ammunition, and food that they feared they would lose to either the destruction of their homes or the door-to-door searches if their attempt to stop the occupiers failed. Many of the residents, including the families of the militia personnel taking part in the ambush, took to the surrounding hills and mountains for safe haven until the threat had passed.

The residents of the confederacy of homesteads were doing the same. Evan, Jason, and Daryl had spread the word throughout each of the properties, to gather in the old mine that they had so diligently been preparing in anticipation of such an event.

As the families had retreated to the safety of the mine, they all gathered out front on a beautiful, sunny day to wish Evan, Jason, and Daryl good luck and to see them off, as well as to go over any final details the group wished to discuss before sequestering themselves inside.

As Evan and Jason were saying goodbye to their families, hugging and kissing each one of their children, Molly and Sarah stood together in tears, wishing this nightmare that kept taking their husbands into harm's way would someday end. Evan looked over and saw Daryl giving Linda Cox a hug, followed by a long, passionate kiss. Evan nudged Jason to get his attention and pointed discreetly.

Jason grinned in reply as several of the others also noticed and were quite surprised to see the extent of the relationship that had been kept so tightly under wraps.

Just as Evan stood up to hug and kiss Molly, Lloyd and Charlie came out of the mine and said, "Okay, the lanterns are lit. Everything looks all set. Lloyd and I will take the first watch at the entrance, then we will rotate through every four hours with Luke, Greg, Jake, Will, and Griff, while the women take care of and entertain the children. Doc Rachel's stuff is all set up in the cleanest area possible, with a cot and a small folding table in the event her services are needed."

"To heck with that," Molly shouted. "I'm taking a rotation in the watch, too!"

"Me, too!" added Sarah.

"Count me in on that!" added Peggy.

"Well..." Charlie said with an embarrassed look on his face. "Then I guess you had better work me into the childcare roster. Looks like we've got plenty people here to get things taken care of. We've got food, ammo, and plenty of medical supplies, so you guys don't worry at all about things here. You just keep your heads on straight and come back to us in one piece." Charlie reached out his hand to Evan.

"Thanks," Evan replied, shaking his hand in return. "Take good care of everyone here. It may have never produced a thing, but you've got the world's greatest riches in this old mine."

Jason and Daryl both shook Charlie's hand as the rest of the homesteaders joined in the final goodbye. Evan, Jason, and Daryl mounted their horses, and with a wave, were off to meet up with the Blue Ridge Militia and the brave residents of Del Rio.

~~~~

Down in Del Rio, at the Baptist Church, Pastor Wallace was busy organizing the group to prepare the best they could. His plan was to ride things out at the church if at all possible, as he did not want to face a night in the mountains with a flock of women with small children if he could help it, but he prepared for such an eventuality just in case.

"Once you've got the extra blankets and tarps gathered together, start putting them into those large laundry bags," he said as he directed the efforts of his volunteers. "Tyrone," he shouted.

"Yes, Pastor," Tyrone replied, coming into the main sanctuary from one of the side rooms.

"Are the weapons and ammo hidden like I asked?"

"Yes, they are. The extra ammo is hidden in the walls. I intentionally stripped out the wood that held the vent screws in place for the large air intake vent for the HVAC system that is in the classroom. All but one, that is. It's a straight slot so a few good turns with a dime, and it will pop right out. The rest are there just for show to make it look as if it hasn't been tampered with at a glance. If you reach into the opening after removing the intake grate, you'll find that the sheet metal on the left, making up the ductwork, is loose. You can just pull that back to
~~~~

access inside of the sheetrock wall where you'll find the ammo boxes. We used masking tape and a marker to clearly label what was in each."

"What about the guns?"

"They are in the false-drop ceiling. See that small stick pin in that one?" he said as he pointed above.

"Yes," the pastor replied.

"A shotgun is lying on top of that panel. You can knock any of the others around it out of place to get to it in a hurry without knocking it down itself. Anywhere in the ceiling you see a small pushpin like that is where you can find a gun in a hurry. All loaded, of course."

"Great work, Tyrone," Pastor Wallace said as he patted him on the back. "Once everyone is done, help me gather everyone together for an afternoon service. I think this is definitely a time where we could all use the soothing feeling that a good worship and prayer service can give you."

~~~~

The militia camp was nestled between two hills, deep in the woods of Teno Hollow and located one mile west of their intended ambush site of the Wolf Creek Bridge. As Evan, Jason, and Daryl approached, they were greeted by fellow militia members, who were all hard at work studying and training on the weapons that were supplied to them for the attack, most of which the members were not familiar with.

"Glad to see you guys could make it," shouted Carl as he jogged down out of the woods. "Tie your horses up right over there and let's get to work. Q is down at the site, selecting the firing positions. In the meantime, I can get you guys equipped and prepped up."

"Roger that," Evan replied.
~~~~

Once the men were dismounted, they joined Carl and hiked up a steep hillside and into the thick brush. They reached a small clearing where he had several equipment cases laid out, as well as numerous metal ammo cans, packs, MREs, and other supplies ready for issue. Once he fitted them each out with their rations and trauma kits, he said, "Okay, I've got three weapons yet unassigned. One of you gets the 'Ma Deuce' and the other two get Barrett M107s. Who has dibs on the Deuce?"

The three looked at each other, and then Daryl spoke up. "I'll take a 107. I think that'll suit my speed a little better."

"I guess I'll take the M2," said Evan. "Jason's quite the marksman; he should have the other Barrett."

"Alrighty, then," said Carl, as he got right down to the business of weapons familiarization with Evan on the M2 .50 caliber machine gun. Once the three had everything they needed, they retrieved their horses and used them as pack animals to carry their heavy weapons and ammunition for the journey through the rugged terrain to meet up with Q a mile east, on the ridge above the Wolf Creek Bridge. All travel via roads was strictly prohibited for the militiamen from that point on, as keeping a low profile from any potential observation was critical to their success, which lay in their ability to maintain the element of surprise.

~~~~

After the rugged and difficult journey through the steep terrain and thickly wooded, vegetated hillside, Evan, Jason, and Daryl met up with Quentin at their assigned rally point on the backside of the ridge, just over the hill from their intended fighting positions.

Quentin greeted them with a smile and a handshake, saying, "Gentlemen, so glad to see you. I see Carl got you all fitted out."
~~~~

"Yes, sir. He gave us everything we need," replied Jason.

"I'd like you to all meet Terry Johnson. He's gonna be your team leader for the duration of the operation. He's got a radio to communicate with the strike leader and me. Terry is in charge of all of the guns at the top of the ridge. We've got additional team leaders in charge of IED detonations, AT-4s, and a mobile team to move rapidly and fill in the gaps as need be. That's four teams total. Keith Harbold, who I believe you may have met last night, will be the strike leader. He will coordinate with each of the team leaders from now through the entire duration of the operation, and direct them regarding their team's employment.

"We also have two trained EMTs who will be with me and the comms folks on the other side of the ridge in the event that someone needs medical attention. As the field commander, I'll be coordinating with the strike leader, as well as our other outside assets, such as the Hot Springs team that is supposed to link up with us behind the convoy, as well as other militia assets in the region.

"I'll leave you gentlemen in Terry's care for now. He'll show you your fighting positions and give you any other pertinent information."

Reaching out to shake each of their hands, he said, "Good luck out there, and thanks again. We really needed you guys."

"The pleasure is all ours, sir," Evan replied, shaking his hand.

As Quentin turned and got back to the business at hand, Terry said, "Well, gentlemen, follow me." He led them to the top of the ridge, where they could get a good view of the scene below. "Do you see that big tree right there, off to the left?" he said while pointing.

"Yep," Jason replied.

"Okay, if you follow that directly across from left to right, you are basically looking at the level your shooting positions are based on. We've ensured that each position has a clear line of sight and an unobstructed firing lane to the target area below. We've also got sandbags in place for the best ballistic protection we could come up with, given the limited time we had to work with, as well as the visual signature we are trying to avoid."

Looking confused, Daryl said, "Maybe I'm just blind, but I don't see anything from here."

"Me, either," added Jason.

"That's the idea," explained Terry. "We have to assume that some sort of aerial reconnaissance will precede the convoy; whether it's manned aircraft or drones, we want to make sure our visual signature is as small as possible. The trees and brush all along the hillside are very thick and we covered the sandbags with natural debris and dirt as best we could. We had guys out here first thing this morning getting it all together."

"Outstanding," replied Evan.

"Anyway," Terry said as he continued, "Evan, I want you in the position just to the right of center. Daryl, you set up to the left of him, and Jason, you take the position on his right. There are three other machine guns and six M107s total along the upper portion of the ridge.

"Once the IEDs and AT-4s stop the convoy, if all goes as planned, the machine guns should keep the enemy's ability to move freely suppressed, while the M107s pick them off one at a time.

"I won't be talking to each of you individually due to our logistical constraints, but you'll know when the operation commences, as it will be upon detonation of the IEDs. I'll try to be as mobile as possible once it all starts going down, directing fire as necessary, but I have faith that you guys will pick good targets."

"We will do our best," Evan said while looking intently over the hill, trying to pick out his shooting position.

"Follow that game trail there and head on down. I've got to coordinate a little more with Q and then I'll be down. Once you get in position and get your gun set up, make yourselves as comfortable as possible. Who knows how long of a wait we will have before the party gets started. Get some rest. You're liable to need it."

With that, Terry turned and began to walk back down the backside of the hill to join up with Q. After a few steps, he stopped, turned back to face them, and said, "Oh, and for the record. I'm honored to have you guys on board. Q told me all about your struggles with him back at the farm and how you guys kept it together. He said he wouldn't have made it out of there without you. That makes me feel good to know that you're on our team."

"We're the ones who are honored," Evan replied. "If not for Q and the Blue Ridge Militia, we would have never made it out of there. More than likely, we'd have ended up swinging from a tree or shot by a firing squad. The honor is truly ours."

Terry smiled and turned to continue his walk down the hill.

Daryl looked at Evan and Jason. "Dang, guys, it sounds like I missed out on a good story. You're gonna have to fill me in on this farm thing."

"I guess you haven't gotten the whole story on that, have you? Well, if we make it out of this, we'll give you all of the details on our way back home," Jason replied with a grin.

"I'll hold you to that."

"Well, guys," interrupted Evan. "You heard the man, let's see if we can carry this stuff down this scary steep hillside without killing ourselves before the commies even get here."

He threw the heavy M2 machine gun over his shoulder while holding onto the barrel. With the M2's tripod lashed to his pack and his VZ58 with its stock folded and hanging by its sling from his shoulder, Evan struggled down the steep hillside with Jason and Daryl following along behind.

Nearing their positions, Evan stopped and turned to Jason and Daryl, gave them both a hug, and said, "I can't wait to tell you the story, Daryl, so stay alive. You, too, Jason. I'm sure you'll have your two cents to add. But seriously, we've been through a lot together. Stay safe and don't make this the last time we see each other. Every single person back home needs us."

"You, too, brother," Jason said, returning the hug.

With that being said, each of the men slipped into their assigned shooting position and began to get themselves set up for both the battle and the wait that precedes it.

Chapter Thirty-Four: The Waiting Game

As the last rays of light from the day's sun peeked over the hills to the west, Evan could not help but sit and think about his family back at the mine, and the struggles they might face until his return. He hoped and prayed that someday, they would no longer have to live in fear of what lay around every corner. He then remembered that's exactly why he was perched high on that wooded hillside. He knew that the actions of individuals such as him, Jason, and Daryl, standing up against tyranny with groups like the Blue Ridge Militia, was the first step in achieving that peace, stability, and freedom they longed for.

As his thoughts continued to drift, he heard footsteps approaching behind him. Reaching for his VZ58, he heard a familiar voice say, "Relax, Evan. It's just me, Terry."

"Oh, hey, Terry. Any word?"

"Yes, actually. Just as our intel suggested, the convoy reached Hot Springs right on schedule. Most of the town was evacuated and safely in their bug-out retreats, so in that regard, it has been relatively uneventful. The disturbing bit of news we've received from our eyes and ears on the ground, however, is that they seem to truly have a list of individuals associated with the militia and any sort of resistance. The homes of many of our key players in the area have been burned and destroyed while all the others were left virtually untouched. I'm not sure how they got their intel on us, but they, without a doubt, have a list and they're checking it twice."

"That's disturbing news," Evan said.

"We've got to stop these guys. If not, they'll burn us all out and keep us on the run, picking us off one by one. And as long as all of the region-wide hits over the next several days go as planned, they'll be spread way too thin to hit back on any one group. On a brighter note, Q said we've received word from out west."

"Really, what's that?"

"The occupiers out that way, mostly Chinese troops flying the UN Peacekeeper flag, have been trounced pretty hard, and they've got them on the run. The Northwestern Defensive Coalition has declared that Idaho is now free of any occupying forces."

"Where did the Chinese go?"

"We didn't get all of the details. We assume west towards Seattle, which was their initial staging area. The important thing, however, is that those guys out there in the mountains of Idaho have proven to us, and to the occupiers, that when Americans stand up to tyranny, we can overcome anything."

As the thunder off in the distance reminded Terry of one of the main reasons he was out making his rounds, he began to dig around in the large camouflaged pack he was carrying. He pulled out several items and said, "Here, from the sound of things, you'll need this. It's a camo tarp and a concealment net. Get yourself set up for a wet and rainy night. It appears thunderstorms may be on their way."

"Thanks, man," Evan said, taking the items. "Oh, and do me a favor. Send my regards to Jason when you're down his way. I assume you already visited Daryl?"

"I will, and speaking of that, Daryl says hey."

As Terry slipped off into the darkness to make his way to Jason's position, Evan once again heard thunder off in the distance. He looked up at the dark cloudy sky and thought, *Just great. That's exactly what we need, sitting on this steep hillside.*

~~~~
~~~~

Back at the old abandoned mine, as Griff and Greg stood watch at the entrance, Judy walked up behind them with two extra blankets and said, “Here, it’s getting cold in here.”

“Oh, thanks, baby,” Griff said. “How is everyone doing? How are the kids handling it?”

“Other than cold, fine. Well, poor little Zack isn’t doing so well. He had another one of his panic attacks about a half hour ago. Peggy has him calmed down for now. Being confined in a dark space is probably the opposite of what he needs emotionally, considering what happened at his grandparents’ home and all.”

“Yes, I can hardly imagine,” replied Griff.

“Why is it so cold in here? You’d think these thick rock walls could keep us warm,” she asked.

“Caves and mines generally stay very cool. The terrain surrounding them is too thick for any of the sun's daytime radiation to warm the air inside. If it was sealed off, I imagine it would be even colder with none of the warmer air getting in from the outside.”

“Is everyone else still awake?” asked Griff.

“Sarah and the Jones boys are asleep. Mildred is telling old-fashioned bedtime stories to the others. She’s such a jewel of a lady.”

“Yes, she is indeed.”

“Everyone else is snuggled together in groups under all of the blankets to stay warm. Oh, and Lloyd volunteered to stay up tonight to keep his lantern going on its lowest setting to give some background light. Most of the kids have probably never been anywhere this dark before. It’s crazy. You can’t even see your hand in front of your face without some sort of lantern or flashlight.”

“That’s why most cave critters, like bats, don’t use their eyes, or have lost their eyesight over time.”

"Damn it, Griff," she said, punching him in the arm jokingly. "Don't get me thinking about bats and cave critters. I'll never sleep now!"

He and Greg both shared a chuckle. "Okay, okay, sorry. Anyway, Greg and I should be relieved in about an hour and a half. As soon as we get off we'll come join you in a snuggle pile."

"Okay, then," she said as she kissed Griff softly on the lips. She then turned and gave Greg a kiss on the forehead. "I'll be waiting up for you. See you soon."

Griff smiled, then turned his attentions back to the darkness of the night outside. As he heard thunder off in the distance, he said, "I wonder if Evan, Jason, and Daryl have a roof over their heads tonight."

~~~~

As the rain came pouring down on Evan's tarp, with thunder seemingly booming all around him, he was thankful for the delivery that Terry had made earlier in the night. Before the rains started, he laid the tarp out flat with the long end going up the hill behind him. He then sat down on the tarp, gathered all of his gear on it as well, and pulled it back overtop of himself. This meant the fold was uphill behind him, preventing water from running underneath him and his equipment. He had also strung his camouflaged concealment net above the tarp, from some branches directly overhead, in order to hide the visible signature of the tarp from above, as Terry had instructed.

As the heavy rain impacted the plastic tarp, the sound was deafening, drowning out all of the natural sounds around him. He could see streams of water flowing to his left and to his right around the tarp. *That entire convoy could roll right in front of us on the road below and take Del Rio, and I'd never*
~~~~

even know they went by! he thought to himself. *I can't see or hear a thing!*

Convinced that staring downhill at the road was a useless endeavor at that point, Evan curled up on the dry portion of his tarp shelter the best he could and returned to his thoughts of his beautiful wife and children in the mine back home. He wished he was cuddled up with them all at that very moment.

~~~~

Early the next morning, Evan was awakened by the sound of birds chirping all around him. The sun was peeking over the hills and mountains to the east. As he yawned and stretched, he pulled the tarp back to reveal a beautiful sunrise moving its way above the horizon. As he gazed at the beautiful sight, he saw something dark coming out of those very same morning rays of light, followed by the sound of several helicopter main rotors, traveling in a westerly direction right toward him.

Holy crap! he thought as the realization surged through his body, rapidly accelerating his heartbeat. Giving his M2 machine gun a quick once over to make sure it was still ready to go, he swung the barrel around to face the threat, knowing that taking on a Russian Mi-24 Hind with a mere machine gun, even if it was a .50 BMG, was suicide.

As the approaching helicopters grew nearer, he could tell they were flying directly up the valley, over the Wolf Creek Bridge and up Highway 9 in the direction of Del Rio. As they flew past, they were at his eye level from his position perched high on the hillside. The two Hinds were an ominous sight as they flew up the valley, seemingly unaware of the men's positions on the hillside as well as along the riverbank down below.

~~~~

As Tyrone walked around the outside of the church, making his morning security sweep, he heard the sound of the helicopters approaching from a distance. Ducking back behind the large heating oil tank, he watched as they flew directly over the church, and then followed the contour of the terrain, peeling off from the valley and heading into the hills to the southwest.

Running for the front door of the church, he saw that Pastor Wallace was already standing outside, watching the helicopters disappear over the hills in the distance. “What do you think they're up to?” he asked.

“They seem to be heading in the direction of the homesteads where Evan Baird and the others live,” the pastor replied with a look of concern on his face. “They must have an interest in the place, considering they already wiped out Mrs. Thomas’s entire herd of cattle.”

“Let’s hope and pray they’re just doing more recon,” Tyrone replied.

“Yes, that we will do. I guess that’s all we can do for now,” said Pastor Wallace as the two men turned to walk back inside the church.

~~~~

As the morning sun began to shine its way through the entrance of the mine, cast through the tree branches outside like a thousand individual rays of light, Will Bailey and Linda Cox had taken the first watch of the day and were admiring the beauty of nature’s magical light show. “It doesn’t look like such a screwed-up world from here, does it?” Will said.

“No, no, it doesn’t. But of course, the only part of this world that is screwed up is the human side. The animals,
~~~~

nature, the earth itself, they're all fine. I'm sure they'd be much better off without us, too."

Will started to reply, but they both went silent when they heard the rhythm of the helicopter rotors as the flight of two Mi-24 Hinds flew up the valley, closely following the contours of the terrain. "Oh, my God, they're back!" she exclaimed.

"Go tell the others," Will said. "I'll keep my eye on them to see where they go."

Linda nodded in agreement and ran back into the mine as Will watched closely with his binoculars.

After only a moment, Griff, Charlie, and Lloyd came out of the depths of the mine with Linda to get a look for themselves. "What's going on?" asked Griff.

"They went over that hill toward—" Before Will could finish his sentence, they heard a deep thump off in the distance, followed by billowing clouds of smoke.

"Oh, my God," Linda exclaimed. "Did they crash?"

Her statement was immediately followed by another deep thump and another plume of black smoke.

"No..." answered Griff. "They're hitting something. I would venture to guess it's our homes."

They all stood speechless as they came to terms with what might be happening to their homes and their livelihoods. After two more explosions and the resulting billowing black clouds of smoke, the helicopters reappeared over the opposing ridgeline and swooped back down into the valley before them.

"Just be thankful no one was home today," Griff said as he watched the helicopters and tried to guess their next move.

To his horror, as he watched them from a distance through the riflescope on an AR-10 he had brought from the house, he saw one of the helicopters land while the other circled overhead. "Ah, crap!" he said.

"What? What is it?" asked Charlie.

"One of the Hinds just touched down. There's only one reason they would do that."

"What?"

"The Mi-24 Hind is a sizable helicopter. It's not only an attack helicopter; it also has an eight-person troop transport compartment in the back. My guess would be they're putting boots on the ground to sweep the area for people who may have fled the homes."

A sinking feeling went through them all as they watched from afar. Charlie turned to Griff and said, "We need to go on lockdown. We need to get everyone else as deep in the mine as we can. We also need to get some guns up here to fight them off, if it comes to that. We can't just die cowering in the bottom of this stinkin' hole in the ground without at least putting up a fight."

Chapter Thirty-Five: The Snake

Not long after the Hinds passed over the Wolf Creek Bridge, Evan and the others could hear the rumble of the convoy's diesel engines approaching from the distance. The militiamen's hearts all began to race as they were preparing to take on a well-armed and well-trained professional military force. Having never fired a Browning M2 machine gun before, Evan went over everything in his head. How to reload. How to address malfunctions. How to accurately predict point of aim versus point of impact with the iron sights of the M2. The machine gunner's belts were not pre-loaded with tracers, in order to avoid being seen, and being inexperienced with the gun, Evan couldn't help but have all of those questions and more racing through his mind.

Evan gripped the spade-style handles of the gun, with his thumbs hovering lightly above the butterfly triggers. As the convoy snaked around the corner and onto the bridge, Evan couldn't help but think of how it resembled a serpent winding its way down the road, on a hunt for food. From what he could see, the convoy consisted of five Humvees, obviously sourced from the U.S. military, as well as three DHS-marked MRAP light-armored vehicles, and two U.S. built medium-duty utility trucks in the personnel/cargo configuration. The two lead vehicles were both MRAPs, as was the vehicle bringing up the rear, with the Humvees and utility trucks filling in as the body of the snake. *They could bring their own helicopters, but couldn't bring their own trucks,* he thought as he watched them work their way across the bridge.

As the last MRAP reached the end of the Wolf Creek Bridge, Evan was startled as the first AT-4 was fired, immediately disabling the MRAP, sending flames and debris flying in all directions, blocking the bridge. This explosion was followed by a cacophony of deafening thuds as several more AT-4s were fired, as well as the detonation of the IEDs placed along the south side of the road, just over the edge toward the river.

Evan opened fire immediately, startled by the power of the big .50 caliber Ma Deuce. At first, the scene was chaotic, with smoke and flames engulfing the convoy, and a deafening barrage of gunfire from the hillside, as the vehicles below were peppered with the heavy rounds from the .50 caliber M2 machine guns, as well as the Barrett M107 precision rifles.

In what seemed like minutes, but in reality was merely seconds, small arms fire from the vehicles on the road erupted, as well as the heavy machine gun fire from one of the MRAP's roof-mounted machine gun turrets that had remained intact from the indirect hit which had disabled, but had not destroyed, the vehicle.

Evan focused his fire on the machine gun down below until his ammo belt ran dry and he was forced to make his first combat reload of the big M2. Struggling at first, but quickly getting a grip on the situation, Evan loaded the belt, cycled the rifle, and re-engaged the target. He could hear bullets ripping through the trees all around him as the UN-flagged soldiers on the road below concentrated their fire on the muzzle flashes of the machine gun operators, as they were the most visible targets to acquire.

One of the machine guns to his left fell silent. Assuming the operator had to reload such as he did, he expected it to resume firing at any moment. Its continued silence, however, gave him a sinking feeling in the pit of his stomach that one of his fellow militiamen had already fallen.

As the return fire from the UN convoy began to lessen in intensity, Evan looked up and was horrified to see one of the Mi-24 Hinds streaking up the valley toward its comrades under fire below. As the Hind neared the convoy, it began a turning climb towards the hillside where the militiamen were positioned, opening fire with its 12.7mm machine gun when one of the remaining AT-4s, held in reserve, fired its anti-tank rocket directly into the flight path of the approaching Hind, clipping its tail rotor, sending it spinning and crashing violently into the hillside, where it erupted into an inferno of burning jet fuel.

As the second Hind made its approach, it made an abrupt turn to its right, avoiding the billowing cloud of black smoke from its smoldering comrade, and fired its S-8 rockets into the hillside, causing massive explosions, sending bits of debris and shrapnel flying high into the air, forcing Evan to dive down onto the ground to avoid being hit while the debris fell all around him. The helicopter then immediately pulled into a steep climb, barely clearing the top of the ridge. It flew directly over Evan's head, disappearing over the ridge and down into the next valley.

~~~~

Tyrone and Pastor Wallace were observing the towering clouds of black smoke from both the direction of the Wolf Creek Bridge, as well as the Homefront and its neighboring homesteads.

"Pastor..." Tyrone said, wishing to ask him a question.

"Yes, Tyrone?"

"At what point should we evacuate the women. I mean... if we wait until we see a threat, a threat can see us as well. And I would venture to guess that any potential threat can outmaneuver and outrun a group of women and children."

"I know; I was thinking the same thing just now. I think we should..." before Pastor Wallace could finish his sentence, a black Ford pickup truck came down the road from the west
~~~~

with several men in the back. "Maybe we're too late," he said. "Let the others know we've got company."

As Tyrone turned to warn the others in the church, one of the men in the back of the truck began waving his arms frantically. Tyrone stopped, and looking closely, recognized Ed and Nate from his encounter in the woods that fateful night when he met them, along with Evan, Jason, Charlie, and Jimmy.

"Wait," he said as Pastor Wallace cycled the action on the pump shotgun he was carrying. "That's them. Those are the men who sent us here. The men who helped save Sabrina."

"What? Oh, my Lord. Thank you, Lord. It's the Hoskins boy and that fellow from up north," Pastor Wallace exclaimed.

Tyrone ran to the truck to greet them as they pulled into the parking lot. "You made it back! Hot damn, you made it back! Evan and Jason told us about what happened. We've been praying every day, long and hard, for your safe return."

Ed jumped out of the truck and gave Tyrone a hug. "So Evan and Jason made it back?" he said with a smile on his face. He turned to Nate. "Nate, they made it!"

"Sorry to interrupt the reunion, guys," said Pastor Wallace, "but there is a lot going on right now that you need to be aware of. You see that smoke off in the distance?" He pointed toward the east and Wolf Creek Bridge. "That's a militia ambush of a UN convoy that's been rolling through each of the towns along its way, causing trouble for anyone associated with a militia." Then he turned and pointed to the southwest. "Do you see that smoke over there? Two military helicopters flew over the ridge into the area of your homesteads, and the smoke has been rising up over the hills ever since."

"Oh, my God!" exclaimed Nate. "Peggy? Mom? Luke? Is everyone okay? What happened?"

"We aren't sure, but Evan, Jason, and Daryl are at the bridge with the militia. Everyone else from your parts bugged out to an old mine back in the hills behind the old Muncie place. Do you know where that is?"

"Not the mine," Ed replied. "But we know where the Muncie place is."

"I really don't know what to tell you, boys. We have no idea the extent of what's happened up that way. We've not received any reports from the militia or the homesteads."

Nate looked at Ed and said, "We've got to get up there. We've got to help them."

Ed looked at Pastor Wallace. "Do you have transportation we can borrow? These kind folks are friends of Henry and Meredith here," he said, pointing to the occupants of the truck. "They brought us all this way and risked a lot, but we can't ask them to go directly into harm's way like that."

"Take the ATV in the back shed. There should be enough gas in it to make it up there and back," Pastor Wallace replied.

"Henry, you and Meredith stay here with Pastor Wallace and the church. They are good people. You can trust them. Nate and I have to go see what happened at home. We'll come back for you."

He then turned around upon hearing the sound of the ATV with Tyrone aboard. "Hop on, Ed," he said. "Nate, you stay here and help guard the church. I'll make sure your family is okay, no matter what it takes."

"Now, Tyrone, we need you here," said Pastor Wallace.

"Look," Tyrone said with a serious voice. "I turned my back and ran when friends of mine were in trouble once before. I'll never do that again. I owe these people my life. Now, Nate, you know you aren't in any condition to go up there with Ed. Where's your leg? I'm going, period."

Henry spoke up and said, "I'm quite handy with a gun, Pastor. I'll help fill in for Tyrone, as well."

Ed climbed onto the back of the ATV with Tyrone, carrying the AK-74 he had acquired earlier in their journey, and Tyrone had strapped his bolt action .30-06 chambered Winchester Model 70 onto the front rack with bungee-style tie-down straps. The two men pulled away as fast as the ATV would go, leaving the others standing and watching.

"Okay, let's get everyone inside," Pastor Wallace said. "I think you should all come in and ride this thing out. It's not safe for you to be driving off anytime soon."

Chapter Thirty-Six: No Challenge Too Great

As Tyrone and Ed arrived at the Homefront, they were horrified to see that all that was left was smoldering ruins and one remaining brick wall. It had been completely destroyed, along with everything Evan and Molly had worked so hard to acquire, which had helped nearly everyone in their homesteading community during the onset of the collapse. The two men didn't utter a word. As Tyrone hit the throttle, Ed pointed the way to the Thomas farm.

As they neared the Thomas farm, they could see the smoke in the distance, and to their horror, they once again arrived to see that Mildred's beautiful old farmhouse had also been burned to the ground. "We've got to get to the mine," Ed said. "If that's where they all went, we need to make sure they are okay. We can't just ride right up to the mine though. We need to check it out from a distance. Otherwise, we may clue someone in on their whereabouts."

"Just tell me where to go," Tyrone replied.

"That way," Ed said as he pointed up ahead, and off they went.

Stopping just shy of a mile from the old Muncie place, which had been slated to become the new Vandergriff home, Ed and Tyrone hid the ATV in the brush, readied their rifles, and set out to make the rest of the journey on foot.

"If the mine is behind the Muncie place, we need to get on the opposing hillside so we can get a good vantage point to see if there are any threats in the nearby area. Then we can—" Ed was interrupted by the crack of several gunshots coming from the direction of the Muncie place.

"Damn it!" he said. "Let's get going."

As they neared the Muncie place, Ed said, "How good are you with that thing?"

"The rifle? I've never really had the chance to shoot it, but Pastor Wallace showed me how."

"Here, trade me," he said, handing him the AK-74. "Here is how this thing works. You cycle the action with the charging handle here to pick up a round from the magazine after you reload, or if it becomes jammed to clear it. This big lever on the side is the safety. Up is safe, the middle is fully automatic, all the way down is one shot for one trigger pull."

"Fully automatic like a machine gun?" Tyrone asked.

"Yes, exactly. I'll take your Winchester up on that opposing hill. I'm a pretty good shot at long range. I used to have my own rifle range in my backyard up in Ohio. Anyway, you creep around toward the Muncie house, but don't give yourself away. I'll get up on that hill, and when I see the threat, I'll start to pick them off from a distance. The AK is easy to use. Point, aim, spray, and pray. What I want you to do is be the last line of defense for the people in the mine if they try to escape, or if someone attempts to enter the mine. Once I start firing, you should get a good idea where the threats are when they return my fire. If they are carrying those things," he said, pointing at the AK-74. "I'll be at an advantage at that distance, which should help even the odds."

"Sounds good. Good luck, man," Tyrone said, shaking Ed's hand before turning to slip off into the woods toward the Muncie place.

Once Ed got himself positioned on the opposing hill, he scanned the area with the 3-9x scope on the Winchester. Starting out at 3x, the lowest magnification setting, gave Ed the widest field of view, enabling him to scan the area quickly. On his second pass across the other hill, he saw several muzzle flashes, followed by the crack of the shot ringing out across the valley. Zooming in on the target with the scope on 9x magnification, Ed recognized the flashes as coming from the same type of Russian troops that had taken them hostage during the roadside ambush of the tractor. "Bastards," he whispered to himself as he continued to scan the area.

Seeing muzzle flashes coming from within the cave, Ed felt some relief, knowing that at least someone from the homesteads was still alive to be putting up a fight. He just had no idea who. For now, that simply didn't matter. His new mission was to eliminate the foreign threat, to liberate his friends who might still be alive.

Taking a slow and steady aim at one of the soldiers from the prone position, concealing himself behind the blades of tall grass that grew on the hillside, Ed thought to himself. *This must be like... three hundred to four hundred yards. I should have never used distance markers and a laser range finder on my range back home. Now I'm spoiled. Oh, well, here goes,* he said to himself as he adjusted his hold for the distance and prevailing wind, took a deep breath, and then gently squeezed the trigger, sending the 180-grain, soft-point hunting round flying across the valley and directly into the back of his intended target. Seeing the man drop from the kneeling firing position to the ground, Ed thought, *That's one.*

Ed adjusted his aim to the next soldier in view, who was frantically informing his fellow soldiers of Ed's shot. Ed could see six men total, one of whom he had already taken out of the fight. Placing his cross hairs on the frantic soldier pointing in his general direction on the hill, he held his breath and let another round fly, ripping through the man's stomach, dropping him to the ground where he writhed around in pain for a few seconds before the movement stopped. *A little low,* he thought.

The other soldiers then began to scatter, and turned to focus their fire on Ed's position. As rounds began to land in Ed's general area, he realized they must have seen the muzzle flash of his last shot. *Thank goodness they have AKs,* he thought, referring to their lack of long-range prowess.

He took his aim and fired another shot, taking another one of the soldiers out of the fight. *That's three.*

As he adjusted his aim for the fourth man, he felt a series of stings impact his right leg. "Damn it!" he shouted in pain, rolling over on his good side to assess the situation. "Crap! Oh, God, that hurts," he said as he watched the blood run from his leg. Removing his belt, he made a tourniquet to stop the bleeding until he was clear of the threat and could take the time to deal with his injuries.

Finding it more difficult to hold his aim with the searing pain in his leg, Ed hovered his cross hairs on the next target, who was now much better concealed, and let a round fly. As he felt the recoil from his rifle, another sharp pain erupted as a bullet ripped through his left arm, causing him to drop the rifle.

Clutching his arm with his hand, Ed moaned in pain and lifted his hand to see a sizeable chunk of his bicep missing. "Oh, dear God," he said aloud. As bullets kept impacting the ground around him, he knew that he must push through the pain and finish the fight. It was his only way out at that point. He was in no condition to retreat from the hillside, and they had a fix on his position.

Letting go of his arm, allowing the profuse bleeding to continue, Ed picked up his rifle and attempted to cycle another round into the chamber, only to realize it was empty. *Damn it!* he thought. *I forgot these things only hold three in the mag and one in the pipe.*

With his only good arm, Ed fumbled around in his pocket for the extra cartridges he had gotten from Tyrone; once he retrieved them, he began to load them, one by one, through the open action of the rifle. It was a slow and painstaking process with only one hand and the distraction of severe pain throughout his body.

Picking up his rifle and propping it up on his dead arm, Ed cycled a round into the chamber, took aim, and fired another shot. Looking through the scope, he could see that the shot hit the soldier he was aiming for, leaving one visible threat. As he cracked a smile, a bullet smashed through his collarbone, sending a shockwave of unimaginable pain through his body. With the rifle still propped up on his dead arm, he struggled to reposition it, as he knew one more threat remained. He attempted to aim the rifle, but his body began to shake; he started to go numb and had trouble simply holding the rifle in place. As his vision began to blur, he saw a series of muzzle flashes through the scope as Tyrone appeared, firing wildly from the hip with full-automatic fire, killing the last of the soldiers. Ed cracked a smile as his vision faded to black, and the world around him went silent.

Chapter Thirty-Seven: Restoring Hope

As Evan looked around at the beautiful day, listening to the birds chirping and feeling the gentle breeze, he could hardly believe it had been three months since the attack at the Wolf Creek Bridge and since Ed's untimely death. So much had happened over the past several years. They had experienced more than their share of both heartache and happiness.

Over the past three months, they had buried a dear friend, had Nate returned to them, and welcomed the addition of Henry and Meredith to their group. Having just completed work on their cabin on the Homefront, which would serve as their home for the foreseeable future, Evan was happy that, as the news kept pouring in over the radio, it seemed the country was finally going to be turning its course back to where it needed to be. He hoped they were entering a period where new beginnings could begin to take root and his children could once again have a future they could look forward to.

As he reflected on it all, he was snapped back to reality as Pastor Wallace said, "Do you have a ring?"

Nate said, "Yes. Yes, we do." He motioned for little Zack, who held the wedding ring. The ring had been given to Nate's mother many years before by his father. "Thank you, son," he said with a smile as he took the ring from young Zack and placed it on Peggy's finger.

Tears welled up in Evan's eyes as he was caught up in the moment, only to be reminded by Daryl's clearing of his throat that he had a job to do as well. "Oh, of course. Sorry," Evan said as he fished the ring out of his pocket and handed it to Daryl.

Daryl then placed the ring on Linda's finger, and after they had each said their vows, Pastor Wallace said, "I now pronounce you Mr. and Mrs. Nathan Hoskins, and Mr. and Mrs. Daryl Moses; you may both kiss your brides."

~The End~

A Note from the Author

What a ride this has been. This completes my fifth book, the fourth in this series, and all I can say is it has been quite a ride. From the beginning of The Last Layover, as I typed it on my Android smartphone, to now, I have truly fallen in love with the characters. To be honest, I find myself wanting to go live on the Homefront and have each of those outstanding individuals as my neighbors.

I would have never made it to book four in this series, however, if my favorite people in the real world, you, my readers, didn't read the books and urge me on to keep the story alive. I thank each and every one of you from the bottom of my heart. I've learned a lot during this journey, and I hope you stick with me as my writing career progresses, both within this series and beyond.

To follow me further, please visit me at the following places. In addition, please sign up for my newsletter at either of my websites:

Facebook: www.facebook.com/homefrontbooks (writing)
Facebook: www.facebook.com/stvbird (personal)
Twitter: @stevencbird
Blog: www.stevencbird.com
Website: www.homefrontbooks.com
Amazon Author Page: http://www.amazon.com/Steven-Bird/e/B00LRYYBDU/
Email: scbird@homefrontbooks.com

Respectfully yours,

Steven C. Bird